The
One Who
Holds
Me

JOAN EMBOLA

THE ONE WHO HOLDS ME

SOVEREIGN LOVE. BOOK 4

JOAN EMBOLA

PRESS

THE ONE WHO HOLDS ME

Copyright 2024 by Joan Embola

Love Qualified Press

All rights reserved.

This novel is a work of fiction. Although the settings and locations are based on fact, the characters, dialogues, and incidences portrayed are either the work of the author's imagination, or used fictitiously. Any resemblance to actual persons, living or dead, are entirely coincidental.

No part of this book may be reproduced in any form or by any electronic or mechanical means, including information storage and retrieval systems, without written permission from the author, except for the use of brief quotations in a book review.

Scriptures used in this book whether quoted or paraphrased are taken from;

Holy Bible, New Living Translation, copyright © 1996, 2004, 2015 by Tyndale House Foundation. All rights reserved.

Manuscript edited by Michaela Bush

Blurb edited by Abigayle Claire

Cover designed and illustrated by Elle Maxwell

For more information, contact;

www.joanembola.co.uk

ALSO BY JOAN EMBOLA

Fiction

The One Who Knows Me: Sovereign Love Book 1

The One Who Loves Me: Sovereign Love Book 2

The One Who Sees Me: Sovereign Love Book 3

Devotionals

Outpourings Of A Beloved Heart: A 30 Day Poetry Devotional About God's Love

The God Who Holds Me: A Companion Devotional & Journal

Also check out the merch store for cute faith-based merchandise such as t-shirts, stickers, mugs, notebooks and so much more.

To my Heavenly Father, the One who holds me.

To the country and people of Ghana, for providing solace for me during a turbulent season in my life. I'll always hold you in high regard.

For I hold you by your right hand—I, the LORD your God. And I say to you, 'Don't be afraid. I am here to help you.'

— -ISAIAH 41:13 (NLT)

NAME PRONUNCIATION GUIDE

Funke (Fuh-n-keh) - Short for Yoruba name Olufunke/Oluwa-funke/Oluwafunmike which means God gave me to pamper/God gave me to take care of

Bolanle (Buh-lah-n-lay)- Short for Yoruba name Omobolanle which means 'child finds wealth at home'

Chidinma (Chi-din-ma)- An Igbo name which means God is good/God is beautiful

Lerato (Leh-raa-t-oh)- Name of African origin which means love. It is a popular name in countries in Southern Africa like South Africa, Lesotho and Botswana.

Chijioke (Chi-ji-oke)- An Igbo name for boys which means God gives gifts/ God is my guide/ God is the custodian for all talents or gifts

Madu (Mma-du)- An Igbo name which means beauty/good exists

Olanna (O-la-nna)- An Igbo name for girls which means 'her father's jewel'

Emeka (Eh-meh-kah)- Short for Igbo name Chukwuemeka which means 'God has done so much'

Kwame (Q-wa-mé)- A boy name of Ghanaian origin which means 'born on Saturday'

Yaw (Y-ow)- Ghanaian name for boys meaning 'born on Thursday'

Obeng (Ob-en)- A Ghanaian name which means brilliant/one who is smart

Abena (Aa-h-b-eh-n-uh)- A Ghanaian name for girls which means 'born on Tuesday'

Kofi (K-oh-f-ee)- Ghanaian name for boys which means 'born on Friday'

Adjei (Ad-jay)- A Ghanaian surname that could mean 'messenger of God' or 'a charming person'

Maame (M-a-a-m-e)- Ghanaian name for girls which means 'Mother'

Mensah (M-eh-n-s-uh)- The most common surname in Ghana which means 'third-born boy'

Nwaeze (Nw-e-zeh)- An igbo name which means 'the king's child'

Adaego (Ah-day-go)- An igbo name for girls which means 'daughter of wealth'

Taiwo (T-ie-w-oh)- A Yoruba name which means 'the first twin to taste the world'

Oluwadarasimi (Oh-lu-wah-dah-rah-see-me)- A Yoruba name which means 'God has been good to me'

Omolade (O-mo-la-day)- A Yoruba name which means 'child of the crown'

Oluremi (Oh-lu-reh-mee)- A Yoruba name which means 'God comforts me'

Shola or Sola (Sh-aw-lah) - A Yoruba name short for Olusola which means 'God has blessed me', or Adesola meaning 'a child crowned with wealth' or Oluwasola which means 'God creates wealth'

Aderinto (Ah-day-rin-tor)- A Yoruba name which means "the crown walks well."

Adaeze (Ah-deh-zeh)- Igbo name for girls which means 'princess' or 'daughter of the king'

Kehinde (K-eh-heen-day)- A Yoruba name which means 'second-born of the twins'

1

OLANNA
NOW

One thing I can't resist doing at Nigerian parties is eavesdropping on the gossip the aunties spread about people they know. Yes, I know I shouldn't, but Nigerian aunties are loud. If Aunty Funke chooses to announce to the entire world that Bolanle dumped Chidinma and moved on to find his next target, I can't walk up to her table and tell her to shut up, can I?

While we all know it's rude to broadcast someone's private business at a public gathering, I know better than to get myself involved. I never know the people being talked about, and if Mom was still alive and here with me, she'd tell me to drink water and mind my business.

What I find interesting is that on my way home from these parties, I never think about the aunties or the people they were talking about. But what always remains etched in my memory is the heartbreaking love stories.

It can never be me, I used to tell my naïve self. How can people who appear to be so in love grow apart and break up? What could possibly go wrong that would cause a relationship to go from a hundred to zero with no warning? How can a love that was once so alive become so dead and cold? I used to wonder about all these things until the day it happened to me.

Thank God I kept my relationship with Alex off social media and I don't regret doing that because, with the way it ended, I wouldn't have been surprised if I heard an aunty narrating our tragic love story at a random Nigerian party.

For the first two months of our relationship, only Danielle and India—my close friends from college—knew about us. Then I later told my brother, Manny, when he suspected I was dating someone. His wife, Heather—who was his girlfriend at the time—was the next person I told and they were so good at keeping it discreet.

My plan was to introduce Alex to Dad on college graduation day, but that plan blew up in my face when Alex broke up with me two months into senior year. I never got closure, and that sucks. Some days, I pat myself on the back for blocking his number and deleting it from my phone. But other days, I chide myself for ignoring his emails for the last two years.

But who cares about that? Certainly not me. I've moved on and that's why I won't spend any more of my precious time thinking about him. It's been two years, for goodness' sake.

A soft knock on the door forces me to lift my head, and Lerato, my personal assistant, pokes her head into my office. "Good morning. Can I come in?"

"Of course." I welcome the distraction while sending a silent prayer up to God. I need him to expel all thoughts of Alex from my mind, so I can focus on being the boss babe I am.

Lerato lets herself in, her notepad and pen in hand and her big curly afro bouncing as she strides in like the South African beauty she is. Only Lerato's hair can wind up my desire to comb out my locs, so I can start wearing an afro again. But I've been at this junction too many times and I know better. Locs suit my busy lifestyle more.

"Here's your cookies and cream Frappuccino as you requested." She places the drink in front of me before settling in the
chair across from my desk.

"Thank you so much. I don't know what I'll do without you."

"Girl, you're the CEO of a multimillion dollar company—
one of the fastest growing healthcare marketing companies in
Jersey City. I'm sure you'll be just fine without me." Lerato
chuckles.

"You can't be too sure about that," I say before sipping on the
cold drink, taking my time to savor its sweet and creamy texture
before focusing on the task at hand. "So, what's our day looking
like?" I open my Filofax planner, and Lerato turns on the iPad
with our daily, weekly, and monthly schedules.

"Well, it's a full day of back-to-back meetings, starting with
the end of week meeting with the managers at nine AM. But you
asked me to schedule some time with your dad. He is already
waiting for you downstairs in conference room A."

"Thanks, girl. Please tell him I'll be out in five minutes."

When Lerato is out the door, I pause and take five deep
breaths in and out. This usually helps, but so far today, it has
done nothing to calm my nerves. It's bad enough that October
is officially my worst month and I don't know what to do with
all these emotions about Alex. But now I also have to worry
about Dad, who randomly decided a few weeks ago he'll be
visiting Nigeria for a month—the same place where Mom
died.

I tip my head back to keep the tears from falling, but it
doesn't work, so I stand up and walk up to my window. Dabbing
on the tears at the corner of my eyes, I stare at the beautiful view
of the Jersey City skyline and Hudson River outside.

It's on days like this that I'm grateful my office doesn't have
glass walls like the offices downstairs. My staff don't need to see
me shedding tears whenever a memory of Mom pops in my

head, or when I remember how hurt I still am from my breakup with Alex. Lord, please help me deal with these emotions.

After counting down from ten, I'm able to think clearly again, so I straighten out the creases on my beige pantsuit, tighten the ponytail on my burgundy locs, and walk out the door, my heels sending click-clack sounds down the hallway.

After making it two floors down in the elevator, I walk out into the open plan office, putting on my brave CEO face again. One thing I love about my team is that they take their work seriously. That's why I'm never disappointed whenever I come down here.

"Morning everyone." I walk over to Yin, Melissa, and Neil, who look up from their group discussion.

"Morning, boss." Yin, Manny's best friend—who is also the managing director here at Madu Health—answers for the group.

"Oooh, I love the pantsuit." Melissa clicks her fingers at me and my cheeks warm up because now I know they're all looking at me.

"Aww, thank you." I reach for a loc strand to flip, but then remember I'm wearing a ponytail today, so I let my hand brush awkwardly against my shoulder before turning to Yin. "I'm going to have a quick meeting with my Dad and then we can meet in my office. Is that okay?"

"Sure thing. I'll get the others ready for our meeting at nine. See you upstairs, boss." He nods and I walk away.

Outside the conference room, I take a deep breath and push open the door to find Dad facing the same view of the Jersey City skyline. He has one hand in his pocket and the other resting on his decorated walking stick. With him wearing his white Kaftan and black cap, you would think he is on his way to a wedding ceremony and not about to spend eleven hours on a flight to Lagos. I've yet to meet an Igbo man who loves his culture more than my Dad.

"Dad?"

He turns around and sends me the warmest smile before opening his arms wide.

I walk straight into his embrace, his warm sage scent saturating my nostrils and providing a safe and familiar space for me. He doesn't know how much I need this hug and how much I need him to stay.

"*Kedu ka i mere?*" He asks in Igbo when we break the hug.

"*Adi m mma,*" I respond, proud that I've finally learned how to respond to some of his questions.

"Are you sure you're okay?" He lifts my chin so I can look him in the eye.

I want to lie, but knowing Dad, he'll only keep pressing until I tell him. "Dad, do you really have to make this trip? One month is too long. Can't you stay for now and go another time?" Or better still, never.

"*Ezigbo m,* it has been four years. I can't keep postponing it. You know, I have many businesses and projects in Lagos. I'm grateful that God helped me find trustworthy people to manage them, but I need to oversee some things myself." He squeezes my shoulders and I lower my head again, trying to keep the tears in.

"It's just that I'm scared and..."

"I'll be fine." He cuts in before my thoughts wander off. "God will take care of me, okay?"

I give him a reluctant nod. I could beg him some more and try using my princess privilege to get him to stay. But being the only girl and the last born of the family can only get you so far. On this one, I'd be fighting a lost battle. Once Chijioke Madu makes up his mind, it only takes a divine intervention to change it. So I have to take a step back and keep praying until he returns safely.

"I'm so proud of you, my dear," he continues. "You stepped

up to this role as a CEO with very short notice and you have done extremely well taking over from me. I have to admit I was a little worried about whether you will handle the workload. But you have surprised me with your strength and determination. You will do amazing. I have no doubt about that."

"Thank you, Daddy." I smile at him, his words calming my anxious heart.

He reaches for his briefcase on the conference table and takes out a folder. "So, I looked through your progress report on your new client—HearCare. You officially start with them on Monday, right?"

"Yes."

He hands me the folder. "Here are my thoughts on some things you should fine tune with the team to avoid any mistakes along the way."

"Thanks, Daddy. I appreciate you always looking out for me."

"Anytime, my darling. Have you spoken to your brother yet?" He asks his favorite question of the week. Dad is very passionate about keeping our family bond strong, so he always checks in to make sure Manny and I are communicating with each other.

"Yes. I'm going over to have dinner and Bible study with them tonight."

"That's very good." He glances at his watch. "My dear, if I don't leave now, I'm going to be rushing and you know I hate rushing." He chuckles as he heads for the door and I follow closely behind him.

"I wish I could come with you to the airport."

"No, I'm a grown man and I can take care of myself. Emeka will bring the car back after dropping me off at the airport. At least now you have the entire house to yourself for a month. Make the most of it." He winks at me before hugging me tight. "I'll call you as soon as I land."

"I love you, Daddy."

"Love you too, my princess," he says before walking down the hallway, greeting the team as he goes.

Lord, please take care of him. I send another silent prayer up to God before heading back to my office for the nine AM meeting. While I need a lot of distraction to keep my mind away from Alex, the downside about back-to-back meeting days is that they are mentally exhausting and I have to rely on lots of coffee to keep me engaged—something Lerato always delivers on.

Hiring her is the best decision I've made for myself so far. I consider myself privileged to have not only a very competent personal assistant, but also a good friend. I knew there was a reason I was so picky during the interview process. God saved Lerato for last because He knew the kind of person I needed.

The icing on the cake was when I found out Lerato is also a Christian. Even though Madu Health isn't a Christian-based agency, my parents built it on Christian principles. After Dad retired and Manny left, Yin and I were the only Christians in the company until Lerato joined the team. After two years of working with her, I can confidently say that there's nothing better than riding with a sister that loves the Lord.

"I'm heading home now, boss." Lerato walks into the office wearing her jacket and her backpack swung over her shoulder. "Is there anything else you want me to do before I leave?"

Wow, how is it already five PM? "No, everything's good here. Thank you so much for your help today. Do you have any plans for the weekend?"

"Yes, Paul is flying down from Portland to visit me." A squeal follows Lerato's words as a massive smile spreads across her face.

"Aww, that's so sweet." Paul is her long-distance boyfriend. They met online two years ago, but the way she talks about him, you would think they've known each other their whole lives. They started dating around the same time Lerato started working for me, and it has been an honor watching their relationship blossom.

"Yeah, he's such a sweetheart. God has been so good to us. We're in such a good place at the moment, and I have this feeling that he's going to propose soon." She places one hand on her chest and bites her bottom lip to quiet another squeal.

"Wow, that's great. I'm happy for you." My voice sounds more strained than I'd like, but I ignore it because I'm genuinely happy for Lerato. Stories like this should give me hope that love doesn't always end in heartbreak. But with my first ever relationship ending the way it did, it's hard to hold on to hope sometimes.

"What about you? What will you be doing this weekend?" Lerato asks.

"Well, I'm taking myself on another solo date and I booked a session at the spa tomorrow. I'm also going to attempt some more of my mom's Nigerian recipes. It'll help me relax." That is all true, except the real reason I need to do these things is so I can distract myself from thinking about Alex—especially now that Dad's not with me. The only thing that'll help me is listening to worship music and praying.

"*Eish*, sis, you've spent the last four weekends going on solo dates. We really need to do something together again soon."

I chuckle and shake my head. "Please, girl, don't be in a rush. I actually enjoy my company, you know?"

"Yes, I know, but you need variety in your social life. We should go shopping and watch a movie next weekend. Are you down for that?"

"Of course. You know I can never turn down a date from you."

"Perfect. I'll put that down on the calendar."

"Amazing. I shouldn't keep you any longer. Get out of here and say hello to Paul for me." I shoo her away.

"Thanks, see you Monday." Lerato heads out and I start packing up all my stuff.

"I'm heading off now, Olanna."

I turn around to find Yin standing at the door. "Oh, great. Is everything set for Monday?"

"Yes, I have a meeting with HearCare's SEO representative first thing Monday morning."

We will set up a search engine optimization team at Madu Health soon and this new SEO representative from HearCare will work closely with us. Manny tried to do the SEO on his own when he was managing director here, but I don't like stress and I certainly don't want to put that pressure on Yin.

"That's awesome. How's Jess doing?" I ask.

"She's much better now. It has been a difficult pregnancy, but God has kept her strong. We only have two more months to go and we will be holding our baby boy in our hands. I can't wait." The sparkle in his eyes as he talks about his unborn baby is unexplainable.

"Aww, I'm so excited for you guys. You're not the only one waiting to hold him." We share a laugh as he runs his hand through his dark silky hair and pushes his glasses close to his face. "Well, please go home and give Jess all the cuddles she needs. I'll see you on Monday."

"Good night, boss." Yin waves at me before heading out, leaving me alone with my thoughts.

I want that—all of that. Someone to do life with, to have babies with, to serve God with, and to grow old with. But how can I have that when I can't get over the crippling fear of having my heart broken again? *Lord, please, give me the strength to survive this season and to learn to be happy for others. Amen.*

2

ALEX
THEN

"What game are you playing, man?" Kwame's voice pulls me out of my thoughts and I peel my gaze away from the one girl who has stolen my attention all evening. Given the amount of chatter that always happens after our Wednesday night Ignite Christian fellowship large group meeting, you'd think I would find something else to distract me, but no. Only one girl knows how to keep all my senses engaged.

"Huh?" I frown at my best friend as my jumbled thoughts beg my brain to remember what he was talking about before I started daydreaming.

"How long are you going to keep playing this staring game?"

"What staring game?" I slurp the last of my diet coke and let out a quiet burp before continuing. "I'm not sure what you're talking about."

"Oh, come on, bro." Kwame rolls his eyes and angles his body toward me. "When are you going to tell Olanna you like her?"

"Shhh!" I press my finger against my lips. "You don't have to be so loud." I turn my head slowly to look at her across the room, my breath hitching at the possibility that she might have heard Kwame. But to my relief, Olanna is still immersed in her conversation with Danielle, one of her roommates and close friends. *Thank God for the loud worship music in the background.*

"Well?" I lift my head to find Kwame still staring at me, his arms crossed against his chest and his head tilted to one side as he waits for my response.

"It's not that simple. You know she's way out of my league." I pick up a bag of chips from the snacks table and tear it open, the chili flavor hitting my nostrils and watering my mouth.

"No, I don't know." Kwame shakes his head as I fill my mouth with chips. "That's something you've convinced yourself to believe. How can you like a girl for over a year without telling her? You're torturing yourself."

I snort and cover my mouth to stop the chips from flying out. "Bro, you want to know what torture is? That'll be me telling her I like her and getting a flat out rejection. Dude, I'll have to spend the rest of college avoiding her on campus. That awkwardness is what you call torture."

"But why are you so sure she'll reject you?" Kwame asks before dipping his hands into my bag of chips and bringing a handful to his mouth. "She might like you, you know?"

I tip my head back as if Kwame's words were a bomb that exploded in my face. "Come on, bro. Look at her." I whip my head around so hard I'm surprised I don't get a whiplash. But it doesn't matter because now my attention is back on her—Olanna Madu.

Everything about her captivates me. Among her friends, she always stands out. Her soft-spoken voice is like a sweet melody to my ears. Earlier during the meeting, she stood up to share what she had learned from the Bible study and I didn't want her to stop talking.

I love the way her beautiful shoulder-length dreadlocks

frame her face. They were perfect before when they were black, but they're even more perfect now that she has dyed them burgundy. Her eyes are the perfect shade of brown and they sparkle every time she smiles.

Her small nose ring sparkles every time she moves her head, and it draws my attention to her. When you top it off with how kind and friendly she is to everyone around her, you get the perfect combo to get any guy's attention. She has certainly had my full attention from day one. *She's so beautiful.*

"Alex Yaw Obeng." Kwame's annoying laughter drags me out of cloud nine and I kiss my teeth before rolling my eyes at him. "Look at you. Should I get you a napkin? Because I think I see a drool...right...here." He points at the corners of my mouth as another fit of laughter erupts from his.

Even though I know he's teasing me, I still touch the corners of my mouth to check I wasn't actually drooling. Instead of wiping anything, I end up getting crumbs on my mouth and beard. "Aww, man." I turn away and grab a paper towel before frantically wiping my mouth and my hands. After sending a death glare in Kwame's direction, I wait for him to quiet down from his laughing fit.

"Listen." I lean forward and take on a serious tone. "Girls like Olanna never say yes to just any random guy." I shrug. "She probably already has a boyfriend."

"Okay, you and I both know that's a cop-out." Kwame wags a finger at me. "If she had a boyfriend, we would've heard about him. Danielle is close to India and you know India tells me everything. There's no boyfriend, so just ask her out."

I open my mouth to protest, but I can't think of any more excuses. Olanna is close friends with Danielle and India. India and Kwame have been dating since freshman year and they are pretty close, so if India says there's no boyfriend, I believe her. That doesn't mean things will work out in my favor, though.

"By the way, where is India today?"

Kwame groans at my pathetic attempt to change the subject. "She had a migraine, so she's resting, but I'm not letting you off the hook." Kwame stands and pulls me up with him. "Bro, you've spent the last two years trippin' over this girl, so you're going to talk to her. Right now."

"Whoa. Calm down, bro. Are you for real?"

"Nah yeah, I am for real. It's a new year, and you promised you would do one thing that scares you this year, didn't you?" He places both hands on his hips and widens his eyes at me.

I want to lie that I never made that resolution, but my best friend knows me too well. "Do I have to do it now, though? We can pick a better time when she's not with her friends?"

"Bro, you and I know there'll *never* be a better time." He turns me around and pats my shoulders before pushing me gently forward. "Lead with her hair. Tell her how beautiful she looks and how well the new color suits her. When you've broken the ice, ask her to do something with you."

"What do I ask her to do with me?" My voice drops to a whisper.

"I don't know, a concert, a movie, bowling, lunch? Anything, bro."

"Okay, but you know I'm not a smooth talker like you. I can't do this."

"Oh, wait, look...you're already doing it."

"Okay, but you gotta stay right behind me, bro. Promise?"

"*Gotchu.*"

A tingling sensation settles on my fingers and toes as we near the group of girls in the corner of the room. I scratch the back of my neck with my sweaty palms before rubbing them on my jeans.

Olanna is talking to the other girls, which means if I want to get her attention, I'll need to alert everyone else involved in that conversation. *Come on, Alex. You have nothing to lose except your dignity if she rejects you in front of her friends.*

I take a step forward and open my mouth to speak when Olanna lifts her head and locks eyes with me.

"Hey, Alex," she says with that perfect smile of hers, which always mesmerizes me.

"Hey." I send her a wave, ignoring the other four pairs of eyes looking at me. "Can I talk to you for a minute?" I ask before turning to Kwame for reassurance, but shock hits me right in the face when I spot him across the room speaking to the large group leader at the snacks table.

Narrowing my eyes at him, I shake my head and accept my fate. I can't believe he left me alone on the battlefield when this was his idea.

"Me?" Olanna's voice pulls my gaze back to her as she points a finger to her chest, her eyebrows raised.

"Yeah, if that's okay?" If she says no, then that would be it. I'll just lock myself up in my room and never come out again. *Ever.*

"Erm...sure." She hands her drink to Danielle, who shrugs and nods for her to go ahead. The other girls immediately fall back into their conversation as Olanna and I walk away from the group.

Rubbing my palms together, I glance at Kwame, who averts his gaze and holds back a laugh. *Traitor.* I bite back the word and turn around to face Olanna, her tropical scent wrapping me up in a new world. Olanna's world. This is it. This is the moment. "So...how have you been?"

"I've been good." Her response comes so easily, it helps calm my nerves. "Did you enjoy the session today?"

"Yes, large group meetings have been the highlight of my week since freshman year." I nod, silently praying that the sweat forming under my arms doesn't seep through my t-shirt. "I love what God is doing here. It's beautiful to witness the strong friendships and relationships we're building."

"Yeah, all my close friends are from Ignite fellowship, so I totally get what you mean." She places her hands in the back pocket of her jeans.

"You have a lovely voice, by the way. I heard you singing earlier during the worship session and you sounded great."

"Aww, thank you. You're so sweet." Her grin spreads across her face and I almost want to pat myself on the back for bringing that smile out of her.

Good one, Alex. Oh, the hair. Don't forget the hair. "I also noticed you got a new hair color over the Christmas break. Burgundy looks great on you."

"Really?" She gives me a broad smile this time and twirls one of her loc strands. "That's great to hear, because I wasn't sure how to feel about it at first."

"Well, if I were you, I wouldn't change a thing because it's perfect." *You're perfect for me.* That's all I needed to return to my daydream again, because the painful few seconds of silence that follow speak for themselves.

"Erm, Alex? Was there anything else you wanted to talk to me about?" It's her voice that pulls me out this time.

Okay, here we go. "Ermm...yeah," I clear my throat before it all comes spewing out of me. "Olanna, I'm sorry if this comes across as awkward, because you and I only see each other once or twice a week. We hang out here on campus with our mutual friends, and we laugh and sing and pray together during these large group meetings, but we've never had a one-to-one conversation lasting this long because why would we?" A nervous laugh escapes my lips followed by an understandable confused expression on Olanna's face.

"Okay, I guess what I'm trying to say is that...I'd like to get to know you better and I wondered whether you would like to hang out with me sometime. We could watch a movie, go bowling, or do whatever you want, really?" I shrug and close my mouth with one hand to stop the spilling before I dig a hole for myself.

At first, she gives me a blank stare and I don't blame her. She's probably getting a headache trying to figure out what I'm saying. *I knew this wasn't a good idea. I hate you, Kwame.*

"Wow, are you asking me out on a date?" The fact that a warm smile accompanies her question gives me the boldness to be daring.

"It depends. If I say yes, then will you say yes?" I drag out my words and squint at her, trying to lighten the mood.

She chuckles and tucks a loose strand of hair behind her ear before glancing at her group of friends and then turning back to me.

Okay, here we go. You have nothing to lose. Rejection is not the end. Rejection is not the...

"Sure, I'd love to."

Shock wounds through my entire body as her words leave me so stunned, I start questioning whether I'm having auditory hallucinations. "I'm sorry, what?"

More chuckles escape her lips again. *A sweet, sweet melody to my ears.* "I said, 'sure, I'd love to.' It'd be nice to get to know you better too, Alex. You seem like a nice guy."

She thinks I'm nice? "For real?" It's taking the grace of God not to burst with excitement right now because what just happened? "Great. I'll text you." I'm about to leap for joy like the lame beggar the disciples Peter and John healed at the Beautiful Gate, when Olanna's voice stops me.

"Wait, don't you need my number?" Her chuckles intensify when I send her a sheepish smile.

"Of course I do," I say before we swap phones and save our numbers. The minutes that follow feel like an out-of-body experience because when Olanna returns to her friends and I walk back over to Kwame, I no longer feel like killing him for betraying me.

He must have noticed the joy in my eyes because, without even saying a word, he pulls me into the hallway and we both jump for joy, followed by chest bumps and fist pumps all the way.

3

OLANNA

NOW

The front door swings open, and Manny's smiling face greets me. "Hey, Trouble." He teases me by going for the nickname I've told him countless times not to call me by.

"Hey, Manny." I push him to the side and let myself into the house, ignoring his out-stretched arms.

"Oh, come on. Don't be like that." He chuckles and closes the door. "What's the point of coming all the way here if you won't give your brother a hug?"

I turn around and raise my brows at him. "And who says I'm here to see you?"

He feigns a gasp and wipes invisible tears away from his eyes.

"Yeah, that's right. Now, you can get a taste of your own medicine." I place a hand on my hip and tap my feet on the carpeted floor. "You know the drill. Go get my princess, please." I raise the plastic bag in my hands to show him the new baby clothes I bought.

Manny lets out a sigh and runs a palm down his face. "You never listen, do you? You don't have to buy clothes for Ayannah every week. She will outgrow them soon and then—"

"Okay, let me stop you right there." I raise my palm, cutting him short. "I'm her god-mother, so I can spoil her anytime I want. I'm also building my reputation as the coolest aunt ever. Stop trying to steal my thunder and go get my niece, please."

"*Ugh*, you're so annoying." Manny whips his head around and takes dramatic steps toward the flight of stairs. "Heather was just giving her a bath. I'll go get them."

"Thank you." I stick my tongue out at him and he rolls his eyes at me before he disappears from my view, leaving me alone in the room. Heather and Manny's spacious three-bedroom house has been my second home since they got married two years ago.

It's much fancier than the two bedroom apartment he was renting as a stressed bachelor and workaholic. It's true what they say, that it's important to marry the right person. Manny has been so much happier since he married Heather.

I place the bag of clothes on the sofa and plop down on it, the soft texture instantly taking away the tension from my muscles. Leaning back and spreading my arms across the sofa, I take a deep breath in, inhaling the delicious aroma of spaghetti bolognese hanging in the air.

One thing I can confidently say about myself is that no matter how rough my day has been, good food usually cheers me up. Heather is a great cook, so I know I won't be leaving this house as sad as I came. Well, I hope Heather's food works its magic because today was *rough*.

Unwilling to let myself go down the dark Alex black hole, I sweep my gaze around the room, focusing on different objects to keep me distracted. But the first object sabotages my mission before it even starts. It's a beautiful framed photo of Manny and Heather on their traditional wedding day.

Even though Heather is not African, she has completely embraced our Nigerian culture, and she killed her looks as an

Igbo bride. For her first outfit, she wore coral beads in her auburn hair and the colors blended so well together. The *gele* she wore for her second outfit was the icing on the cake that day and I'm sure their wedding was the topic of discussion for a lot of Nigerian aunties for months—as it should've been—because it was nothing short of beautiful.

Alex and I used to talk about marriage so much that I was sure he was going to be the one I end up with. I can't count the number of times I imagined our Nigerian-Ghanaian wedding, the blend of colors, delicious food, glorious outfits, incredible dances, culture, tradition, and, of course, the drama that comes with it.

It seemed too good to be true that the first man I ever fell in love with would end up being my husband. But I believed it was true because God never revealed otherwise every time I prayed about it.

But maybe I was wrong. Maybe what I thought was God's approval was really His disapproval. Maybe it really was just what it was—too good to be true.

Phoebe, Heather and Manny's ginger cat, scurries across the living room as she chases after a ball of string. Her fascination with the object is so cute to watch and it draws a chuckle from my lips. But then the sound of approaching footsteps zaps my attention away from the cat and back to the present moment.

"Look who's here," Manny says as he comes into full view, holding his nine-month-old daughter in his arms.

"Hello, my love." I stretch my arms out to Ayannah and the big smile that appears on her face at the sight of me warms my heart. She wiggles in her father's arms and leans forward until I'm able to scoop her up in a big hug. She wraps her arms around my neck and rubs spittle on my forehead as she plays with my locs. She loves me.

"Aww, thank you so much for the clothes, Olanna." Heather walks in wearing an oversized t-shirt over black leggings. Her auburn hair is up in a sleek bun and her bangs are almost covering her eyes. "You can see she's returning all the love you're pouring on her." Heather nods to the baby, who is still playing with my hair.

"I know, right? My plan is working." I grin at Manny, and he rolls his eyes for the umpteenth time today.

"Yes, and it's giving rich aunty vibes." Heather clicks her fingers and we both chuckle.

"That's right. You're going to be the most spoiled baby ever, aren't you, Ayannah?" I kiss her forehead and run my hands through her soft, curly brown hair, which smells like coconut. She's the light-skinned spitting image of Manny, but she clearly has Heather's green eyes. *Magical.*

"Alright, let me try to take her to bed and then we can have dinner." Heather stands up and takes the bag of clothes from me before pausing again. "By the way, I was on the phone with Amara and Teeyana earlier today."

I gasp, sitting up in my chair. "Really? How are they doing?"

"They're doing great. Amara's bump has popped now. She says the twins are very active."

"Aww, that's awesome. I can't believe Amara will be a twin mama. More kids to shower my love on."

"I know, right." Heather takes Ayannah from me and after another round of cuddles and kisses, she takes the baby upstairs, leaving Manny and me alone in the living room.

"So, how's everything going at Charis?" I ask Manny as he sits next to me on the sofa. He doesn't like talking about work at home, but it's the only thing I can do to distract myself right now.

"It was a very busy few weeks. You should have seen Heather

and I running around like headless chickens." We both chuckle. "Our staff was brilliant, and they sacrificed so much to help with the move. But we have finally settled into our new office space and I'm excited to see where God takes us."

"Aww, I'm so proud of you, Manny." I squeeze his hand. "Can you imagine that two years ago, you were so afraid of taking that leap of faith? Look at how far God has brought you and Heather."

"Yeah, I know. But you don't have to keep reminding me about how much of a coward I was. Cut me some slack, please."

"If I cut you some slack, would you have a reason to call me *Trouble*?"

"*Aha*, I knew you secretly liked that nickname." He pushes me with his shoulder and we both laugh.

Manny and Heather have come such a long way. Dad thought Manny would be the one to take over Madu Health as the CEO. But God had other plans for him. Manny and Heather set up their own business—Charis Charity Marketing shortly after they started dating and they've been doing amazing work helping Christian charities in Nigeria, Africa, and all around the world.

"By the way, Heather and I are planning another trip to Nigeria in December. We'll be meeting with Mr. Nwaeze and the team at AWC. Have you changed your mind about coming with us?"

Okay, someone give me a break, please.

"No." The finality in my tone sends silence stretching between us. I know Manny wouldn't press any further because he understands. He has his own way of grieving Mom's death and he respects mine.

A Widow's Comfort is a charity that was founded by Mom in Nigeria to support widows, single mothers, and their children.

Since setting up their business, Heather and Manny have been heavily involved in running the charity and they plan yearly trips to Nigeria to catch up with the team.

"Speaking of Nigeria," Manny breaks the silence. "I see you couldn't change Dad's mind about going, huh?" He turns his head to meet my gaze.

I sigh and cross my arms against my chest. "Of course I couldn't. You know your father. I'm trying not to worry about it, though. God will take care of him, right?"

Manny nods. "Of course He will. There's nothing to worry about." He pauses before continuing. "Are you okay?"

And that's all he needs to ask to have my thoughts held captive again by memories of Alex. I shake my head and open my mouth to lie because I didn't plan to talk about this tonight. I just wanted to come over here and have dinner and Bible study, before going back home to cry myself to sleep. But the tears are saying no as they blur my vision.

Manny must have recognized the shift in my mood because, without asking, he takes my hand and leads me across the living room, past his plant sanctuary and outside to the balcony—my favorite place in this house. He urges me to sit in one of the chairs and takes the seat across from me. The chilly October air is enough to make me shiver, but Manny throws a blanket over my shoulders, so it's bearable.

"Talk to me, Olanna. What happened? Did someone say or do something to you at work? Just give me a name and I'll deal with them right away." His serious, big brother, protective persona bursts forth and his jaw tenses as he balls his hands into fists.

A tear rolls down my cheek and I swipe it away before taking the box of tissues from Manny. "It's October." I sniffle and dab my face with tissue paper. "Next week will be two years since

Alex broke up with me. Last year was horrible because I spent the whole day in bed looking through our messages, listening to our voice notes, and going through all the photos we took." My bottom lip quivers and I swallow the lump in my throat.

"This year, I thought it would be different, you know? I thought I had moved on, but clearly not." I shake my head as more tears fall. I lower my head and fidget with the tissue box in my hands because I don't want to see the look of pity in Manny's eyes.

"It's been two years and the emotions are still as fresh as the day he let me walk out of his life. Why do I feel like I did something to push him away? It's been two years and I still feel the ache in my chest—the same way I did when Mom died. If only I could see her again or hear her beautiful voice singing to me, then perhaps everything will be okay. What is wrong with me, Manny?" The sobs explode from me as I cover my face, my shoulders shaking violently and my hands trembling like someone who has had twenty cups of coffee.

"Nothing is wrong with you, sis. I miss Mom too...every day." Manny sits on the arm of my chair and wraps his arm around me, before letting me cry on his chest. "It hurts because you're human. God gave you the ability to feel all these emotions. It hurts because you love Mom." He lifts my chin up so I can look at him. "It hurts because you loved Alex, too.

"Please, don't blame yourself for what happened. Alex is a grown man and he should've taken responsibility for his actions. He had the opportunity to redeem himself and spare you a lot of pain, but he didn't. I know it hurts, but you can't control other people's actions. So let yourself feel these emotions. But know that someday, you will meet someone much better.

"Someone who will treat you right and be your answered prayer. Let yourself feel these emotions, but know that God will heal your heart. It doesn't matter how long it takes. Go at your own pace. God will give you the peace that your heart is longing for." Manny holds me tight and rocks me back and forth until my sobs quiet down. That's when I hear the soft whispers from his lips and I look up to find his head bowed and his eyes closed as he silently prays for me.

4

OLANNA
THEN

A frustrated sigh escapes my lips for the umpteenth time as I stare at the display of clothes on my bed. I was so sure I wanted to wear the white off-the-shoulder top, but now the purple halter neck looks more appealing. Don't even get me started on the gorgeous, black one-shoulder blouse. *Ugh, why is this so hard?*

For someone who has never had a problem choosing an outfit, this is beyond me. It's just Alex. Alex, who I see at our large group meetings every Wednesday night and who I sometimes hang out with on campus, mainly because of India. I've never cared about how he perceives me, so why has everything changed?

I pause as the answers come flooding into my brain. Of course, he's no longer just Alex from large group meetings. He is now Alex Obeng, the guy who likes me. My stomach twists into knots and I take deep breaths before lowering myself onto the bed. *Lord Jesus, please help me.*

"I'm back." My bedroom door swings open as Danielle strolls in with her backpack slung over her shoulder. *Is she the answer to my prayer?*

Danielle, India, and I met at Ignite in freshman year, and we became inseparable. We got an apartment together in sophomore year and we've been living together since then. India majors in education, Danielle in marketing, and I in business management. Our difference in majors has never affected our bond and we've been supporting and encouraging each other since the beginning.

Danielle stops in the middle of the room and takes in the surroundings before raising her brows at me. "You haven't chosen an outfit yet?"

I drop my shoulders and cover my face with my hands. "No, I'm so confused. I don't know what to wear and...and..."

"Okay, okay, okay. Calm down. Danielle to the rescue." She places her backpack on my bed and rushes to my side. "Do you know where he's taking you?"

I shake my head slowly. "He just called to say he'll pick me up at six. I should've asked him where we're going or whether I should dress casual or smart, but my brain wasn't working properly because of all the stupid butterfly feelings in my stomach."

"Aww, you're so cute." Danielle chuckles and flips her curly blonde hair to the side. "I don't blame you, though. If a cute guy asks me out too, I think I would react in exactly the same way."

There's a soft knock on my door and India pokes her head in. "Did someone send for reinforcements?" She enters the room showcasing the bag of chocolate cake balls she bought.

"Oh, God bless you for that." Danielle grabs the bag from India's hand and starts tearing through it.

"So...have you picked your outfit yet?" India asks, placing both hands on her curvy hips.

"Nope," Danielle says before stuffing her mouth with two white chocolate balls. The girl has such a sweet tooth.

"Well, what are you waiting for? You have to start trying them on. Alex will be here in..." She taps her phone screen.

"Three hours, seven minutes and twenty-three seconds, and he will not find us slacking, so come on."

"Yes, Ma'am." I grab the black one-shoulder blouse and start putting it on. India has always been the organized one in the group. Danielle can be too, but she gets easily distracted by everything—like a bag of chocolate balls. India hates time wasting, and she's always prompt. I owe my ability to make it to eight AM classes to her.

"You want one?" Danielle offers me a peanut-butter-covered chocolate ball and I shake my head, drawing a gasp from both girls.

"Is everything okay? That's your favorite snack." India takes a few steps toward me, concern etched in her features.

"Yeah, she's just nervous about the date, that's all," Danielle responds on my behalf.

"Really?" India raises her brows. "Why?" she asks, fixing the bangs of her teeny weeny afro.

I shrug. "It's my first date and this whole situation came to me as a surprise. What if I mess it up?"

"Trust me, honey. You won't mess it up." India turns me around to look at my full-length mirror. She tilts her head and says, "This looks cute, but maybe not for a first date? What do you think?"

I nod. "Yeah, I prefer color."

Danielle nods too, in between bites.

"Girl, if you finish those chocolate balls, I promise you, we'll fight." India squints at Danielle, who lowers the bag on the bed and scoots forward to sit on the edge of the bed.

"Why are you so sure I won't mess it up?" I ask India as I take off the black top.

"Because Alex likes you too much to change his mind," India responds casually, as if this information was general knowledge.

"Really? How do you know this?"

"Because Kwame told me everything," India responds. "Alex has liked you since freshman year. Kwame says he thinks highly of you and always thought you were way out of his league. That's why he was scared to ask you out. Last week at the large group meeting, Kwame literally had to force him to speak to you. I wish I didn't have a stupid migraine that day because I would have *loved* to see the whole thing go down."

Why does he think I'm out of his league? It's only me. Olanna Madu. "How long have you known that Alex likes me?"

India shrugs and lowers her head. "Since Kwame told me a year ago."

I gasp. "A year?"

"Yes, but..." India raises a hand. "You know I don't like meddling. I didn't think it was my place to tell you. I hoped and prayed Alex would come to his senses and tell you about it, so thank God for Kwame." India and Danielle giggle.

"My sister once told me about a guy at her workplace who liked her for five years, but he didn't tell her until she handed in her notice," Danielle says.

"Really? What did she say?" I ask.

"She didn't have a boyfriend at the time, so she agreed to go on a date with him and they've been married now for two years," Danielle responds.

"Aww, that's a cute love story." India places both hands on her chest. "Olanna, that could be your story, too."

"Yeah, that's true." I put on the purple halter neck top and turn to face the mirror. "I'm glad Alex didn't wait five years. I might be nervous, but I have to admit I'm also excited. He seems like a nice guy. Right?" I turn to face the girls and they both nod.

"He's very sweet, and it seems like he genuinely loves God," India adds.

"Yeah, and don't forget about the fact that he's *very* good-looking." Danielle giggles.

"Yeah, and very funny. I like guys who are funny." A warm sensation explodes in my abdomen and spreads down my feet before curling my toes. "This is nice," I say, smoothing the purple top.

"Yeah, I like it." The girls agree, but by the time I try on the white off-shoulder top, we all agree by the way our eyes sparkle that it's the one to go for.

"Now, about your hair," India says, "do you want to wear the locs down, do a half up, half down, or bangs and a bun?"

I tilt my head and tap my chin with my finger. "I never do bangs, so let's go for that and give the boy an element of surprise, shall we?"

"Yeah, baby." India grins and in less than an hour, I'm all dressed, hair and makeup done and ready to go.

India clicks her fingers as I turn around to show them my complete look. "If Alex doesn't gawk when he sees you, then sis, he ain't the one."

"Amen to that," Danielle adds, and we all burst out laughing.

When the doorbell rings at six PM on the dot, Danielle and India have to pin me to the sofa in the living room, so I don't go flying to the front door.

"Relax, honey. You don't want him thinking you've been desperately waiting for six PM, do you?" India says.

"But I *have* been waiting desperately for six PM to come around." My voice comes out more high-pitched than I'd like.

"Yeah, true, but he doesn't need to know that." India winks at me before walking to the door and leaving me with Danielle, who squeezes my hand.

India disappears round the corner and the door clicks open shortly after. "Hey, Alex." India's voice fades to the background and all I can hear is the deep husk of Alex's voice, which sets off the butterflies in my stomach again.

"Sure, come on in," India says and the door closes.

Danielle and I stand and she pulls me close to her as if she's trying to stop me from running away. I'm still grateful for her supportive hand squeeze because it stops me from squealing when Alex walks round the corner looking all handsome in his white sweater and black jeans.

"Wow." He stops in his tracks when his gaze lands on me and in the intensity of that moment, I don't realize when Danielle lets go of my hand and she and India go back to sit on the sofa. Alex steps closer and holds my hand, the warmth of his grasp sending tingling sensations through my body.

"You look great," he says and heat flashes up my cheeks.

My words elude me, so I just stare at him, smiling like a fool, until India clears her throat and wakes me up from my reverie.

"Thank you." I finally respond and avert my gaze, trying to hide my embarrassment.

"Well, she's all yours," India says, linking arms with Danielle.

"Enjoy." Danielle waves at us as we close the door.

Outside in the cold, Alex places one hand on the small of my back and opens the car door for me. *Ooh Alex, the gentleman. We love to see it.*

Not long into our car ride, the nerves take over me and while Alex focuses on his driving, saliva dries out from my mouth. I resist the urge to pull down the car mirror to check that my bangs are still in the right place or that my lipstick is not smudged. *Calm down, Olanna. You look great.*

I take a deep breath in and close my eyes for a few seconds. That's when the calming beats of the worship music gets to my ears. "Ooh, I love this song," I say out loud, expelling the silence.

"You do?" A wide grin spreads across his face. "Me too." He turns up the volume and we sing the lyrics out loud, waving our hands in the air and Alex occasionally doing beatboxing inter-ludes, which makes me chuckle.

"Do you beatbox to worship songs at church, too?"

"Not out loud, or I'll probably get death glares."

"No doubt." We both laugh and for the rest of the fifteen minute drive away from campus, our conversation flows so effortlessly that I'm disappointed when the ride ends.

"Here we are," Alex says as he pulls into a parking lot.

"Wow, I don't think I've ever been in this part of the city."

"Really? I've been here a few times with Kwame and some other boys from Ignite."

"Cool. So where are we?"

He lets out a sharp exhale before speaking. "Okay, before I tell you, I have a confession to make."

My heart sinks at the word *confession*, but I shake away any negative thoughts, trying to pry their way into my mind. "Okay? What is it?"

He fiddles with the car keys before angling his body toward me. "I've never been on a date before."

"Aww." I lean forward. "Me neither, so we're good."

He smiles and relaxes his shoulders. "That takes some of the pressure off." He nods. "I wasn't expecting you to say yes to me last week, so I freaked out a little because I had no idea what sort of things you like to do. I went on the internet and printed out an A-Z list of fun date ideas." He pulls out the folded piece of paper from his pocket. "For today, I thought we'd start with number one on that list," he says, pointing to the sign in the building in front of us.

I crane my neck and squint my eyes to read the letters on the sign and when realization dawns on me, I gasp. "We're at the arcade center?" I turn to him with a wide grin on my face.

"Yeah. Do you like it?"

"Are you kidding? I *love* arcade games. My dad used to take my brother and I when we were kids and we used to be so competitive that we would fight each other."

Alex laughs. "You won't fight me if I win, will you?"

I tilt my head. "Well, you'll have to beat me first though, won't you?"

He narrows his eyes and nods. "Bring it on." He gets out of the car and walks around it to open the door for me. Then he extends his hand and helps me out of the car. His lavender scent wraps around me as we both walk toward the building. *I love it when a guy smells good.*

"Hope you're not cold?" he asks as I try to keep up with his strides.

I shake my head and wrap my jacket around me. "No, I'm okay. Thank you."

Inside the building, nostalgia hits me as I glance at all the different games. It's just like I remember it; several coin-operated entertainment machines, lights, colors, music, crying children, laughing, and lots of cheering.

When Alex asks what game I want to play first, I'm spoiled for choice. Starting with pinball, we move on to Pac-Man, then air hockey, basketball, and foosball.

"How does it feel to be beaten by a girl?" I gloat at Alex while we're waiting for our order at the food hall.

He shrugs and turns to me. "I don't mind. I'm still a winner because I'm here on a date with you. That's my prize."

Aww.

My mind hasn't finished savoring his words when the server calls out our order. He declines my offer to carry one of the trays and instead leads me to a table for two and places both trays on them.

I take a seat across from him, enjoying the princess treatment I'm getting, even though part of me feels guilty that I'm letting him do all the work. But if he's doing it with all his heart, then I won't feel guilty about letting him be a gentleman.

"Hmm, that smells so good." I inhale the aroma from the burger, curly fries, and chicken filets.

"It tastes even better," Alex says after a bite into his double chicken and cheese burger.

I pick up a fry and swipe it on the blob of barbecue sauce on my plate before putting it in my mouth. "Can I ask a question?"

"Sure." He sips on his orange juice.

"Why do you like me?" I meet his unwavering gaze and the smile that spreads across his face is so charming I can watch him smile for the rest of the evening and I'll be satisfied.

"Because you're beautiful, inside and out. You have a kind heart. Your friends love you."

"Okay?" I touch the nape of my neck as a warm sensation travels up. "Keep talking," I respond with a smile.

"I've been watching you for over a year now, but not in a creepy way. I'm not a stalker or anything like that. I've just seen the way you interact with others, how proactive you are at Ignite and how the love of Jesus radiates through you. It's beautiful to see and I've found it really difficult not to be drawn to you."

Aww. How many times can this guy make me blush in one evening? "Where did you learn these sweet talks from? Was it Kwame?"

He sits back and laughs. "My best friend is a well-known sweet talker, I'll give him that. But actually, I learned this from my dad. From the years of watching him continuously woo my mom."

"That's adorable. How long have they been married?"

"Twenty-five years. But if you see the way he makes her laugh, you'd think they are high school sweethearts. My mom always tells me stories about when my dad used cheesy pickup lines to get her to marry him when they were in Ghana."

"Really? Like which one?"

"Like calling her the *jollofiest* jollof rice and the sweetest plantain he has ever eaten. He also once told her that her beauty is so tantalizing that he wants to buy her a sewing machine."

"Huh?" I snort. "Is she a fashion designer or something?"

"No. She has no interest in sewing, but apparently that's what her beauty does to him."

"Wow." The laughter and cackles that follow our conversation are so intense, tears leak from the corner of my eyes. "Your dad is so hilarious. I can see where you get your sense of humor from."

Alex gives himself a pat on the shoulder before rubbing his beard. "It's my pleasure, Ma'am."

At the end of our date, Alex parks in front of our apartment and disappointment weighs on my heart because the night is over. I have nothing to compare this date to, but this has set the bar really high. "I had so much fun tonight. Thank you."

Alex walks with me to the front door and I stop him from getting too close because I know India and Danielle have their ears pressed against the door right now.

"So, did I pass the test to earn a second date?" Alex places his hands in his pockets as his gaze drops to the floor. It's so adorable when he does that.

Of course. The words leap to the tip of my tongue, but I hold them back, so I don't sound desperate. Instead, I tilt my head and tap my chin with my finger. "Hmm. I'll have to think about that."

When he lifts his head to look at me, his pleading gaze reminds me of Danielle's puppy when he wants to play fetch.

"Just kidding." I lean in and touch his arm. "I'd love to go on a second date with you."

"Yes!" He lifts his fisted hands above his head.

"So, what will the next date be?"

"Don't worry, I can pick a random one from the list for the element of surprise," he says. "Or we can go through the list together and pick one?"

"No, I trust you and I love surprises."

"That's good, because I love surprising you." He smiles and takes my hand in his. "Goodnight, Olanna." He leans forward and closes the gap between us, and this is the moment where everything changes.

The guy standing in front of me is no longer just Alex, the guy I see every week at large group meetings, but Alex, the first guy who kissed my cheek. *Oh, and did I mention the goosebumps?* That's right. Alex, the first guy who kissed my cheek and gave me goosebumps.

5

ALEX
NOW

I believe in second chances, but I can't figure out whether God created this second chance for me. While I'm looking forward to seeing Olanna again, it would be selfish of me to expect her to take me back after how much I hurt her. But my selfish heart can't help it.

I'd give anything to hold her in my arms again, but since I hurt her so much, she's probably better off without me. Either way, I can't let this answered prayer go to waste. I need to give Olanna closure. She deserves it.

"Here's your key, sir. I hope you enjoy your stay with us." The receptionist smiles at me as she hands me the key to my apartment.

"Thank you." I force a smile with the last bit of strength left in me and swing my backpack over my shoulder before dragging my suitcase toward the elevator.

Up on the third floor, I'm relieved to find that my apartment is the first one on the left. That'll save me the energy of walking all the way down the hallway on days when all I want to do is get back quickly to rest.

Inside the studio apartment, the smell of fresh fragranced

sheets hits my nostrils and the warm air wraps around me like a hug. The gray comforter matches the gray sofas leaning against the window, while the yellow pillow covers match the yellow lamps and curtains.

The living area has a smart TV, and they furnished the kitchenette with a microwave, a stove, and some kitchen utensils tucked away in the cupboard. At least I have all the necessary tools if I crave a home cooked meal. I'll just need to shop for groceries later and I'll be sorted.

I turn on the bedside lamp and the lamp above the desk area before putting my suitcase in the wardrobe. After placing my backpack on the desk chair, I lower myself on the bed, the softness of the mattress promising me a good night's sleep. Hear-Care must be paying a lot of money to keep me here for three months, but I'm not complaining. I'm exactly where I need to be because I'll be seeing Olanna soon.

Olanna Gloria Madu. Just thinking about her right now brings back all the memories that have taunted me for the last two years. To this day, I chide myself for letting her go the way I did. She didn't deserve it. That's why I tried to make amends. That's why I tried to meet up with her so many times in our senior year of college. But she was always with Danielle or India and they all made it clear Olanna didn't want to see me.

After she blocked my number, I emailed her so many times and even tried reaching out to her on different social media platforms after college graduation. But some things are better said in person, and perhaps that is what God is trying to teach me in this season.

It wasn't a coincidence that out of everyone HearCare could've picked for this project, they chose me to come to Jersey City even though I've only been working in their SEO department for a year. It also wasn't a coincidence that out of all the companies they could've sent me to, they picked Madu Health.

I still remember the shock on my face when my boss told me about this project. Olanna mentioned the name of their family business a few times while we were together. I knew she was looking forward to working with her dad and brother, but finding out she's now the CEO of Madu Health makes me so happy for her.

I should've been there with her to celebrate all her achievements, but I chose otherwise, and it sucks. Reliving those moments is the last thing I want to do. But it's important that I remind myself of everything I did, so I can understand her reaction when I finally explain everything to her.

I let out a sigh and walk to the desk before putting on the kettle. After making myself a cup of hot chocolate, I tear open the packet of cookies and take it over to the sofa. After one sip of the hot beverage, I add more sugar before leaning back and staring at the view outside my window.

Being in this apartment and looking at this view feels like a glimpse into the future, where I'm running a successful SEO business, living in my own penthouse apartment while following God's lead and sharing that journey with the woman I love. It would be a miracle if that woman turns out to be Olanna.

The last time Olanna and I looked at the New York skyline and the view of the Hudson River together, we hoped that our future would be filled with laughter and never-ending friendship—a friendship I destroyed because of my selfishness. I didn't expect my life to take a turn for the worse like it did in senior year. I never imagined myself making Olanna suffer because I couldn't handle the events of my past.

The look in Olanna's eyes on college graduation day will forever be etched in my memory. Her brown eyes have always been my favorite feature about her. It was so easy to make her laugh and bring out the sparkle in them. But on that day, as she stared at me across the crowd of celebrants, there were no sparkles left in them. She only stared at me for five seconds, but it was long enough to notice the tears that formed in her eyes before she averted her gaze and continued speaking to her family.

I should've been there with her, celebrating with her and getting to know her brother and dad. She was so excited for me to meet them. But I take responsibility for everything that happened because I put those tears in her eyes. I have to do everything I can to make it right.

"Please, Jesus. Help me obey You." I close my eyes and whisper to my God—the One who has shown me the error of my ways. "I don't want to cause Olanna any more pain."

Alex, my beloved. I am with you. Trust Me.

I trust You, Lord. I don't know what You have planned, but I know Your hand is in this. Please help me not to give up when the road gets rough.

6

ALEX
THEN

I f I had known it would be this easy to make Olanna laugh, I would've asked her to go out with me the first day I set my eyes on her. I can't get enough of her perfect brown eyes and I could get lost in them without caring much about finding my way back.

I've looked forward to this moment for so long that it now feels like a dream that's too good to be true. But I know it's not a dream because every time she leans in close to me, the scent of her tropical perfume wafts into my nostrils, alerting me to the realness of her presence.

I know it's not a dream because every time she laughs at my jokes, the happiness in her voice is so contagious it makes me laugh too, even though I don't think my jokes are funny. If this was a dream, I wouldn't be able to feel her warmth when she holds my hand. I can't believe at one point in my life all I could do was wonder what it would be like to be this close to her. God has answered my prayer ten thousand times over.

"This one looks interesting." Olanna tugs on my arm while pointing at a painting on the wall. Our first stop today is the art gallery. We both have never been to one before, but since we're still on the A section of our A-Z date ideas list, we thought this would be a cool thing to explore together.

The gallery has white walls all around, which makes the paintings, photographs and sculptures stand out more. We initially started our tour with a group, but as time passed, we lagged, trying to figure out the meaning behind the art ourselves instead of listening to the tour guide. It has been more fun that way, if I do say so myself.

"I love the pastel colored squares," Olanna says, still looking at the painting.

"Yeah, the colors might look random, but..." I take a step back and tilt my head. "Maybe the artist was intentional about the position of each color to convey a specific message?"

She takes a step back too and tilts her head, her locs grazing my shoulder. "Hmm. Nah, the position of the colors looks quite random to me." She giggles. "But the pattern is very pretty. I think I have a rug with a similar pattern, actually."

"Really?" I smile and rub my beard before lowering my voice. "Do you think you can bring your rug so we can swap it and sell this original piece for millions of dollars?"

She gasps and swats my arm. "Alex Obeng."

"Ouch." I rub my arm as we both laugh out loud.

"Are you trying to recruit me for a heist operation?" She leans in and rests her hand on my chest.

"Well, am I convincing you?" I wink at her, waiting for her giggles to settle.

"You are, but I have to warn you. Mr. Chijioke Madu will be waiting on the other side to send you to jail for being a bad influence on me."

I shrug. "I'll go to jail for you any day, girl."

"*Ugh*, there you go again with your cheesy lines." She rolls her eyes and walks ahead of me, and I follow closely behind her.

Come on Alex, come up with something less cheesy now, will you?

"I think this is the last one." Olanna points at the black-and-white photograph of a woman and a child playing in an open field. "This was more fun than I thought it'd be," Olanna says after we agree the artist was probably trying to capture the love between a mother and her son.

I take her hand in mine as we make our way toward the exit, meandering our way through the crowd of people who are all fascinated by the artwork. "Do you think it was fun because of the artwork or the company?"

She flips her loc strands over her shoulder and smiles. "I'd say both...but most especially the company."

"I'm very relieved to hear that, because I feel the same way." We step out of the art gallery and take a left turn, making our way to the next stop for today—the ferry ride. I thought we'd go down the A-Z list in a chronological order, but where's the fun in that?

Some things you're sure to find on the streets of Manhattan are the yellow cabs, newsstands, and power-walking pedestrians. While many people might not be a fan of the busy way of life in the city, it's this fast pace that reminds me to slow down and focus on God. I can't imagine myself living away from this buzz. But I was born and raised in New York, so you can't blame me.

"It's so cool that the ferry ride is free," Olanna says when we're on the subway.

"Yeah, and I can't believe you've never been on it."

"I can't believe you've been on it twelve times. Don't you ever get bored with the scenery?"

"Mmm hmm." I shake my head. "When you see the view for yourself, you'll understand why."

Half an hour later, we get out of the subway and make our way to the Whitehall terminal just in time for the next departure. The iconic orange ferry shuttles people back and forth from Manhattan to Staten Island and I can't wait for Olanna's reaction when she has a closer look at the Statue of Liberty.

"This is my favorite spot." I point to a space at the metal barriers when we arrive on the top deck. People are already filling up the empty spaces along the barrier, while others are sitting in the chairs behind us.

When the ferry starts moving, the sun's rays reflect on the ripples of the water below and God has smiled on us today by blessing us with blue skies at the end of January. Olanna shivers as a gust of wind travels past, so I stand behind her and wrap my arms around her waist, pulling her close to my body.

"Better?" I ask and she leans her head back and rests it on my shoulder.

"Much better," she responds, and we soak in the skyline's view in silence.

While watching the sun set in the distance, I grab the opportunity to find out more about her family. "So, are you and your dad close?"

She nods. "Yes. He and my older brother, Manny, are very protective of me. As the only girl and my father's princess, they could literally break bones on my behalf." She laughs.

"Wow, so I have a lot of work to do to get on their good side, then?"

She shrugs before turning to look at me. "Well, not really. You're a good guy, and it wouldn't take long for them to see why I like you."

"Hmm...so you like me now, huh?" I grin.

"Come on, if I didn't, I wouldn't be here, would I?" She raises her brows at me as if to say that was a ridiculous question.

"That's true. What about your mom? Is she protective of you, too?" I ask and the smile fades from Olanna's face as sadness replaces the sparkle in her eyes.

"My mom died in a car accident when she visited my home country, Nigeria, two years ago."

"Oh. I'm so sorry." I take her hand in mine.

"It's okay." She exhales, and then her smile returns. "It still hurts, but I'm choosing to look on the bright side. Grief has strengthened my relationship with my brother and my dad. Manny is working hard to take over our family's healthcare marketing company when my dad retires. The plan is for me to work with them too, after I graduate."

"I'm glad you're counting your blessings." I plant a kiss on her hand. "I'm here to cheer you on every step of the way."

"I appreciate that, Alex," she says. "Enough about me. What about you? I know about your parents, but do you have any siblings?"

I lean against the metal bar so I can protect her from the wind blowing into her hair. "No. I'm the only child of my parents. I was born in Ghana, but my parents moved to New York when I was only a baby, so I don't remember anything about Ghana. My parents promised me a vacation trip to Ghana after college graduation, so I can get the chance to connect to my African roots. I'm really looking forward to it."

"Yeah...good for you." She drops her gaze from my face. "I wish I could relate to your enthusiasm," she whispers.

"What was that?"

She lifts her head again and shakes it. "Hmm? Oh, never mind. I'm happy for you. Look." She points in the distance as the view of the Statue of Liberty gets bigger and then she whips out her phone to take photos. I want to press in a little further, because I can't shake the feeling there's something bothering her. But I choose to hold my peace for now. If it's something diffi-cult for her to talk about, then I don't want to ruin this beautiful moment with my questions.

I take a few photos of her for her social media platforms and after finding the one she is happy with, she takes a few of me too. Then we take some selfies together with the Statue of Liberty as our backdrop before spending the rest of our time talking and, most importantly, laughing.

"I see what you mean," she says when we're staring at the view again. "It's very beautiful."

The time passes by with the blink of an eye and soon, we're back at Whitehall terminal where we started. We stop by a taco truck to buy dinner before getting the subway back to campus.

"I had an amazing time today, Alex," Olanna says as we hold hands, walking to her apartment, which is ten minutes away from campus. "Thank you for showing me what I'm missing in New York. It's amazing how much you can still discover about a city you've been studying in for two years."

"Yeah, that's why you have me." We stand face to face at her front door when my nerves take over me. As I try to pick the right words out of the jumbled thoughts in my brain, Olanna's charming smile and sparkling gaze calm me down.

When I think about godly marriage examples, I think about my mom and dad and how much they love each other. I want to share that kind of love with someone someday. But if I want to have a marriage like Mom and Dad, it has to start from somewhere—this very moment.

"Olanna..." I squeeze both her hands and stare into her eyes. "I don't know about you, but these last few weeks have intensified feelings I've never felt for anyone before." I take a deep breath and continue. "These feelings didn't start when I asked you out on a date. I've liked you for the last two years."

"Yeah, India told me about that." She smiles. "She said Kwame told her."

"Of course he did," I mutter under my breath before smiling back at her. "Look, Olanna, I don't know what love is supposed to feel like or what people mean when they say they are falling in love with someone. But I know I care deeply about you and I want the best for you. I'm not sure what God holds for our future, but I would love for you to be in it. So if you think these feelings sound like love...then maybe...maybe I love you."

"Aww, Alex." Her gaze softens as she looks at me and there's something about the emotion in her eyes that makes me believe she understands what I'm saying. "I'll be honest and say that before you asked me out two weeks ago, I never saw myself being in a relationship with you. But after finding out that you've liked me for so long, a veil has been lifted from my eyes and I can now see qualities about you I truly admire.

"I love how close you are with your parents, how much you love your culture, how caring you are, and how you treat me like a princess. I would love to meet your parents one day, so I can tell them they did a good job raising you."

"I'm sure they'll love to meet you too." I laugh and she takes a step closer before continuing.

"We've only been dating for two weeks, but it feels like we've been together for much longer. I love talking to you every night and reading your text messages when I wake up every morning. I'm always excited to have lunch with you and whenever I'm on my way to see you after class, my heart does this weird dance in my chest, like it's going to explode if I don't hug you or hold your hand. The thought of being around you always makes me feel so happy, and I love going on all these adventures with you."

My smile broadens at her words and my heart does the little dance she just described. I lean forward until our faces are only inches apart before saying, "So I have feelings for you and you have feelings for me?"

She nods slowly as I bring my hand up to her neck and lean in closer.

"Olanna?"

"Yes?" She licks her lips and looks me in the eye.

"Can I kiss you?"

She nods and parts her lips before wrapping her arms around me and pulling me close. Her soft lips meet mine and I'm not sure how long the kiss goes on for, but I savor every second of her tropical scent, kissing her slowly, softly and tenderly until we naturally break away.

We both smile at each other before hugging again. "Can I safely say that you're my girlfriend now?" I whisper in her ear, and she chuckles.

"Yes, I think it's safe to call me that," she responds before leaning in and kissing me again.

7

OLANNA
NOW

The dreaded weekend is finally over and I've concluded that I'm done with falling in love, and I'm done with men. I refuse to let anyone trample on my heart again. From here on out, I'm only focusing on God, the assignments He has for me, and how I can serve Madu Health better as the CEO.

I did a video call with Dad yesterday evening and apart from some drama with the customs officers at the airport about his bags, he has settled into our family home in Lagos. The last time I was in that five-bedroom mansion in Lekki was when we all traveled back home four years ago to bury Mom.

According to the Igbo culture, when a woman dies, she has to be buried in her husband's village. But Dad chose to bury Mom at our family home in Lekki instead of Bende village in Abbia state, where both Mom and Dad are from. Of course this decision ruffled the feathers of the elders of the village, but Dad couldn't care less. He wanted his wife to be laid to rest in a place where she called home.

I still remember those summers when Mom and Dad would take Manny and I back to Nigeria and we would host parties for different family members at our house, play in the swimming pool, and go on various touristic expeditions with our cousins.

Those days brought me joy because my family was complete. But what's the point of going back there now and seeing her grave every day, reminding myself that she's really gone and never coming back? Why would I put myself through that?

I've been praying that nothing happens to Dad while he's over there. I'm taking everything one day at a time and today is going to be a good day. No more worrying excessively about Dad and certainly no more thinking about Alex.

Lord, please take control. I turn to look at myself in the elevator mirror. I always cherish the alone time I have in the elevator every morning, as it gives me the chance to pray and motivate myself for the day.

Today, I went for a yellow pencil skirt, a one-shoulder yellow and blue Ankara top, and matching yellow stilettos. Bright colors make me feel like a ball of sunshine. My top bun and half down look was a last-minute decision, but the black lipstick is always my Monday choice. I'm all set to face the day. I'm ready for whatever comes my way.

"Good morning." Lerato's face welcomes me as I step out of the elevator, but instead of her usual cheery smile, she greets me with worry lines etched across her forehead, fidgety hands, and a shaky voice. Lerato never gets nervous unless something has gone wrong. *What could possibly go wrong before the day even starts?*

"Is everything okay?" I ask as she falls in step with me and we both walk down the hallway toward my office.

"Not really." She swallows and clutches her notepad close to her chest before continuing. "Yin called ten minutes ago from the hospital to say that Jess started having early contractions, so the doctors have admitted her."

"Oh, no. Is she okay?" I ask as we enter my office and I settle behind my desk.

Instead of responding, Lerato takes out her phone and dials. The phone rings once and Yin's voice comes through from the other side. "I'm really sorry to bail on you like this, Olanna. Jess' due date isn't until another eight weeks, so this was unexpected."

"Please, don't be sorry, Yin. You're prioritizing your family, as you should. Don't worry about us over here. Take as much time off as you need. We'll be praying for you and Jess. Please update me when the baby is here, okay?"

"Sure thing. Thank you so much," he says and ends the call.

Breathe, Olanna. God's got you, so you've got this. I take a deep breath in and out before holding Lerato's hands, and we say a quick prayer together for Yin and Jess. "Okay, what do we have to sort out today while Yin is away?" I ask, before turning on the iPad on my desk.

"Yin was supposed to have a meeting with the HearCare representative at 8:30 this morning."

"Of course. Can one of the other managers meet with him instead?"

Lerato enlarges the diary on the iPad screen and scrolls up and down before responding. "Actually, they are all in meetings this morning, too." She pauses. "But you're free for the next hour and the gentleman is already here."

"Oh, okay. I can see him then. Yin already briefed me about this meeting and it's just an introductory session, anyway. Where is he now?"

"In the waiting room downstairs."

"Please apologize for the delay, inform him about the change of plans, and take him to conference room B. I'll be with him shortly."

"Got ya." Lerato grabs her notepad and pen and scurries out of the room, almost tripping over herself.

You can do this, Olanna. Hiccups happen all the time and I can fix it. Even if we get a complaint from the client, I'm competent. I know my job and I can deal with it. There's nothing to worry about.

I walk out of my office and make my way to the first floor, where the conference rooms are. In the open-plan office, I wave at Melissa and Neil, who are already arriving for the work day. I like to come in earlier than everyone else, so I can make sure everything is ready for the day. It also helps to straighten out kinks like this one.

Lerato is standing in front of the conference room with her hand on the doorknob as she beckons me over. "He's inside," she whispers, and I nod before stepping into the room.

Here we go. The back of our client's head is the first thing I see through the glass doors, and even though I get the strange feeling the back of his head looks familiar, I shake it off.

"Good morning, sir. I apologize for the delay. I'm Olanna Madu, the CEO of Madu Health, and you are?" The client turns around as I extend my hand, but when I lock eyes with him, I freeze in my spot.

If I wasn't staring into the same brown eyes I came to cherish for nine months, or the same smile I used to look forward to seeing every day, then maybe I would've convinced myself this is all a dream.

"Alex Obeng." He stands and takes my hand in his before shaking it. A warm, tingling sensation travels up my arm and into my chest before setting off a lump in my throat.

If I didn't know his voice so well as the one that prayed over me or sang for me on the days I felt low, then I would've convinced myself this is all a dream. Except it's not. Alex Obeng is really standing in front of me.

The sound of Lerato closing the door jolts me into my

current reality, and I remove my hand from his loose grip. A million and one questions flood into mind. All those questions I asked myself over the last two years, and the questions I wished I asked him.

A wave of sadness takes over me as we stand there, staring at each other in silence, but with so many unspoken words passing between us. This sadness is about what we lost and what could have been if he hadn't been a selfish jerk.

When a small smile forms on his lips, all that sadness turns to anger as I grit my teeth and ball my hands into fists. If looks could kill, Alex would have dropped dead right about now.

How dare he think he can just show up here and pretend everything is fine? Is that smile supposed to be a peace offering, or is he smirking? With everything that has gone wrong today, why did God choose this day for my past to come knocking? *This is not fair.*

Tears gather in my eyes and blur my vision as Lerato walks into the room. I turn my face away, smiling at Lerato as I dab the corner of my eyes. I refuse to let him see me cry. I refuse to let him see how much of an effect he still has on me. I have to get out of here.

Taking a step back, I straighten out my skirt and clear my throat. "Lerato, I just remembered there's something I need to sort out quickly first. Please, could you provide Mr. Obeng with some refreshments? I'll be back shortly."

"Okay?" Lerato frowns, her facial expression letting me know she suspects something is up. "Is everything okay?" she asks, her gaze shifting between Alex and I.

"Yeah, sure." I force a smile. "Refreshments, please."

Alex's eyes follow me as I walk toward the door. "Actually, I think I'm okay, Miss Madu."

"No, please, I insist." I hold open the door. "It's the least I can do for the inconveniences caused." Without waiting for his response, I shut the door behind me and power-walk to the end of the hallway before taking the next left into the ladies' room.

Finding an empty stall, I lock myself in it before slumping on the seat and letting the sobs out. *This is too much, Lord. I can't take this anymore. Help me, please.*

8

OLANNA
THEN

Her soft voice wakes me up from my slumber with the Igbo version of the famous Nigerian morning devotion song 'Good morning, Jesus. Good morning, Lord.' It's the first of many Igbo songs she taught us as children to help with our pronunciations. Even if you placed me in the middle of Times Square, I would still recognize that beautiful voice of hers.

She pulls me in for a hug as I rub the sleep from my eyes and her vanilla scent takes over not just my nostrils, but my entire room. "Gloria, my darling." Her voice whispers my name as the sleep clears from my eyes and I wrap my arms around her, holding her tight and refusing to let go.

"Mom? Where did you go? I've missed you so much." A lump builds in my throat as she kisses my forehead and leans her head on mine. She's wearing the same beautiful ankara blouse and matching fishtail skirt she wore the last time I saw her—the day she flew to Nigeria.

It's the same outfit from the family photo a stranger took of us at the airport. The same photo I've had as my screensaver for the last two years.

"Oh, Gloria. I missed you, too. But I can't stay any longer." She starts pulling away, but I tighten my grip around her waist.

"But Mom, you just got here. Please don't leave me here alone. I need you." I shake my head as she holds the sides of my face, tears falling from her eyes.

"I can't stay, my princess." She sniffles. *"But God is with you. You are never alone. I need to go."*

"No, Mom, please. You can't leave me again. Mom!!!" I scream at the top of my lungs as her hands slip away from mine and then I jolt awake.

Sweat trickles down my forehead and chest, and soaks through my t-shirt. I take off my comforter and get out of my bed before rushing to the window. My chest heaves and my throat closes up as I open the window to get some fresh air.

When my breathing slows down, I turn around to meet my empty room. "Mom?" I'm already halfway to the door when realization dawns on me. It was just a dream—the same dream I've had so many times over the last two years. I haven't had one in the last six months and this is the first time I've had it during the day.

I glance at my open books on my desk before lowering myself onto the edge of my bed. I was only two hours into my study session when a migraine hit me and I couldn't concentrate anymore. It was meant to be a power nap, but I went into a deep sleep as soon as my head hit the pillow. It's only six PM, but it feels like midnight with the gloomy darkness that comes with February's longer nights.

It was just a dream, but it felt so real, like she was really sitting on my bed, hugging me and kissing my forehead. It was just a dream, but I can still feel the warmth of her hug and her vanilla perfume teasing my nostrils. It was so vivid—as if she was actually right here in my room.

"Oh, Jesus. Please help me." The lump in my throat returns

and I sob into my pillow. After a few minutes pass, my phone vibrates on my bed and I lift my head to find several messages pinging in from Alex. I push the phone away, not wanting to engage in any conversation, but when the messages keep pinging in, I pull the gadget toward me.

Alex: Hey babe 😊 *I just came back from my shift at the library and I thought I'd check on you. How is your study session going? Have you had dinner yet?*

I wipe the tears from my eyes and put the phone away. Alex and I have only been dating for a month, so the idea of opening up to someone who is not family feels strange. But he has been an amazing boyfriend and I love how he always makes time to see me between his classes, even if he has a busy schedule.

Sometimes we have lunch with India, Kwame, and Danielle, but most times, it's just the two of us, talking about everything and anything. He has made it his life goal to make sure we cross off every activity on our A-Z list before graduation and I'm here for it.

I love how he notices the little things, how he's always asking how I'm doing, whether I've eaten or if I'm okay. He never stops making me laugh, and being with him helps distract me from thinking about Mom. So maybe telling him about Mom will help because these feelings are eating me up.

I pick up my phone and dial Manny's number twice. It rings both times with no response, so I send him a text to call me when he's free. Then I try Dad's number next and I can't get through to him either.

Danielle and India are working on some important assignments, so it would be unfair to burden them with this. They wouldn't understand. In moments like this, the only person who would've been the first to pick up my phone call would've been Mom.

My phone rings and I immediately pick it up without looking at the number. "Hello?"

"Hey, babe." Alex's voice comes through from the other end of the line.

"Hey." I sniffle and wipe my nose.

"Are you...are you okay?"

I bite my lip to fight back the tears, but they betray me when they come pouring out of my eyes. "No...no, I'm not okay."

"Do you want me to come pick you up? Take you somewhere, so we can talk about it?"

I pause for a moment, thinking about his question. Alex has been nothing but kind to me. So maybe I should give him the benefit of the doubt. After all, honesty is important in a relationship. "Yes, babe. I'd really like that."

Twenty minutes later, Alex arrives outside my apartment like he promised and he drives us to Chicken Nugget Palace—our new favorite place. "What do you want me to get for you?" he asks as we walk into the fast-food restaurant, the smell of fried chicken hanging thick in the air.

"Just a peanut butter and banana milkshake, please." It's my comfort flavor, and it always puts me in a good mood. While Alex goes to place our order, I take off my jacket and take a seat at the table.

Ten minutes later, Alex arrives with two large peanut butter and banana milkshakes and their special box of spicy chicken nuggets. I never said I wanted chicken, but he knew I would change my mind, so he bought it anyway. He just gets me.

"Olanna, what's wrong?" Alex holds my hand and pulls his chair closer, narrowing the space between us. "You know I hate to see you like this. Please talk to me."

A sigh escapes my lips as I prepare to recount the story without crying. But even the thought of talking about it blurs my vision with tears. "Can you promise me that whatever I tell you will remain between us?"

He nods. "Of course, babe. I'd like you to trust me, please."

I exhale deeply and start talking. "Since my mom died two years ago in that car accident, I've been struggling. She was my best friend and I still miss her so much." I sniffle. "I keep getting these dreams where she comes into my room, sings to me, and sometimes she even prays for me. She always hugs me tight and gives me temporary comfort. Her hugs feel so real, as if she's really there with me, but then she tells me she can't stay and she leaves me alone despite my pleading and crying.

"The last time I spoke to her was the night before she died. That morning, she was traveling from our village called Bende to Lagos. It was a few days before the annual campaign event of the women's charity she set up, which is called A Widow's Comfort. She promised to call me that morning before she traveled, but I missed her call because I had already left for class. She left me a voice message to say that she was leaving for Lagos, that she missed me and that she would call me again when she was in Lagos. That was the last time I heard from her.

"I still go back and listen to her voice messages, praying that it's all a dream, that she'll tell me she is on her way home. Sometimes, when I miss her, I send her number a text message to tell her how much I miss her. I know it won't happen, but I keep hoping that one day she'll respond and tell me this was all a prank, and she's coming back home." The sobs come out of me, my shoulders shaking and my nose all bunged up.

Alex wraps his arms around my shoulder and hands me some tissue paper to blow my nose.

"Some days I blame myself for letting her go to Nigeria. I should have convinced her to stay. That's why I can't relate when you say you're looking forward to going back home to Ghana. To me, whenever I think of Nigeria, I think of the place that took my mom from me. That, to me, can never be home."

I bury my head on Alex's shoulders, grateful for the music playing from the overhead speakers and also the empty restaurant, so I don't have to worry about other people watching me.

Alex kisses my forehead and thumbs a tear away from my eyes. "I'm so sorry that you've been going through this alone. Thank you for being honest with me. Have you spoken to Emmanuel or your dad about how you feel?"

I shake my head. "No, I tried to call them today, but they're busy. Manny is still trying to adjust to his new role as the managing director at Madu Health, and my dad is busy trying to make sure he hands everything over to Manny before he retires. They are both so busy with their own lives and I don't want them worrying about me."

"Hmm." Alex squeezes my hands. "One thing I've learned recently is that the devil loves to make us believe that we're alone when we face challenges. That can make us withdraw from others to deal with everything alone. But you're not alone, babe."

"Yeah, that's exactly what Mom always says in the dream before she leaves."

"And it's true. God is trying to remind you that you're not alone. You weren't meant to process these feelings alone. God has placed you in a community that loves you. But He's also able to help you through it. You believe that, right?" He places his palm on my jaw, his warmth providing a comfort my heart craves for.

"Yes, I do." I lift my head to look at him. "I want to work through these feelings, so they don't consume me."

"Have you considered a bereavement counselor?"

I hold his gaze for a few seconds before shaking my head.

"No, I don't think I'm comfortable speaking to a stranger about my feelings. Plus, I already feel better talking to you about it, so it's all good."

"I'm glad you feel better now." He kisses my hand. "But I'm not a counselor and I don't have the professional skills to help you deal with all these emotions. It's something you'll be able to process with time, but you need the strategies to help you do so. We'll be praying about it, but will you promise you'll at least think about speaking to a bereavement counselor?" He tilts his head and pleads with his eyes. He looks even cuter when he does that.

I finally smile. "Okay, fine. I promise I'll think about it." *That's the best I can do for now.*

"That's my girl. I'm glad your smile has returned," he says as his phone vibrates. He taps on the screen to read a text message pop up and I catch a glimpse of his screensaver.

"Aww, are those your parents?" I point to the older couple in the photo with him.

He nods and opens the photo from his gallery. "Yes. The photo was taken last year."

"You kinda look like your mom, you know?"

Alex snorts. "Really? You're the first person who has ever said that. I don't think I look like any of them."

"You have the same dark complexion as your mom and the shape of your noses are also the same, see?" I bring the phone closer, but he still gives me an unconvincing nod.

"Okay, then. If you say so."

"I also love the matching Kente outfits. You could pass for a royal family."

"Thanks. My mom bought the Kente clothes when she traveled back home to Ghana two years ago and..." His voice trails off and he purses his lips, as if he's physically trying to hold the words in his mouth.

61

"What?" I ask as he scratches the back of his head.

"I'm sorry I brought up traveling to Ghana when you *literally* just unburdened your trauma about visiting Nigeria. That was a bit insensitive of me."

"Oh, no please, don't apologize for loving the place you call home. I'm the one with the trauma, not you."

He raises his eyebrows. "Are you sure?"

"Of course. I want to hear the backstory for this beautiful photo."

"Okay." He clears his throat before continuing. "That Sunday was cultural day at church, so it seemed fitting for us to wear the outfits."

"Aww, that's so cute. What about that necklace your mom is wearing?"

"Erm…" Alex zooms in on the photo. "I remember her saying she bought it from a local market in Accra. It's an African map with a cross in the middle. She says it reminds her of her identity as a child of God."

"Aww, that's really nice. Your parents sound like amazing people. They've raised you into an amazing young man."

"You're not just saying that because I'm your boyfriend, right?"

"Of course not. Look how you took time out of your busy day to get me out of my sour mood. Alex, you're amazing and I mean it." I reach out and touch his beard. He only started growing it out a few months ago, but it already looks so good.

"Well, I'm glad you think so, because I wouldn't want to be anything but kind to you." He presses my hand to his face. "When I visit Ghana next summer after graduation, I'll buy you that same necklace," he says before quickly adding, "*Ugh*, I'm sorry. I can't believe I did it again. I promise, I'll shut up about Ghana starting now."

I chuckle as my cheeks warm up. "It's okay, babe. I'd really like that actually."

"Great," he says before his gaze drops to my milkshake on the table. "Are you going to have any of that? You know I have space for two in my belly, right?" He smirks.

"Oh, you think you're smart, don't you? Let's see if you're still smiling when I finish my milkshake before you."

"Aww, man. That's not fair. You know I get brain freeze when I drink too quickly."

"Loser," I say, but the wide grin on his face only lets me know he has a cheesy comeback brewing.

"I'll be a loser for you any day, baby girl." We both laugh before drinking our milkshakes and eating the spicy chicken nuggets in between.

9

ALEX
NOW

My throat is parched, but that is not enough reason for me to drink the coffee in front of me. The guilt rising in my chest has taken over my whole being and I'd rather die of thirst than do anything that would give Olanna a false perception of my intentions.

She left the room because of me. She has shed tears today because of me. Her whole day might be ruined because of me. I knew she'd be angry, but I didn't know she'd still be in so much pain. *This is worse than I thought.*

"Is everything okay with your coffee, sir?" Lerato walks into the room and nods at my now lukewarm beverage on the table. It has been thirty minutes since Olanna left the room and a part of me wanted to run after her, let her know how sorry I am, and let her take out her anger on me. I thought playing it cool and sending her a smile would break the ice, but obviously, that backfired. *Lord, this is harder than I thought.*

Alex, my beloved.
Don't worry about her.
She is clay in My hands.

I am working on her.

Trust Me.

"Sir?" Lerato's voice pulls me out of my thoughts, reminding me I haven't given her an answer.

"Erm...no. I mean, yes, everything's fine. Thanks, Lerato." I take a sip of the coffee before pushing it away from me and she exits the room again.

My gaze sweeps through the conference room briefly and then to the glass walls. The employees are at their workstations in the open plan office, minding their business, but I won't be surprised if they're whispering to themselves.

They've probably made me out to be the villain in this story and they're not wrong about that. But if the vilest offenders can be redeemed, then there's still hope for a villain like me. If only I can get Olanna to believe that this story might have a happy ending.

The door opens again, and Olanna walks back into the room. This time, no tears, no smile and a look of determination on her face—stern and almost venomous. I rise to my feet as she settles behind the chair at the head of the table.

"You can take a seat, Mr. Obeng," she says without looking at me, and her jaw tenses as Lerato hands her an iPad and a pen. "Once again, I apologize for the delay this morning. As you're already aware, Yin, our managing director, had to take emergency leave, so he couldn't be with us today." She finally looks at me and sends me a smile that doesn't reach her eyes. I've seen that smile so many times in movies. She's frontin' and wearing a mask to hide her true feelings about this situation.

"Welcome to Madu Health. We're excited to be working with you on HearCare's next launch. Please, you can proceed with your presentation as planned. The rest of the team managers will join us shortly."

"Oh, I thought the presentation was going to be later this afternoon?"

"Well, plans have changed and I'm sure the team can spare ten minutes of their time to listen to your presentation," she says before her eyebrows furrow. "Unless your presentation isn't ready?"

"No, it's ready. I'm happy to proceed." I walk to the front of the room and connect my laptop to the projector before loading my presentation.

In less than five minutes, the other managers flood into the room and take their seats around the conference table with Lerato sitting on Olanna's right-hand side.

"Good morning, everyone," Olanna addresses the group. "I'm sure you've already heard Yin couldn't be with us this morning, but I wanted to introduce you to Mr. Alex Yaw Obeng, who is HearCare's SEO strategist."

Wow, she still remembers my middle name. I think I only mentioned it to her once.

"Alex will be working with our team over the next three months to ease us into the exciting world of search engine optimization, so we can set up our own team here at Madu Health. But before we get into that, Alex is going to give us a presentation about how we will work together." Olanna introduces everyone seated in the room.

"Alex, this is Neil, our PR manager, and Melissa, our digital marketing manager. Sarah is leading the content marketing team, James—branding, and Carolina is head of advertising." She points to all the managers as she goes around the room. "Everyone, please welcome Alex."

"Hi, Alex." The crowd responds before I start my presentation.

"Thank you, everyone. I'm so happy to be here. As you know, my name is Alex Obeng and I'm the lead SEO strategist at Hear-

Care. Over the next three months, I'll be working closely with each department to show you why implementing organic SEO success is an important long-term marketing strategy that will help increase the discoverability of your clients' products." I go through my slides and finish in ten minutes.

A round of applause follows the end of my presentation, followed by Olanna's closing remark. "That was a very interesting presentation, Alex. I think I speak for everyone when I say that we're all excited to work with you." She smiles.

"Lerato will take you on a tour around the facility and inform you of the next thing on your agenda." She hands her iPad back to Lerato and stands up. "I believe we're done here. Thanks, everyone, for coming," she says, her gaze moving around the room, looking at everyone but me.

Following her lead, everyone stands and makes their way out of the room. I walk up to Olanna and extend my hand to her, but she ignores it. "When will our next meeting be?" I ask.

"If you want any more information, then please liaise with Lerato, who knows my schedule," she says with a straight face. That's all she gives me and I deserve it. All of it. But God sent me here for a reason and I refuse to be defeated on the first try.

As she walks toward me, heading for the door, I step out onto her path and grab her elbow gently when she is about to walk past me, bringing her to a halt. "It's so good to see you again, Olanna," I lean in and whisper into her ear. Her tropical scent fills my nostrils and transports me back all those days when she buried her head on my shoulders and allowed them to be her safe space.

Her gaze drops to my hand on her elbow and it slides upward slowly as I pray earnestly that she'd look me in the eye, allowing me the pleasure of beholding the sparkle that was once there when she looked at me.

But her gaze stops just above my shoulder and after what

seems like forever, she exhales a sharp breath and says. "I'm afraid I can't say the same." She jerks her elbow away from my grip and walks out of the room, with Lerato trailing behind her.

10

ALEX
THEN

The end of summer break always feels like the start of a new year for me. Senior year of college is finally here and soon, we'll be out of here and facing the real world. I have so many things to be grateful for—one of them being Olanna, of course. It's our seven month-iversary today and I would have felt more joyful if I didn't have this recent development pressing on my mind.

I lean forward and rest my head on my hands. My coffee and brownie remains untouched and my eyes are begging for sleep that is far away from me. The fresh breeze coming in from the library's open windows counteracts the hot weather outside. Apart from my weekend shifts as an assistant, I like the library because it's my space to think and get rid of the nerves.

"Yo, bro." Kwame appears behind me and we shake hands and pat each other's backs before he joins me at my desk in my favorite section of the library. Olanna will join me later this afternoon, but I need to have this conversation with Kwame before she comes over.

"Your text sounded urgent when you used those exclamation

points." Kwame laughs and sets his backpack on the table. "I had to leave India to come to you."

"I'm sorry, man. I didn't know you were spending time with India this afternoon. It just wasn't something I could talk about over the phone."

"Nah, don't sweat it. I'd love to take a break from her K-Drama marathon, anyway." Kwame chuckles and turns his snapback hat to face backwards. "Bro, is everything alright? Are you and Olanna having problems?"

I shake my head and lean my elbows on the table. "No, actually things with Olanna are going great. It was our six month-iversary last month, but since we couldn't see each other face to face over the summer break, we'll be celebrating that and our seven month-iversary next week."

"Wow, seven months, huh?" Kwame intertwines his fingers on the table. "For your first relationship, you've done really well. I didn't even need to give you any tips after that first day. I'm proud of you, man."

"I didn't do anything much. She's fun to be with. I'm never bored when I'm with her. Our conversations are effortless and she's so kind. I love her, man."

"Yo, that's what I'm talking about." Kwame flashes me a grin before giving me a high five. "Have you met her family yet?" He lowers his voice when the guy in the sweatshirt and headphones on our right-hand side sends a glare in our direction.

"Not yet, but I know a lot about them. She always talks about her dad and her older brother, but her mom died two years ago. She says she met her brother's potential girlfriend over the summer break and apparently she's planning double dates for us or something along those lines."

"Bro, that's how it's gonna be. You better get used to it." Kwame laughs before his facial expression becomes serious again. "Okay, if things are going great with Olanna, then what's the problem?"

My smile fades and I lower my head before letting out a sigh. "Kwame, please, can you promise that what I'll share with you today will remain between us?"

"Oh, come on, bro. You know me."

"Not even India."

"You have my word, man." Kwame extends his hand and I shake it.

"Okay, it's a health issue and I just need your advice because..."

Kwame shakes his head before I can finish my sentence. "Bro, I'm only a pre-med student and not a doctor. You know I can't give medical advice."

"I'm not asking for medical advice. I just want your opinion as my friend, please."

"Why didn't you just Google it?"

"Dude, seriously?" I tilt my head and narrow my eyes at him. "Don't you remember what happened the last time I Googled a symptom? The internet told me I only had ten days to live."

We both laugh as memories of freshman year come rushing back. After struggling with abdominal pain for months, I was so sure my whole world was crumbling. But when Kwame finally convinced me to see the doctor, it turned out I was just very constipated and had to stop eating junk food every day.

"Man, the internet is a wild place." Kwame crosses his arms against his chest and shakes his head. "Okay, fine. You win. What's up?"

I look over my shoulder and urge him to lean forward before whispering in his ear.

"I noticed a...erm...I noticed a lump."

Kwame's eyes widen and his jaw drops open. "A lump? Where?"

I lean forward and whisper in his ear, afraid of someone else hearing.

"When did you notice it?"

"About two or three days ago." I scratch the back of my head. "What do you think I should do?"

Kwame shakes his head. "I still think you should speak to a doctor. It's probably nothing serious, so don't worry about it, alright?"

Phew. I let out a sigh of relief and nod. "That's all I needed to hear. I'll be going home next weekend and I'll tell my dad about it."

"What about Olanna?"

I rub my forehead and pull on my beard before sighing. "Like you said, it's probably nothing serious, so I don't want her to worry. Besides, it's kinda embarrassing."

To this, Kwame shakes his head. "From my experience with India, I'd advise you not to keep Olanna in the dark."

"Yes, Mr. *Steve Harvey,* I've heard you." I bump Kwame's fist before he leaves. It feels like Kwame has taken a huge weight off my shoulders, but maybe he's right. Maybe I should see a doctor. I'll tell Olanna after I've gotten the all clear because I don't want her to worry about me.

Lord, Jesus. I hope Kwame is right, and this is nothing serious.

11

OLANNA
NOW

"My goodness!!! Olanna, are you okay?" Manny's eyes widen after he responds to my pounding fists against the door. Unable to get my words out, I throw myself at him, tears leaking out of my eyes and my chest heaving as I struggle to get my words out.

"You're soaked." He glances over my shoulder at the pouring rain outside. "Please come in before you catch a cold." A flicker of lightning passes, followed by a rumble of thunder as he helps me inside the house.

Heather rushes to my side and wraps a large towel around my shoulders before rubbing them. I don't know how I drove all the way down here in the rain and the tears blurring my vision the whole way through. I just knew when I left the office that I couldn't go back to the empty house after seeing Alex again today.

Rain on my scalp is one of the triggers for my seborrheic dermatitis and I know Wendy—my loctician—won't be pleased at my next appointment. I can already feel the flakes building up, but that is the least of my worries right now.

Heather and Manny help me sit on a chair in the dining room. "I'm...so...sorry for making a mess in your house." I point to the puddles of water and mud on the floor. "I promise I'll clean it up." My words come out in between the clattering of my teeth and shivers.

"Honey, please don't worry about that," Heather says. "Let's get you into some dry clothes before you catch pneumonia." She leads me up the stairs into the guest bedroom, which is much warmer. After changing into comfortable sweatpants and a sweatshirt, I slip on some fluffy slippers before making my way back downstairs, where Manny and Heather are waiting for me.

"Here you go, hun." Heather places a cup of hot cocoa on a stool in front of me as I lower myself on the sofa in the living room.

I take several sips and let the warm cup transfer the heat to my hands while Heather and Manny sit quietly on either side of me. They don't say a word and they don't push until I'm ready to talk. After what seems like forever, even for me, I finally open up.

"You remember our new client from HearCare?" I stall to give myself time to steady my breathing.

"Yeah?" Heather and Manny say in unison.

"They sent a representative to work with us for the next three months and...that representative is...Alex."

Manny and Heather look at each other briefly before realization dawns on Manny, and he turns to me.

"Alex Obeng?" Manny frowns and I nod. "He has got some nerve showing up there after everything he did to you," he says through gritted teeth and pushes himself up.

"Baby, please calm down." Heather's soothing voice calms both Manny and me as she gets him to sit down again before turning to me. "Did Alex say anything to make you upset?"

"No, but he didn't need to. His mere presence brought back all the emotions I thought I'd buried. I spent fifteen minutes crying in the toilet because I just couldn't hold myself together when I saw him. He told me it felt good to see me and I had to restrain myself from slapping him across the face. He was the one who hurt me, but he seems to be handling it really well while I'm the one who can't sleep, or eat, or concentrate because of him."

Heather wraps her arm around my shoulders and Manny stands up again and paces the room. "Do you have to work with him?" he asks. "Can you ask HearCare to send someone else?"

I shrug. "I suppose I could, but I'm not sure what reason I would give them without bringing up my personal business. HearCare speaks highly of him and his work ethic. They think he is the best person for the job. I have to think about the company and be professional about it instead of letting my feelings get in the way, but I don't know how I'm going to do that."

"What interactions have you had with him so far?" Manny continues his line of questioning.

"Well, we had the introductory meeting with him this morning, but because I needed distraction, I invited the other managers in so Alex could give his presentation. I left immediately after the meeting was over and Lerato and I worked out his schedule, so we have as little one-on-one interactions as possible."

"That's good. Do you want me to have a word with him?" Manny asks, and I shake my head. With all the pent up anger he has toward Alex, I don't want him to actually fulfill his promise of breaking Alex's face.

"No, I don't think that would be necessary. I can handle it." I send Manny a weak smile.

Heather clears her throat and her green gaze meets mine.

"Olanna, I understand you're hurt and angry, but...what if Alex asks to speak to you and explain what happened? Would you give him a chance?"

"He had his chance, and he ruined it," Manny responds for me, and Heather shakes her head at him.

"Babe, please. Just give her a chance to think about it," Heather says to her husband before turning back to me. "The reason I ask is that I've been in this exact position before. When my mom returned a few years ago and tried to explain to me why she left, I refused to speak to her for months because I was still holding on to so much anger. My therapist encouraged me to speak to her and get some closure, and my healing really started when I did."

I sigh. "Heather, I don't think this is the same situation."

"Of course, it's an entirely different scenario, but it's very similar. You still have anger and hurt eating you up inside and you need to forgive him before moving on. Do you really think God brought him back into your life for nothing? He is a God of intentionality, remember? Please, all I ask is that you think about it. Not for me or Manny or even Alex, but for yourself."

A few minutes pass as I consider Heather's words. I open my mouth to speak, but I don't even have the strength to continue with this conversation or to think clearly. A tight band of pain squeezes my head and radiates down my neck, letting me know it's time to rest. "Thanks, Heather, but I think I'm going to call it a night. Is it okay if I crash here tonight?"

"Of course," Manny says. "You can stay here as long as you want."

"Thanks, guys." I finish my hot cocoa and hug Manny and Heather good night.

Back in the guest bedroom, I take a shower, brush my teeth, and change into some pajamas Heather laid out for me. It's pouring rain outside, so I pull the curtains closed and climb under the comforter. After listening to my daily dose of my audio Bible, I turn on my Spotify playlist of worship songs as I lie on my bed.

When sleep refuses to come, I pick up my phone to respond to my messages. The first one at the top of my list is Dad's. He has been giving me daily updates about his Lagos adventures, so I don't worry about him. Yesterday, he had lunch at a restaurant with two of his business partners and he sent me mouthwatering photos of his *amala*—a staple swallow food served with *ewedu, gbegiri* and *Buka* stew. The fantastic presentation of the meal makes me want to reach into my phone and taste it.

Today, he has sent me videos of the places he visited, including a history lesson about the Third Mainland Bridge— the longest bridge in Nigeria, which connects Lagos Island to the mainland. I chuckle at his commentary about Lagos traffic and for a moment, I wish I was right there with him, experiencing the craziness for myself.

To stop my thoughts from wandering far, I close my messages and open my photo gallery. I saved all the photos of Alex and me in a folder because I couldn't bring myself to delete them after the breakup. Starting from the beginning, I flip through all the photos we took during our nine months together.

I still remember our dates at the arcade, the ferry ride with the Statue of Liberty behind us, and at the sip and paint event. The painting he gave me is still somewhere in a shoe box tucked underneath my bed. He gave it to me as a gift and I couldn't bring myself to throw it away either.

The smiles on both our faces were so promising. We looked so happy and so in love. Maybe Heather is right. If Alex asks to speak to me again, maybe I should give him a chance to explain himself because I don't understand why he gave up on us.

He destroyed everything we built and it wouldn't be my fault for turning my back on him the same way he turned his back on me. Not knowing what else to do, I turn off my phone, bury my head in my pillow, and whisper my prayers to God until sleep finally comes.

12

OLANNA

THEN

"**B**abe, what do you think about my painting so far?" I turn my board around to show Alex, but instead of the *ooh* and *ahh* reaction I was hoping for, he shields his eyes with his hands and turns his face away.

"Hey, I'm not supposed to see your painting until the end. Don't ruin the surprise for me," he says with his back to me, and I roll my eyes.

"Come on, don't be like that. I really need you to see it."

"No, we're sticking to the rules this time."

"Okay, fine." I turn my paint board back around to face me. "If you want to follow the rules, then okay." I sip on my glass of non-alcoholic wine before placing the glass on the table in front of us.

Alex sticks his tongue out at me and then continues with his painting. The president of Ignite recommended this sip and paint event when Alex and I told him about our A-Z list. The first session involved us all trying to draw a fruit bowl. For the second session, the instructor asked us to focus on individual awareness and growth by playing our favorite music and painting the first thing that comes to mind.

The instructor also told us not to share the painting with anyone else until the very end and to prevent anyone from cheating, we're using paint boards with shields on the sides. While Alex is the patient one out of the two of us, I can't help myself.

"Can I see your painting?" I crane my neck toward him, but he turns his board away from me.

"No, you can't. Stay right there." He points his paintbrush at me, but instead of deterring me like he intended, his action draws a chuckle from my lips.

"You think I'm scared of getting paint on my clothes? Well, think again, mister." I step down from my stool, but Alex raises his hand to alert the instructor's attention and I sit back down.

"Oh, you're such a tattletale." I squint at him and he laughs.

"You're no fun." I kiss my teeth and tighten my apron around my neck and waist.

"Oh, I'm sure you don't mean that," he responds with a confidence I love.

"Of course, I don't." I send him a sheepish smile before going back to my painting. My gaze sweeps through the room as I watch the other people working on their paintings. There's a mother-daughter duo, a group of three best friends and a husband and wife who could be in their late twenties.

A sip and paint date has been on my to-do list with Danielle and India since freshman year, but it's much better that I'm doing it with the man I love. Yes, I know I just said *love* and I mean it. It has taken me seven months to fully accept that my feelings toward Alex go deeper than surface level. We connect in a way I've never connected with anyone before, and that is something I can't even explain.

"What's the best thing you love about our relationship?" I ask, and he turns his head to meet my gaze.

"It's simple. You get me. I get you. You're my best friend."

"Aww." My smile probably makes me look like a fool now, but I don't even care. "You're so sweet."

"Well." He pats his shoulders and clears his throat. "A beautiful young lady has told me that a lot over the last seven months, so I believe you." He winks at me, and I playfully push his arm.

When we're done with our painting, the instructor, a twenty-something year old brunette woman, goes round the room asking us to showcase our paintings and talk about the inspiration for it.

When it's Alex's turn, he stands and takes off his apron before clearing his throat. "Hi everyone. My name is Alex, and this painting is dedicated to someone who has made a huge impact in my life since the first day I set my eyes on her."

My cheeks warm up as I struggle to contain my smile. He looks at me and finally turns the painting around to show me. It's a faceless painting, but with all the right features to confirm it is in fact me. He included my favorite hoop earrings, my burgundy locs, and the words *Girl Boss* written in cursive writing at the top.

Alex turns to the class and continues talking. "My girlfriend over here is called Olanna, and she loves teasing me about using clichés to express my feelings, so this public display might make her wish the earth would open up and swallow her." A wave of laughter passes across the room before he turns to look at me again.

"But when I tell you that you've been a blessing to me, I mean that in every sense of the word. You're so incredibly beautiful, so strong, so resilient, and even though the last few years have been hard on you, you still grace everyone around with your lovely smile. Thank you for seven months of being my best friend and making me believe I can do anything. I love you."

"Aww." The word comes out of the crowd, followed by a round of applause.

I'm not even sure when I left my seat and threw my arms around him in a tight hug, but he plants a kiss on my lips and wipes the tears on my face I didn't even realize were there.

"Now I feel embarrassed to show my painting." We all laugh as I brace myself to showcase mine. I turn the paint board around, so everyone can see. It's more of a cartoon version of Alex and I holding hands on a sunny day, with lots of blue clouds, green grass and love hearts scattered around.

"I did a similar drawing like this when I was ten years old because I was fortunate enough to grow up in a functional family with a mom and dad who loved each other." I sigh before continuing. "Unfortunately, I lost my mom two years ago, but one thing I can take away from her incredible life is that true love is possible. I'm a hopeless romantic and I'm incredibly blessed to see that God has smiled on me like this." I turn to look at Alex, who walks up to me and squeezes my hand, something I definitely needed.

"Thank you, Alex, for being an answered prayer and for not destroying my belief in true love. I love you." I lean in and kiss him again as the crowd applauds.

After the event, we stopped by an Italian restaurant as I've been craving some really good pasta for a long time. The food was delicious, the music and atmosphere set a romantic scene, and it was a perfect way to end the evening. Well, it would've been the perfect end if I didn't notice the change in Alex's mood during our drive back home.

In between the silences in the car, we usually either sing along to the music playing, or talk about anything and everything. But today is different because during these pauses he sends me glances and opens his mouth, as if he wants to say something, but when I turn to look at him, he just smiles and focuses on the road again.

"Everything okay, babe?" I reach for his free hand that's not on the steering wheel, but before he can respond, my attention switches to the constant buzzing on my phone. Text message notifications from Manny chime in, asking me if I'm okay and if I'm back home from my date yet.

Since I told him about my relationship with Alex back in March, he has been checking in constantly to make sure Alex is still treating me like the gentleman I've made him out to be. Every time we have a conversation about Alex, Manny makes it his duty to remind me that if Alex ever breaks my heart, he'll break his face.

At first, I worried about the possibility of that happening because I know Manny is not bluffing. But after the last seven months and the amazing day Alex and I had today, I have nothing to worry about. He's my one.

"Sorry, it's just Manny checking on me," I say after sending a quick reply and putting my phone away.

"No need to apologize. He cares about you."

I nod. "He sure does. That's why I can't wait for Manny and my dad to meet you. When they see how lovely you are, it'll ease any worries or reservations they have." I relax in my seat and silence stretches again between us before I speak again. "By the way, I forgot to tell you I finally contacted the bereavement counselor."

"Really?" He glances at me briefly, a smile crossing his face.

"Yeah, I have my first session next week. I'm very nervous, but I've been doing a lot of research and apparently many people find it useful, so it won't hurt trying." It took me six months to decide, but at least I got there.

"That's my girl." He reaches for my hand and squeezes. "I'm so proud of you."

Even though he's smiling and responding to my questions, there's still something off about his body language I can't put my finger on, so I push one last time. "Alex, are you sure everything is okay? You've been quiet since we left the restaurant."

This time, he sighs and says, "Yeah, sorry, babe. There's just a lot on my mind right now."

"Like what?" I prod some more. *Was it something I said or did?*

"Erm...it's my dad. He has some health challenges, so I need to go home and visit them this weekend," he says without looking at me.

"Oh, I'm sorry to hear that." I sit up and lean toward him. "I'll be praying for him."

"And just say a prayer for me too while you're at it, will you?" he adds in with a smile.

"Of course. Thanks for sharing with me. I appreciate it." His free hand finds mine again and we don't let go of each other for the rest of our journey.

13

ALEX
NOW

I tap my pen slowly on my desk and rub my forehead as Melissa wraps up her presentation and takes a seat next to me again on the conference table. Today, I've been meeting with each of the managers individually to get a better idea of what their team does and how I can help.

All the meetings so far have been insightful and I'm excited to get to work and show them what I know how to do best. What I'm not so excited about is the fact that I haven't seen Olanna at all today. I know her office is on the third floor, and only Lerato can tell me her whereabouts at any time during the day, but I was hoping she would come down at some point.

Is she so swamped with work that she can't leave her office for one second? Or is she just avoiding any possibility of seeing me?

"Thank you, Melissa. I'll look at the analytics and schedule another meeting with you. I think you're doing a great job here."

"Aww, thank you." The middle-aged woman flashes me a grin before tucking a strand of her curly brown hair behind her ear. "I'm glad you said that. When I first got the promotion to digital marketing manager two years ago, it seemed very daunting to fill Yin's shoes, but I think I've found my bearings now."

"That's good to know." I return her smile. "If Yin used to be the digital marketing manager, and he's now the manager director, who was the managing director before Yin?"

"Oh, that was Emmanuel, Olanna's older brother. Have you met him before?"

My body stiffens, and I straighten my back. "No, I haven't." And maybe now is not the right time to meet him, as I hear I have a punch waiting for me.

"We all thought he was going to take over the company after their father, but he now runs a fast-growing charity marketing agency with his wife Heather."

Ah, that makes sense. So he ended up marrying Heather like Olanna predicted. I'm glad at least one of the two siblings had a happy ending for their love story. "Good for them."

"Yeah and for us too, because now we have Olanna as CEO. Don't get me wrong, we all loved Mr. Madu as the CEO, but Olanna is just awesome. She's the best, don't you think?" Melissa sends me a sly smile, almost wiggling her eyebrows as she speaks.

Wait a minute? Does she know about Olanna and me?

"Yes, she's the best indeed," I respond before changing the subject. "Well, thank you again. I'm going to study your analytics on your social media pages and come up with suggestions on how we can use SEO strategies to increase your reach, especially when you start posting about HearCare's upcoming launch."

"That's exciting. I'm looking forward to it." Melissa packs up her folders before making her way to the door.

At least one person is happy I'm here. I'll count that as a victory.

"Oh, Melissa?" I call out to her before she opens the door. "Have you seen Olanna today?"

"No, I haven't, but I think she'll be in her office. She usually comes down in the morning to greet everyone before the start of the day and she didn't do that this morning, so I'm not sure. You can ask Lerato, though."

"Sure. Thanks." I nod and Melissa leaves.

I rub my beard and pack up my folder before returning to the office allocated to me yesterday. After dropping my folder on the desk, I make my way to the third floor to find Olanna. I don't even know what my game plan is, but all I know is that if anything, I need to make sure she's okay.

The third floor, which I've gathered is for senior management, is much quieter than the second floor which has the open plan office. It has a reception, which I was told is manned by Lerato, but today she, too, is not there.

I press the bell at the reception and wait for someone to pop out and after a few seconds, the sound of approaching footsteps saunters into my ears. I turn around to meet Lerato's approaching silhouette because of the dimly lit corridor, but her big afro gives her away before she steps into the light.

"Hi, Alex." She sends me a smile before walking around to her desk. "Can I help you?"

"Hi, yes. Sorry to bother you. I just wanted to find out whether Olanna is in today?"

"No, she's not. She called this morning to say she'll be working from home today, so I came in to pick up some files for her."

"Oh," I say, unable to hide the disappointment in my voice. "Is she ill?"

"Well, I don't know the details, but I'm on my way to see her. Did you want me to pass on a message?"

No, but I'd like to have her house address. The words slip to the edge of my tongue, but I hold them back, because I'm not about to start raising eyebrows around here. Especially since it seems no one knows about my previous relationship with Olanna. *At least not yet.*

"No," I say, after realizing Lerato was still waiting for a reply. "Never mind, I'll just send her an email. Do you know when she'll be back at the office?"

Lerato shrugs. "No, it could be tomorrow, or later this week. I'm not sure."

I nod, wondering whether I should leave a message. Should I ask her how she is? Or ask her to call me? Or should I tell her to get well soon? That would be really awkward if she's not ill.

"She seems really busy," I say, as Lerato and I walk toward the elevator. "Does she have time for her boyfriend outside of this place?" I sneak in an attempt to find out about her relationship status, and Lerato jumps in with an immediate response.

"What boyfriend?" She shakes her head. "The girl has no time to date."

"Is that so?" I wasn't expecting Lerato's response to bring me so much joy.

"Yeah. I have a feeling someone broke her heart before and now she just shuts down any opportunity of dating."

A pang of guilt rises in my chest, followed by jealousy at the thought of Olanna considering any other man but me. But what right do I have to think that way? I was the one who broke her heart after she begged me not to.

"Well, we can hope and pray for our boss, right?" I say as Lerato steps into the elevator.

"That's right. I know someday she'll find true love." Lerato slips in before the elevator door closes shut and I stand there, staring at it and considering her words.

I can't help but wonder how different things would've been if I hadn't walked away. Being here and experiencing the aftermath of my selfishness is soul-destroying. *Lord Jesus, please soften Olanna's heart again.*

I return to my office and sit at my desk before letting my head drop in my hands. I don't know why I hoped today would be the day I speak to her. Of course, she's the CEO and she can work from home as long as she pleases. But she blocked my number and I can't send personal emails using my work email address, so I basically can't reach her. This is proving to be more difficult than I thought.

A knock on the door causes me to lift my head and Neil—the PR manager—pokes his head into my office. "Hey, man. Everything okay?"

"Yeah, thanks. We have a meeting at two, right?"

"Yup, that's right. I might be a little late because I have to rush home. It's a family emergency."

"Yeah, sure. That's okay." I nod. "Family comes first."

"Cool. Thanks, man." He closes the door again.

After another ten minutes of questioning all my life choices, I pick up my jacket and walk out of the office to get some fresh air.

"Going out for lunch?" Melissa's voice stops me in my tracks and I turn to look at her.

Lunch. Of course, that's a brilliant idea. "Yeah," I say, glancing at my watch. "I thought I'd take a short walk to check out some places."

"You should definitely try Rosa's Café across the street. Their sandwiches are to die for." Melissa literally lights up as she spends another five minutes talking about their panini, as if they were the greatest discovery ever known to man.

"Wow, thanks for the recommendation. I'll head there now." I smile at her and make my way to the elevator and out of the building.

The instant calming aesthetic of the café welcomes me as I walk in, followed by the soothing saxophone music playing from the overhead speakers. The aroma draws me in further and I take a minute to admire the plant wall decor before making my way to the counter. I'm the only one in line, but there are approximately a dozen people seated in the café eating their meals.

"Hi, can I have a steak and cheese panini, a side of fries, and some diet coke, please?"

"Yeah, coming right up. Please take a seat."

I pay for my food and walk further into the café to find a seat. Shortly after settling down into a turquoise velvet tub chair next to the window, the server brings my order and I say a quick prayer for the food before digging in.

The steak and melted cheese blend in really well, but the combination of the caramelized onions and horseradish sauce causes an explosion of flavor in my mouth. I'm definitely coming back here again because Melissa was not exaggerating.

My phone rings in my pocket, giving me a break from my meal as I take it out to answer Kwame's call. Between him navigating his second year of med school and keeping his flourishing relationship with India afloat, it's difficult to know the best time to call him. But he always makes time out to call me back. "Yo, bro."

"How's it going, my brother? You good?" he asks, and I swallow the food in my mouth before responding.

"Yeah, I'm good...I guess." I know even a child would not find my response convincing enough.

"Yeah, I wish I could believe you, but you're a terrible liar, so start spilling. Have you spoken to Olanna yet?"

I dab the corner of my mouth with a napkin. "No, I haven't."

Kwame's sigh on the other end of the line mirrors mine. "What happened?"

"I messed up before I even got the chance to speak to her." I rub my beard and stare out the window. "There was a change of plans yesterday, so instead of meeting their managing director, I had to have a direct meeting with Olanna and boy, I gotta say, she was not happy to see me."

"Well, you expected that, right? We knew it would take some time for her to come around, given how things ended between you two."

"Yeah, but she didn't turn up to work today. I spoke to her assistant, who said she's working from home, but I have a feeling she's avoiding me." I sip on my coke before continuing. "You should've seen the look on her face yesterday, Kwame. She hates me. She even left the room for about thirty minutes shortly after I arrived, and I saw the tears in her eyes. I've only been here for two seconds and I've already made her cry. I don't see how I can ever get through to her. It's impossible."

"Of course, it's impossible...with your own thinking and your own strength." Kwame's subtle reminder cuts deep into my soul, and I sigh.

"Yeah, you're right. It's just that it's hard to see how much pain I caused her without chiding myself for it. Sometimes I wish God hadn't opened a door for me to come here. Maybe it would be best for everyone if things stay as they are. Maybe I should let her be, so she can move on with her life. Telling Olanna the truth will require me to reopen the old wounds on my end, too, and I'm not sure I want to relive those memories."

"But this is not about you, Alex," Kwame cuts in. "It's about what God is planning for both of you. God instructed you to tell Olanna the truth. Shutting your mouth now will mean disobeying God, and you know you'll have regrets about that. Doing the right thing doesn't always come easy, but just because you don't feel comfortable doing it doesn't mean you should give up. You already gave up on this relationship once before and you're still facing the consequences. You can't let history repeat itself. If you love Olanna, you'd at least try."

He's right. I do love her. I still love her. I've never stopped loving her, and that's why this process hurts so much. "Okay, I guess I'll just have to wait for when she's back at the office and then I'll find a good time to talk to her."

"That's my man," Kwame says. "Just send me a text anytime. You know I'll always respond...even if it takes me a day or two." We both laugh and Kwame ends the call.

Lord, please. Give me the strength to obey. No matter how hard it is.

14

ALEX
THEN

The moment I step into our four-bedroom family apartment in the Upper West Side, Mom engulfs me into a hug, followed by her usual one million questions about college and how classes are going even though I only just resumed two weeks ago. She never gets bored with my one-word answers and somehow, she always comes up with new questions every time.

"*Eii*, look at your cheeks. You've been listening to me and eating well, haven't you?" She pinches my cheeks and ruffles my hair before settling on her favorite line. "*Herh*. Beard gang. It's growing well, oh." She touches my beard.

"Thanks, Mom." I hug her before she slips in one last question.

"What about Olanna? When do we get to meet her? *Dɛn na ɛregye wo bere tenten saa*?"

"Okay, Abena, I think the boy has had enough questioning for one day." Dad swoops in and saves me.

"Hey, Dad." I hug him, grateful he doesn't have a list of questions waiting to throw at me.

"How are you, Yaw?" He squeezes my shoulder. "I wasn't expecting you to be visiting us so soon."

"Yeah, about that." I lower my voice and lean close to him. "I'll speak to you after dinner, but please keep this between you and me." I thought I'd speak to Dad first since my problem is related to 'men's business,' but I also know Mom is likely to get anxious and the last thing I want to do is make her worried about nothing.

Dad's graying eyebrows crease up into a frown, but he nods and doesn't ask any further questions. I carry my suitcase to my room and sit on my bed for a few minutes with my head in my hands.

Welcoming the silence with open arms, I listen to the ticks from the wall clock which is next to the Ghana map on my wall. I bought it shortly after Mom and Dad told me we would travel to Ghana. I thought it'd be a good idea to familiarize myself with the places we'll be visiting and color them in on the map when I return.

Excitement was my only emotion the last time I was in the room. But now, everything I feel is dread, even though I'm trying to remain as positive as I can. I pick up my phone to check my unread messages and, like I expected, at the top of my list, Olanna's message is staring at me.

Olanna: Hey, babe. Are you home now? How's your mom and dad? Hope they're okay? Please let me know. I love you. 🤍

I shouldn't have lied to her. I should've told her the truth, like Kwame advised. My plan was to tell her after our dinner date, but I couldn't bring myself to make her worry about me like that.

I hope this turns out to be nothing serious, so I can finally tell her.

Dad knocks on my door and pokes his head in. "Come on, son. It's time for dinner."

"I'll be down in two minutes." I smile at him and when he leaves, I send a quick reply to Olanna to put her mind at ease.

Me: *Hey, babe. I arrived not too long ago. Mom and Dad are doing great and Mom can't wait to meet you someday. I miss you so much. I can't wait to see you soon. I love you.* 🩶

Placing my phone in my pocket, I rush down the stairs to join Mom and Dad at the dining table. I settle in the chair opposite Mom while salivating over my plate of *waakye* served with *shito*, red stew, *gari*, spaghetti, fried plantain, salad and, of course, a boiled egg.

Mom loves spoiling me with food whenever I come home because she has this idea that I don't eat well at college. She may be right, but I won't complain because this food is delicious.

While we eat, Mom and Dad fill me in on their adventures as property owners in Ghana. They always have stories to share about their tenants—from late rent payments, to broken toilets, and endless renovations.

With Dad working as a senior accountant and Mom a nurse, they've both experienced challenges juggling their full-time jobs and running several businesses in Ghana over the years. But their resilience has been so inspiring. If I can become half as successful as they both are, I'll consider that a huge blessing.

After dinner, I help Mom wash the dishes before heading to Dad's office. But instead of walking straight in, I stand outside the door for a few minutes, trying to steady my breathing and racing heart rate. I've spent all day trying to convince myself everything will be fine. But what if it won't?

"Yaw, what's wrong?" Dad asks as I enter the room and take a seat on the couch next to him.

I exhale and rub my forehead before forcing the words out of my mouth. "Dad, I found a lump."

His eyes widen, and he straightens his back. "What do you mean, a lump? Where?"

I lower my head and fiddle with my fingers.

"Son, talk to me. Where did you find it?"

"Erm..." I look over my shoulder before lowering my voice. "My...my testicle."

Dad remains silent for a moment before pulling himself close to me. "When did you notice it?"

"I think a week ago...or longer. I don't know."

"Does it hurt?"

I shake my head. "No, it doesn't bother me. That's a good sign, right?"

Dad doesn't answer my question, but he takes his phone out of his shirt pocket and dials a number. "We need to get you to see a doctor urgently."

After watching Dad's reaction, panic settles into my chest. "Urgently?" I ask as I push myself to the edge of my seat. "You think it's something serious?"

"Son, I'm not a doctor," he says calmly. "But things like this have to be dealt with urgently before they get worse."

Get worse? But I only noticed it a week ago. Did I leave it too late?
"Okay." I swallow the lump building in my throat before gathering the strength to speak again. "What do I need to do now? Who are you calling?"

"Just stay right here." He brings his phone up to his ear. "I'm calling Kofi. He is the only urologist I know. I'll ask him if he has time to see you today."

15

OLANNA
NOW

Back-to-back meeting days are my favorites now, not only because they keep me distracted, but because they keep me hidden in my office, so I don't have to bump into Alex. One thing Manny advised me to do when I first took over Madu Health was to take a break from my computer. As an ex-workaholic himself, he only had to list out what stress did to him when he was the managing director and I took his advice seriously.

I used to spend my break going downstairs to check in on everyone in the open plan office, but since Alex showed up last week, I've been spending my breaks on the first-floor balcony instead. Not many people know about it because it was the secret hangout spot for Manny and Heather when they used to work here. It has the best view of the Jersey city skyline and Hudson River, so that helps calm my nerves.

I'm on a mission to be a girl boss and still live a soft life—which means I need to identify stress triggers and avoid them. Trigger number one—aka Alex Obeng—is already being dealt with, as my avoidance technique is working.

But with today being a Saturday, I couldn't settle for my

usual routine of Bible study, workout, bath, and cooking all day. My scalp has not recovered from my rainy day shenanigan last week, so I called Wendy and booked a hair appointment for this afternoon.

"There's my favorite girl." Dressed in a cute puff-sleeved black blouse tucked into a floral red skirt, Wendy, my loctician, greets me as I step in through the doors of Luscious Beauty hair salon. The customers and stylists turn their heads to face me as I do my walk of shame across the shiny wooden floors to give Wendy a hug.

No matter how long I'm away from this place, my favorite things are still the same when I come back; the white walls and the gold chandelier on the ceiling, which is surrounded by drawings of black women with afros.

The smell of tropical fruits and coconut wafts into my nostrils and the sweet melody of the old school R&B songs playing from the overhead speakers grazes my ears, transporting me to my childhood days when Mom used to pin me down between her legs to comb my hair while I screamed my lungs out. *Sigh.* Those are bittersweet memories, which Wendy helped me expel because she taught me that taking care of my hair doesn't have to be painful.

"Hi Wendy." I only have a few seconds to show her my bright smile before she engulfs me in a big hug and lifts me off the floor with her petite but strong arms. *What kind of weights has she been lifting at the gym?*

"Girl, you had me trippin,'" Wendy says as she sets me back on the floor. "How you go'n up and leave me like that for months?" She leans back and places a hand on her hip as she twirls her own locs with her fingers.

Wendy was the reason I started my loc journey five years ago. I used to complain about how much of a chore it was to look after my natural hair, but I didn't want to chemically straighten it. I grappled with the guilt for a long time, but when Wendy suggested I loc my hair, I was too chicken to do it alone, so she did it with me and we have not looked back ever since.

"I'm so sorry, Wendy." I hide my face with both hands. "Work has been busy. You know your girl is still getting used to this CEO thing." I rattle out my excuse as Wendy pulls out the seat close to the shelf of hair products.

"That's right, boo." Wendy takes a step back, her block-heeled boots pounding against the floor. "Did y'all know this young lady right here is not just beauty, but brains?" She turns to her attentive audience. "She's the CEO of a multimillion dollar healthcare marketing company and she has been bringing it on."

"Wow. Girl, you're on fire." A stocky woman says with her hair inside the hair dryer and a magazine on her lap.

"I love to see people like us win." One stylist clicks her fingers at me before returning to washing a woman's hair at the sink. This stylist must be new because Wendy tells this story every time I come here.

"Yes, and especially us women," Wendy adds. "I love it when we win. I'm so proud of you, Glo." Wendy is probably the only other person who refers to me by my middle name, Gloria—the other person was Mom.

My cheeks warm up as I struggle to keep up with everyone's kind words. *Man, I missed this place.* "Aww, you flatter me too much, Wendy."

"But girl, you deserve it for all the hard work you do. So relax and let me give you a pampered hair day." She chuckles before running her hands through my hair and doing her assessment.

Unlike me, who likes to try every hairstyle under the sun with my locs, including deciding to change the color to burgundy while I was in college, Wendy keeps hers simple—gold hair cuffs and always wearing it in a half-up and half-down style. I keep waiting for the day when Wendy will tell me off for not following our agreed hair care regime, and today might be that day.

After what seems like forever, Wendy sets my loc strands down and walks to the shelf to get some hair products. For a second, I convince myself I've gotten away with it, but when Wendy lets out a heavy sigh, I realize at that moment that her experienced eyes and hands must have found something.

"Girl, have you been stressed? Coz your scalp be looking all crusty," Wendy says, and if it was any other person, embarrassment would've ravaged my being. But it's Wendy, and I braced myself for this. I nod and lift my head slowly until our eyes meet in the mirror.

"Kinda."

"What's been stressing you out?" she asks. "Talk to Mama Wendy."

I shrug before taking a quick glance at the others in the room. The woman next to me seems to be engrossed on her phone, typing away with her long pink nails as the stylist does her single braids. The other customers are reading magazines or singing along and swaying their hips to Alicia Keys' "This Girl Is On Fire" blasting through the speakers.

"Okay, let's just say an *old flame* recently came back into my life and it has thrown me off my game."

Wendy raises her perfect penciled eyebrows and purses her lips, which have red lipstick that matches her skirt. "Oooh, girl. Don't tell me it's the same brother who broke your heart in college."

Wow, this woman's memory is good. I remember mentioning the story to Wendy during one of my appointments here a year ago, but I didn't think it was a story that would stick. After all, which girl doesn't have a heartbreak story to tell? The fact that she remembers only goes to show how much she cares.

"Wow, I can see why that has gotten you all riled up." She continues before I can respond. My facial expression must have given her enough information to start ranting for five minutes about how men need to be more considerate of women's emotions.

Being in her late thirties and unmarried was not a deliberate choice for Wendy. But after a failed engagement and two further heartbreaks, she has decided to take a break from men. I don't blame her because I'm in the same boat.

"Do you think God brought this *old flame* back to restore your relationship?" the woman with the pink nails asks. Apparently, she wasn't so engrossed in her phone after all.

I turn to her. "Erm, I don't know about that. I can barely bring myself to have a conversation with him because I'm so angry. He hurt me too much, and it'd have to be a miracle for us to end up together again."

The woman places her phone on the table and turns to face me squarely as the stylist starts another section of braids. "You know, I used to think the same thing about me and my fiance. Three years ago, our relationship was in a mess and we broke up. During the year when we were apart, we matured, we grew closer to God, and He brought us back together. We're getting married next week." She thrusts her hand forward, showing us the big, shiny rock on her finger and everyone around the room *oohs* and *aahs*.

"Wow, congratulations. I'm glad to know that it's not all doom and gloom for everyone," I say to her. "If you don't mind sharing, why did you guys break up? What did he do?" I don't mean to compare, but I'm curious to know what struggles other couples have.

The woman smiles to herself before answering. "He didn't do anything. I did. I cheated on him...with his friend."

Gasps travel around the room and my jaw drops.

"Yeah, I know. It was only a kiss...nothing else. But it was enough to break us up. It was the biggest mistake I could've ever made, and I never thought we could recover from it. God worked on me because I had a lot of issues to address—issues that were dating back to my childhood. But once I dealt with all that, Justin and I started talking again, and God restored our relationship. It was a miracle, and an answered prayer because I can't imagine myself being with anyone else."

"I'm so happy for you. I have to admit, that's a very encouraging story." I turn to look at Wendy, who gives me a nod to show that she agrees with me.

"Yeah, so don't be too quick to discard your *old flame*." The woman makes air quotes with her fingers as she says the last two words. "Ask God why He brought him back into your life. It couldn't have been a coincidence, right?"

For the rest of my appointment, the woman's question lingers in my mind, forcing me to ask myself and God serious questions about the purpose of all the recent events. I have to admit that as much as I dread being in the same room as Alex right now, I still want to know why he broke up with me.

Did God really bring him back so He could restore our relationship? Can I really get through all this pain in my heart and look at him the same way I used to in college? I believe in miracles, but I just don't see how that can happen.

Olanna, my beloved. Trust Me.

Yes, Lord. I trust You. But show me the reason for all this. Please show me what Your plan is.

After deciding to give up the battle of wrestling with my thoughts, I let myself relax as Wendy delivers what she planned for my hair.

With my head leaned back over the sink, she soaks my loc strands for thirty minutes in detox solution. Then she washes with a residue-free shampoo and conditions with a natural oil.

After gently massaging my scalp and removing all the buildup, she rinses out the strands and re-twists them, leaving my scalp feeling fresh and clean.

Being the caring person she is, Wendy gives me another detailed hair regime and recommends products that won't irritate my scalp. "Thank you so much, Wendy. You're seriously a lifesaver."

"Aww, don't flatter me, girl. Please, don't be a stranger. Stick to our regime and I'll see you in three months."

"Yes, Ma'am." I hug her one last time before making my way out, feeling like a new woman.

The sun's rays hit my face and I embrace them fully to get a dose of vitamin D as I walk to the parking lot. I swing my bag over my shoulder and walk past a car pulling out. There's a man parked on the other side of the road, bending over, and reaching for something in his car.

As I'm about to cross the road, the sound of my name causes me to stop in my tracks. I slowly turn my head around and with the good sense of humor God has, the man who was bent over reaching for something in his car is no other than my *old flame*— Alex Yaw Obeng.

16

ALEX
THEN

Walking into Dr. Adjei's office feels like I've just stepped into the most suspenseful part of an action thriller. I have no problem with the office's white walls, or the poster of the human urinary tract, or the picture frames sitting on the shelf with laminated certificates.

The problem is the pounding of my heart beating against my chest, my shallow breathing, and the perspiration dampening my underarms, which are all indicators that I'm not handling this situation as well as I thought I would.

After telling Dad about my predicament, it only took one phone call, and we were out of the house and driving half an hour to Dr. Adjei's clinic for a consultation. The fact that hearing my story prompted Dad's childhood friend to give us an emergency appointment today means this is serious. On our way here, I sent several prayers up to God to ease my anxiety, but I can't shake the feeling of dread hanging over me like a dark cloud.

"Thank you so much for seeing us, Kofi." Dad shakes Dr. Adjei's hand.

"Daniel, please don't thank me. It's the least I could do, my brother. It's one perk of having a private practice. How is Abena?"

"She's fine. Although she doesn't know about this yet. We thought we would assess the severity of the situation before breaking the news to her," Dad says and the two older men turn to look at me.

"How are you, Alex?" Dr. Adjei extends his hand.

I shrug. "I'm okay, thank you." I shake his hand and we all take our seat at the desk.

Apparently, the two men—who I sometimes refer to as the mustache twins—grew up in the same neighborhood in Accra, Ghana, and they even went to the same primary and secondary school. But Dr. Adjei got a scholarship to study abroad and left Ghana years before Mom and Dad met. When my parents finally moved to the U.S. years later, the two men reconnected and their friendship has remained strong ever since.

Over the years, our two families have visited each other most summers and in my freshman year of college, we took a trip to the Dominican Republic along with Dr. Adjei's wife and their high school twin sons, Daniel and David. I always thought it was cool to know someone personally who is a doctor and runs a private practice, but I never thought I would one day need his services.

Dr. Adjei clears his throat and pushes his glasses close to his face before firing questions at me. "Okay, Alex. You said you found the lump a week ago, right?"

Although I'm now ninety percent certain it has been longer than a week, all I do is nod, because that's the only action my body permits me to do.

He leans forward and rests his forearms on his desk. "Has it grown bigger since you found it?"

"I...don't think so." Now I'm even questioning my memory.

"Does it hurt?"

I shake my head and he moves on to ask about my sexual health history as well as whether I have any urinary symptoms. I shake my head at all his questions. Then he asks Dad about whether there is any family history of urological cancers and my body stiffens as my head turns in Dad's direction.

Dad adjusts in his seat and fiddles with his hands before shaking his head. "Not that I'm aware of."

"Okay, good." Dr. Adjei sighs before continuing. "If you don't mind, Alex, I'd like to perform a physical examination. Your dad can stay in the room and act as your chaperone."

"Yes, please." I turn to look at Dad, who pats my shoulder before Dr. Adjei stands up and picks up a box of gloves.

He leads us to the exam table, pulls the curtains, rattles out instructions about what he is going to do, and within five minutes, the physical examination is complete with us sitting back at his desk.

Trying to read Dr. Adjei's facial expression is a waste of time because it's still as neutral as when we first got here. I'm not sure if that's a good or bad thing, but rather than projecting my fears onto him, I wait for him to talk.

"So, there's definitely a lump there." He rolls the sleeve of his white coat. "It could be something as common as a cyst, which is just a sac of fluid. Those are harmless and don't cause any trouble." He pauses and lets out a breath. "But what would be useful to exclude, especially in someone your age, is...testicular cancer."

My breath hitches in my throat and before I can get my thoughts together to make a coherent sentence, Dad asks. "How can we exclude that?"

Dr. Adjei adjusts his glasses and rubs his mustache. "We would first need to do some blood tests to check for tumor markers. We can do them today and we'll have the results ready to interpret by next week."

"Okay, and what about a scan?" Dad asks again.

Dr. Adjei nods. "Yes, we can do an ultrasound scan next week as well to check whether this lump is a fluid-filled sac or solid."

"Next week?" Panic sets into Dad's voice. "Can't he have a scan today as well?"

"I'm sorry, Daniel. I already checked the schedule, and we didn't have any ultrasound appointments today. If there are any cancellations during the week, though, I'll let you know."

"No, that's okay. Next week should be fine." Dad responds. "Yaw is going back to college tomorrow, anyway. He can come back for the scan. Right, son?"

I lift my head up to look at the doctor as I didn't even realize I'd been staring at the floor the entire time. Again, with my thoughts too jumbled to think about the right words, I nod and drop my gaze again to the floor.

"Great. I'll go get the nurse who will take your blood sample today," Dr. Adjei says before stepping out of the room, leaving me alone with Dad.

He reaches for my hand. "Don't worry about it, son. God is in control. You hear me? He is in control."

I nod and let out the breath I'd been holding to calm my breathing. *Lord, please. Help me.*

Dr. Adjei re-enters the room, followed by a nurse dressed in blue scrubs and a straight weave tied in a low ponytail. "Here's Amanda. If you follow her, she'll do your blood test and I'll speak to you next week."

"Thank you so much for your help." Dad shakes his friend's hand again and we follow Amanda out of the office, down the hallway, and into the third room on the right.

There are cubicles on either side of the room, some of them occupied by nurses taking blood samples from patients, while others just have patients chatting with their friends and family, or sitting on their own.

"Please take a seat here." Amanda points to the cubicle at the far end of the room. "I'm just going to take care of something quickly in the next room and I'll be back to take your blood sample."

"Thank you so much," Dad says to her, and she smiles before walking out of the room.

"Son, I'm going to get some water from the fountain and update your mom. Do you want me to get you anything?"

I shake my head, so he squeezes my shoulder again and leaves the room. Turning my head slowly to look out the window, I watch the nurses and doctors walk past. I want to pray, but I don't know what words to say. In my panic, I take out my phone from my pocket and dial Olanna's number. I don't even know if I want to tell her what's going on, but I need to talk to someone.

"Hey, baby." Her soft voice comes through from the phone, already providing me some relief.

"Hey," I respond as a lump builds in my throat.

"Is everything okay?" she asks, concern etched in her voice. "Is your dad okay?"

Here's the perfect opportunity to tell her that this is not about Dad. Here's the moment to tell her I'm so scared and I don't want to take any tests and I prefer to live without knowing. But instead of correcting the mistakes I've made so far, I choose cowardice and give in to fear.

I shake my head as a tear falls. "Not really." I sniffle and wipe my eyes. "He...uh...he has some vague symptoms and they're going to do some blood tests and a scan. He'll have results next week, so I'll have to come back again."

"Aww, I'm so sorry to hear that," Olanna says. "I wish I was there with you right now."

"Honestly, me too."

"Baby, is there anything I can do to help?"

I pause for a second to steady my breathing before responding. "You can pray for me...I mean for him. That all these tests would come back normal."

"Of course," she says and for the next few minutes, I close my eyes and listen to her pray for healing and strength, while I claim all the prayers for myself in my heart.

17

ALEX
NOW

Who says God doesn't answer prayers? Definitely not me, because my God is too good. After sending my petitions up to Him this morning, begging Him to provide an opportunity to speak to Olanna without it seeming like I'm harassing her at work, He showed up for me.

Here's the moment where I find someone to do my happy dance with, which includes some fists pumps and chest bumps. But Kwame isn't here, so I'll respect myself and not let this opportunity go to waste.

"Olanna," I call out and she stops in her tracks before turning her head slowly to look at me. Instead of the irritated and stony look she has been giving me so far, Olanna's eyes soften when our eyes meet and, dare I say, there's even a faint sparkle in them.

Lord, please, don't let her walk away.

I wait a few seconds and when she doesn't move, I take that as my cue and inch toward her, getting close enough to inhale her hypnotizing tropical scent. I'm close enough to notice she has re-twisted her locs and looks refreshed and relaxed. I'm close enough to notice the smile forming on her lips accompanied by a slight shake of her head, which I recognize as a gesture she makes when she's feeling amused.

Is that...is that really a smile? Or am I now imagining things?

"What are you doing here?" she asks, and if I hadn't already convinced myself that this was really happening, I would've pinched my arm to wake me up from my dream. She's actually talking to me and attempting to make a conversation? *Hallelujah.*

"I ran out of food at my apartment, so I thought I'd make a quick trip to the grocery store." I nod toward my car.

"Okay, then. I won't keep you." She takes retreating steps onto the road as a car approaches her from the right.

"Olanna, wait..." In one swift motion, I run toward her and wrap my arms around her before lifting her off the ground and turning her away from the car.

The driver swears at us before honking multiple times and driving off, but time stands still as we both stare into each other's eyes, her hands planted firmly against my chest and her warm breath mingling with mine.

She adjusts her feet on the ground to gain her balance and that's when I realize I'm still holding her really tight. "I'm sorry." I let go of her and take a step back as she smoothes out the creases on her jacket.

"Thank you," she says under her breath. "I didn't see the car coming and—"

"Olanna, please, can we talk?" I cut her off because if God has started out my day by throwing blessings my way like this, I'll go straight to the point and not waste any more time.

When she shakes her head, I step even closer. "Please, I need to explain." I lift her chin up with my finger, so her eyes meet mine because I know she can also feel the electricity that courses through our veins when we look at each other.

"I can't," she whispers.

"You can't or you won't?" I press in, holding her hand, and just when I start getting used to her warmth, she pulls away.

"No, don't do that." She raises her voice, letting me know I've overstepped my boundary.

"I'm sorry." I raise both hands in the air and step back again. "But Olanna, please..."

"Why are you begging me, Alex?" She looks at me again and the sparkles in her eyes are long gone, replaced by hurt threatening to consume them. "You remember what I told you the day I came to your apartment?"

"Of course I remember, and I beat myself every day for letting you walk away."

"You had a choice." Her voice breaks as another car drives past us. "But you let me walk out of your life without thinking of the consequences." She turns around and starts walking across the road.

Desperate to make her stay, I blurt out, "I had health problems." And it works.

On the other side of the road, Olanna stops and turns to look at me. "What?" Her forehead creases up in confusion as I walk across to meet her. "Are you...are you dying?"

I shake my head vigorously to relieve her worries. "No, I'm not, but there's so much I need to tell you. Please have lunch with me. I'll explain everything." I extend my hand to her and after holding back for a few seconds, she finally lets me hold her hand.

I never found another branch of Chicken Nugget Palace apart from the one close to the NYU campus, so you can imagine my excitement when Olanna and I find one inside the mall. Her silent gasp followed by a wide grin tells me she's as excited as I am, so with our shared and unspoken consent, we make our way toward the fast-food restaurant which—if we say so ourselves—makes the best chicken in the whole wide world.

This one is smaller than the one we frequented in college, but it doesn't matter because the menu is still the same. With Olanna's hand still in mine, I guide her to a window seat because she always loved sitting on the high chairs and letting her feet dangle from them as she challenged me to our milkshake drinking race.

She always won—or shall I say, I always let her win—because she was the queen of my heart and it was my duty to give her what she wanted. Two years have passed, and a lot has happened between us, but she's still the queen of my heart and I need her to believe that.

"The usual?" I ask when she takes a seat and places her bag on the table.

"Yeah, medium, please."

"Yes, Ma'am." I make my way to the counter, ordering us both spicy chicken nuggets, fries and large peanut butter and banana milkshakes. I pay for our order and five minutes later, I'm walking back to our seat with our food.

Olanna's face lights up when I place the food in front of her and the milkshake is the first thing she tries. "Hmm, it still tastes so good." She closes her eyes and tips her head back.

"You can say that again." I chuckle and she follows suit.

"Honestly, I can't remember the last time I had Chicken Nugget Palace food."

I place a nugget in my mouth. "I don't remember the last time either, but I remember I was with you."

Her gaze moves from her burger and she locks eyes with me for the first time since we've been here. She holds the gaze for a long time and I wait patiently, hoping that if not for anything, at least for the sake of the good times we shared, that she'd engage with me.

"Yeah, so much has changed since then, hasn't it?" She clears her throat and picks up some fries from her plate before putting it in her mouth.

"Yeah, but you still look as beautiful as ever," I respond, choosing not to play it subtle.

She looks at me again before a smile breaks on the corners of her lips. "Thank you. You don't look too bad yourself."

Thank You, Lord. She's finally engaging. Now I just need to make sure I don't say or do something stupid that'll ruin this beautiful moment.

"So, CEO, huh? How did that happen?" I lean back in my seat and rest my hand on my jaw.

She shrugs as she takes another sip of her milkshake. "Well, I guess you could say we can make our plans, but eventually, God's plans always prevail." She picks up a nugget and continues. "Manny never wanted to take over Madu Health. My dad wasn't happy about it at first, but he realized Manny was called to do something different. He and Heather are doing great running their own charity marketing agency called Charis Charity Marketing. They've made a huge impact across the globe over the last two years, especially in Nigeria and other African countries."

"Wow. That's amazing. So I'm guessing Emmanuel and Heather got married then?"

She pulls her brows together. "Yeah, how did you know?"

I lean back and scratch my head. I can't let her know that I've been going around asking about her. "Erm…Melissa might have slipped something out after our last meeting. You know how excited she can get, right?" I let out a nervous chuckle, but Olanna seems to be buying it.

"Yeah, they got married and they have a beautiful daughter —Ayannah. I can't believe I'm an aunt. I'm so blessed."

"Indeed, you are." I smile at her as she dabs the corner of her mouth with a napkin.

"What about you? How did you get this position and how did they come to trust you so quickly?"

I slurp the last of my milkshake. "Well, in senior year, I became really interested in the SEO world. So after college graduation, I built a website and did some work on my own to build my portfolio. Then I pitched my ideas to a few companies and a year ago, HearCare hired me. When it comes to them sending me to you, though, that's all on God. I had nothing to do with that."

Her eyebrows furrow. "What do you mean?"

I pause as my gaze drops to her hand on the table. I know I shouldn't, but I can't help myself. Being this close to her does things to me I can't explain. One of them is finding it difficult to keep my hands away from her, like I'm trying really hard to do right now.

"I mean that for two years, I prayed for God to give me an opportunity to sit down with you again." I give in to my urge and reach for her hand. When she doesn't pull away, I cover her hand with mine.

"So you got an answered prayer. Now what?" Her tone is neutral, yet her expression is as serious as I've ever known it to be.

Now is not the time to beat around the bush. I prayed and God came through for me. He did what He promised and brought me back to Olanna. Here is the part where I obey and tell her everything that happened, even at the risk of her thinking the worst of me.

"Alex?" The sound of my name in her mouth is like a balm that soothes my heart. But it pulls me out of the black hole of my thoughts, reminding me about the important task at hand. I can't mess this up.

"Yes, baby." Her body stiffens at my use of the term of endearment, but I'm not even sorry. I've hidden so many things from her before, but one thing I never intend to do is hide the way I still feel about her.

"What happened?" she asks. "What health problems did you have?"

Okay, here we go. Lord, please take control. I let out a huge breath and start talking.

18

ALEX
THEN

When Dr. Adjei mentioned the diagnosis five minutes ago, it felt like an out-of-body experience, like I wasn't sitting there when he told me I have cancer at twenty-one years old.

For the last week, Dad, Mom and I have prayed about this. Kwame joined me in praying and even Olanna—even though she didn't know the entire truth—has been praying that these results will be favorable. *How can this be?*

"Alex?" Dr. Adjei's voice, starting out distant, becomes louder and finally zaps me out of my daydream when Dad's hand squeezes my shoulder.

Tears blur my vision as my gaze moves from my trembling hands to the desk that separates me from the doctor. He's still looking at me, waiting for me to answer the question I don't remember him asking.

"*Nyame boa yɛn o.*" Mom places her hands on her head and wails. The tears stream down her face as she fidgets in her seat and calls on God to help us.

Dad, who has been silent since the news, lets out a sigh, then lowers his head and shakes it. "I know this is a lot to take in, son, but..."

"Am I going to die?" The words don't feel like mine, but they weigh heavily on my tongue as tears escape from my eyes. "Please, be honest with me."

Dr. Adjei leans forward and places his arms on the desk. "Testicular cancer is the most common cancer among adolescent and young adult males, but it is also very treatable. The good news is that from your ultrasound scan and blood tests, we think the cancer is only stage 1A. This means it hasn't spread outside the testicle. Your tumor markers were also normal, which is very reassuring. Of course, the staging process will continue after the surgeon removes the tissue, but so far, our hope is still alive," he says with an upbeat tone, which does nothing to cheer me up.

"So, Kofi, what options do we have? Where do we go from here?" Dad asks.

"Well, I have to refer to the hospital's oncology team so they can discuss the treatment options in more detail. Alex, you may not need radiotherapy or chemotherapy because surgery to remove the testicle is usually the first treatment."

"What?" My eyes widen at his response. "Remove the whole testicle? Won't that...won't that affect my ability to have children in the future?" Mom's wailing increases, and this time she stands up and paces the length of the room, sending prayers up to God in Twi.

I turn to Dad and send unspoken pleas his way. He takes the hint and clears his throat.

"Erm...Kofi, please, is there a less invasive way to do this? Can they just take out the cancerous cells themselves without taking out the whole testicle?"

Dr. Adjei shakes his head before responding. "I'm afraid not. Because of the size, it will be more effective to take the whole thing out, to reduce the chances of leaving any cells behind, which may cause a relapse in the future."

"A relapse? So even after surgery, there's a chance the cancer could come back?" My voice breaks as I swipe tears away from my face.

"That's the risk the surgeons will try to minimize as much as possible," the doctor responds. "Also, removing one testicle rarely affects fertility, but there's a small risk that the remaining one might not work as well. It's only a small risk, Alex, so everything could turn out fine."

"And what if it doesn't?"

Dr. Adjei sighs. "We have to keep hope alive, son."

I can't believe this is happening. This has to be a joke or a dream. It better be a bad dream. I can deal with a bad dream as long as I wake up from it. This wasn't how this was supposed to turn out. It was meant to be good news. I was hoping Dr. Adjei would give us good news, so I can finally come clean to Olanna. What do I tell her now? *Oh, Lord. Please help me.*

I push myself up as Dr. Adjei and my parents' voices fade into the background. The throbbing of my heartbeat intensifies as my feet carry me to the corner of the office, where I slide to the floor and let my sobs out while Dr. Adjei and Dad's arms try their best to console me.

I've never felt as helpless as I do now. With my behind glued to this hospital bed, I've watched nurse after nurse walk in here to perform different procedures—drawing blood samples, doing an ECG, checking my blood pressure and checking my weight. The anesthetists and the surgeons have also been throwing lots of information at me—most of which I can't remember.

The worst part of all this is that I have to sit here and watch

Olanna's messages ping in from time to time, sending me words of encouragement for Dad. I still haven't had the courage to tell her because...I just can't. I should've listened to Kwame and never lied to her. What is she going to think of me if I mention all this now?

It's not enough that there are already risks associated with this surgery, but now I also have all the potential post-surgical complications to add to my list of worries. Apart from praying that the surgery goes well, I can't stop thinking about the possibility that this could affect my fertility.

Mom and Dad have been so supportive, staying by my side and keeping me distracted. But it's moments like this, when I'm alone, that the worries flood in again and take over me. Most times, I lose the battle against these thoughts and allow them to consume me.

My phone vibrates on my bed and I turn my head slowly to look at it, silently praying it's not Olanna because I don't know what to say to her. When I turn the phone over, Kwame's smiling face is on the screen, alerting me to a video call. I swipe right and put my headphones on.

"So this is really happening, huh?" Kwame asks, and I nod before leaning back. "Hope they're treating you nice, at least." He cracks a smile to lighten the mood, but when I don't return his smile, I'm sure he gets the memo.

"I'm really sorry, man," he says. "I can only imagine how difficult this is for you. But please, if anything, try to look on the bright side. It could've been a lot worse."

"Yeah, of course." I nod before pulling on the neckline of the hospital gown, and Kwame throws his head back and laughs. "What's so funny?"

"Could you look any more uncomfortable in that gown?"

"Well, it's a good thing fashion is no one's priority here." I glance around my room before watching a nurse walk past to the other end of the ward.

"Have you spoken to Olanna yet?" Kwame's question makes me groan internally. I don't even need to respond and Kwame gets his answer. "Come on, man. Seriously?"

"It's not that simple." I drop my head and try to find the words, but I can't. "I'm the one going through this, so I know how it feels. You don't, so please don't judge me."

Kwame opens his mouth to say something, but then shuts it again. "You're right. I'm sorry, man," he finally says after a brief pause. "Let's focus on praying that the surgery goes well, alright?"

"Thanks, man."

"By the way, where are your parents?"

"The doctors asked if I wanted either of my parents to donate blood to me in case I needed a transfusion during the surgery. I agreed to that, but unfortunately when they tested my parent's blood samples, neither of them were a match for me. Both of them are AB positive and I'm O negative, so we'll have donor blood on standby. My parents went to get something to eat, but they should be back soon. My surgery will be in two hours. The doctor says if all goes well, I should be able to go home today."

"That's cool. So by the end of today, everything could be over?" Kwame asks and I nod. Then, after a few seconds, he tilts his head and looks at me. "Wait a minute. If both your parents are AB positive, then shouldn't you be an A, B, or AB? How did you end up being O negative? Dude, you're weird." Kwame chuckles, but when I maintain my straight face, his smile disappears.

"What is that supposed to mean?" I ask, trying to decipher his medical jargon. But Kwame waves a dismissive hand.

He scratches his head and averts his gaze. "Erm...never mind, bro. You know I'm always trippin'. You shouldn't be talking this much. You go in for surgery soon, so you need to rest."

"I've done a lot of resting for one day." I grunt. "There's no difference between this place and a prison."

"A prison you will get out of soon, by the grace of God."

"Amen," we both say, and Kwame ends the call.

I swipe through Olanna's recent messages where she's asking if I'm okay and I type a quick response with all the emojis she loves to let her know I'm doing well. It's the best I can do, so she doesn't suspect anything—at least until I can get my thoughts together and figure out how I want to tell her.

As much as I'm trying to stay hopeful, I can't shake away the feeling that this situation is a ticking time bomb waiting to explode. I just hope that when it eventually does, the damage will be salvageable and I'll still have Olanna in my life.

19

OLANNA
NOW

"Cancer?" My eyes widen as I stare at Alex. "Wow. I...I had no idea. I'm really sorry that happened to you."

"It's okay, baby." He holds my hand and squeezes gently. "You didn't know because I didn't tell you."

With those words, the reality of what really happened hits me and I move my hand away from his grip. "Wait a minute. Did you hear what you just said? You were diagnosed with cancer and you didn't tell me?" My voice comes out more strained as I struggle to keep my emotions in check.

Heat rises in my chest and a lump builds in my throat as a mixture of anger and sadness turns my stomach sour and threatens to open the floodgates of tears. Remorse washes over his face as he lowers his head. I want to empathize with him, but his actions have sent out betraying daggers into the same heart that loves him.

"So, all those times you told me your dad was sick, *you* were the one who was going to the hospital?"

He sighs and nods.

"Was your dad ever sick at all?"

He doesn't need to respond because his expression exposes his lies. "Olanna, I..."

"I can't believe this." I cut him short, my voice trembling. "How could you keep such information away from me? Did you think I wouldn't understand? That I wouldn't care enough to stand by you?"

He opens his mouth to speak, but I cut him off again.

"Was I not a good girlfriend to you? Was I not a good *friend* to you? Did you find me so appalling that you didn't trust me enough to open up about what you were going through?"

"No, it's not that I didn't trust you."

"Then what was it, Alex? I'm sure you told Kwame everything, right? You told Kwame, yet you claimed I was your best friend. What excuse could you possibly give to explain why you lied to me?"

"I was scared." Tears wet his eyes as he stares straight into mine. "I'm sorry, but it's the truth. I was scared of what you would think of me. I was ashamed that..." He pauses and lowers his head again before wiping his tears with the sleeve of his shirt. "I was ashamed to tell you that there was a possibility my fertility would be affected. I was scared that you wouldn't look at me the same and that you would leave me."

An unintentional snort escapes from my mouth, but it doesn't mask the tears flowing from my eyes. "Well, isn't that ironic?" I lean back in my chair. "You were scared that I would leave, but you were the one who broke up with me."

"I had too many things going through my mind." I reach for her hand again, but she pulls away. "After the surgery, I wanted to tell you everything, but I wasn't okay, Olanna. The physical ailment was out of my body, but my mind was not in the right place. For months, I kept checking and rechecking because I kept convincing myself I had found another lump.

"Every time I had a cough, I convinced myself it was lung

cancer and every time I had a headache, I was sure it was a brain tumor. It messed up my head because even though God healed me, there was always that feeling of uncertainty hanging at the back of my mind about whether it'll come back. I didn't want to dump that on you. I didn't want to be a burden to you." He presses his lips together as another tear falls.

I want to step forward and wipe his tears, but I'm rooted to my spot. "You should've told me, Alex. If you had said something, you would've spared me a lot of pain."

"Yes, but the story doesn't end there. Something else happened and I…"

"I'm tired of your lies, Alex. I'm tired of your excuses and your explanations. You know I would've stood by you, but you shut me out. You were only thinking about yourself, weren't you?"

"Olanna, it was a difficult time for me, but I never stopped loving you and you know it."

I get off the high chair, my feet landing firmly on the ground. "No, I don't know anything. I don't know you. The man I fell in love with trusted me. He would've *never* treated me the way you did and you're *not* him."

Alex steps down from his chair too and holds my hand, the warmth of his touch sending tingles up my arm. "Olanna, it's still me," he says, rubbing his thumb over the back of my hand. "I'm still the man you fell in love with, but a much better man who will make it up to you. Just tell me what you want me to do and I'll do it, please."

My heart melts at his soft gaze and the more he caresses my hand, the more I want him to pull me close. As I stare at his hand on mine, for a moment, I let my guard down, my heart remembering the old times, when his arms felt like home.

But even if I pull him close, even if I let him hold me, his daggers are still wedged deep into my heart. Since the day he let me walk out of his life, I've only seen him as Alex—the guy who broke my heart.

"I gave my heart to you and I loved you in every way I could. Every day, I stood by you, but when the going got tough, you chose yourself and I no longer mattered to you. You ran away and guess what? You lost a good thing, so deal with the consequences. I've spent the last two years trying to get over you, and I will not put myself through this again. I'm sorry that you had cancer and I'm glad God healed you, but I can't do this." I close my eyes and remove my hand from his grip. "I'm sorry."

"Olanna…"

"Nothing you say or do will change my mind, Alex. Please, leave me alone." I grab my bag from the table and walk past him.

"Olanna, please wait. There's something else I need to tell you. Please." His voice calls out to me, but I don't stop. My determined steps take me all the way back to the parking lot and when I'm safe in my car, I let the uncontrollable sobs break free.

20

ALEX
THEN

Sleep. Water. Pain relief. That's how I spent my entire night. The doctors made a last-minute decision to keep me overnight to monitor my blood pressure, which kept dipping, so Mom and Dad went home late last night after I was moved to the post-surgical ward.

Waking up from surgery with an oxygen mask on my face while feeling dizzy and sluggish was the scariest moment I've ever had to live through. Even though the doctors said the surgery was successful, Mom couldn't stop herself from worrying. She asked if I was okay every ten minutes and although I appreciated her care, it became annoying because all I wanted to do was rest.

Dad, as usual, didn't say much, but he made his presence known by squeezing my shoulder from time to time. I drifted in and out of sleep and every time I opened my eyes, my gaze landed on Dad reading his Bible. They said they'll be coming back at noon and hopefully it'll be time to go home then.

"Knock-knock." A red-haired nurse pokes her head into my room as I return from my toilet break. "Good morning. Did you sleep well?"

I nod and take slow steps to the bed, making sure not to strain the lower half of my body. "Yeah, it could have been worse."

"Do you need any more pain relief this morning?"

"Erm...maybe some Tylenol for later, if that's okay." I'm so glad I'm stable enough to no longer need the regular pain relief.

"Here you go." She places a small cup with two pills on the table before scrolling through the mobile computer she brought in with her. "Your vital signs have been stable all night, which is reassuring. Hopefully, the doctors will let you go home today. I'll be back later with a breakfast sandwich."

"Thanks. I appreciate it."

She types something quickly and then smiles at me before wheeling the computer out of the room and closing the door behind her. After slowly getting myself freshened up and changing out of the hospital gown into some new clothes, my body starts feeling much better.

A soft knock comes from the door again and this time, Mom and Dad walk in. They look well rested with a change of clothes. "Son, how are you doing?" Mom rushes to my side and snuggles me like a five-year-old.

"I'm much better."

"Oh, *aseda nka onyame*." She sits next to me on the bed while Dad hovers on his feet. "Have you eaten anything?" Mom asks, and I shake my head.

"Do you want us to get you some food?"

"No, the nurse said she'll get me a sandwich. I'll just eat that and if I don't like it, I'll eat the food at home." I smile at Mom, who presses her hand against my cheek.

"I made you some *jollof* rice, just the way you like it."

Thinking about Mom's delicious spicy *jollof* makes me feel much better. "Thanks, Mom."

"Has the doctor been around this morning?" Dad asks and shoves his hand into his jacket pocket.

"No, not yet. The nurse said they'll be making their rounds soon."

"Okay, I'll see if I can find them." He nods and then leaves the room while Mom lingers behind.

She turns my face, so I'm looking at her. "Are you sure you're okay, honey?" she asks, her eyes searching mine. She might be the first one to get worried, but one thing Mom has always been is intuitive.

I want to tell her everything—about Olanna, about my jumbled thoughts, and about the fact that I can't stop thinking about the comment Kwame made yesterday. But like all the other times, the words catch in my throat and instead of speaking up, I nod. "Yes, Mom. I'm okay."

"Alright then. I will join your father so we can find out what the plan is." She plants a kiss on my cheek and then heads out the door.

That's when I take out my phone and start Googling about blood group types. A part of me cautions me not to, but my curiosity gets the better of me. Page after page, my eyes scan through the paragraphs of texts and the more I read, the more unsettled I become.

Apparently, sometimes AB parents can have an O child, but it is extremely rare according to studies. I should find that information comforting, but instead, my brain focuses on the *extremely rare.*

Scrolling through my contact list, I put through a video call to Kwame and he picks up on the third ring.

"Yo, bro, are you okay? You look kinda pale."

"Yeah, I'm fine. The pain is controlled," I respond. "I can't stop thinking about the comment you made yesterday."

"About the blood groups? I knew it." Kwame groans and rubs

his temples slowly. "Listen, bro. I'm only a pre-med student. I know nothing at this point. You shouldn't listen to me."

"I figured you were going to say that." I tilt my head. "So I did some Googling."

Kwame rolls his eyes. "I thought we agreed not to Google symptoms. The internet always tries to convince you it's the worst-case scenario."

"Or it could just tell you facts." The tone in my voice is serious as I glance at Mom and Dad speaking to the doctor out on the ward. Kwame pauses and looks me in the eye. I know he's thinking the same thing, too.

"Hang on, bro. I think it's very dangerous to make assumptions like this." He shakes his head. "You should speak to your parents directly. I'm sure they'll clear any doubts you have."

"Or I could just check my medical chart or something. Shouldn't I have a file at the foot of my bed?" I shuffle to the edge before looking around the room for my medical notes when Kwame starts laughing at me.

"What's funny?"

"I don't think you'll find any paper charts in your room. Most hospitals have advanced to electronic notes now. "

"Aww, man. I knew I should've looked when the nurse came by earlier."

"Dude, stop it, please. Instead of sneaking around and doing all this digging, don't you think it'll be better to ask your parents directly?"

I swallow to wet my dry mouth. This day is just getting weirder and weirder. I'm probably overthinking this, but if there's something they're hiding from me, then I believe I deserve to know the truth. "Yeah, you're right, man. I'll ask them when we're back at home because I don't think this is something we should talk about in the hospital."

"Bet," Kwame says. "Aigh't, man. I'm out. Talk to you later, man."

We end the call and a few minutes later; the nurse comes back in with some food, which she places on the table. I push the tray away, not because the sandwich and ice cream don't look appealing, but there's so much going through my mind right now and the last thing I want to do is eat.

21

ALEX
NOW

I used to have dreams that the cancer came back. These dreams intensified the weeks after my surgery. While I was in hospital, I had faith that God is a healer and He came through for me and healed me. But as soon as I got out of the hospital, I looked for every single opportunity to make myself believe I was going to end up in the hospital again.

For a long time, there was nothing my parents or Kwame could say to make me believe otherwise. I just couldn't shake off the feeling that if it had happened once, then it could happen again. Living in that constant fear wrecked me. I went from living my life for God to doing things because of the fear of the unknown. The fact that I had so many uncertainties about myself was the reason I started pushing Olanna away.

I thought she would understand when I told her yesterday, but of course, I thought wrong. This is something I should've told her two years ago. I see that now. It would've made more sense if I had opened up to her then. No matter how hard I try to explain now, she won't be able to get past the fact that I hurt her. I shot myself in the foot and this is me paying for it.

Trust Me, my beloved.

Lord, I do. I trust You, but nothing I've done so far has helped. I don't see how this can ever work out. Olanna hates me.

Is there anything impossible for Me to do?

No, Lord. There isn't.

Then trust Me, My beloved. I am still at work. Trust Me.

The sound of my ringing phone forces me to open my eyes and my gaze lands on the golden chandelier hanging down from the ceiling of my studio apartment. After watching Olanna drive off yesterday from the parking lot with tears in her eyes, guilt ravaged my being as I drove back to my apartment. As soon as I got in, I jumped into the shower and lay on my bed because I didn't have the motivation or the appetite to cook anything. I didn't realize when I fell asleep.

My phone rings again, and I lean over to grab it from the nightstand. It's eight AM. I rub my eyes as I stare at the photo of Dad and me on my phone screen. "Hello?" My voice is groggy, so I clear my throat and speak again. "Hey, Dad."

"Good morning, Yaw. Are you okay?" His voice comes through the phone and I place it on speaker as I walk over to the couch next to the window.

"Yes, I am. How's Mom?"

"I'm doing well, my darling." Mom's voice takes over and I know they have me on speakerphone. "We're about to leave for church, but I was worried about you as we hadn't heard from you in a few days, so I asked your dad to call you to make sure you're okay."

I smile and rub my forehead. She'll never change. Always a worrier. "I'm fine, Mom."

"*Wow ɔ awer ɛhyem?*" She asks in Twi.

"Yes, Mom. I'm very sure."

"No, I'm not convinced because you sound low. Does this have anything to do with Olanna?"

I let out a sigh as I forgot how intuitive Mom gets. She's not going to give up, so there's no point prolonging this conversation. "Yes, Mom. It does. I finally spoke to her yesterday." I explain how it all went down and one blessing that has come with being an only child is that the attention has always been on me.

My parents are both so approachable and I've never had issues with telling them about my personal problems. They always tell me the truth, correct me if I'm going the wrong way, and encourage me when I feel discouraged.

"The frustrating thing is that she didn't let me finish my explanation. I didn't get the chance to tell her about my trip to Ghana and I don't know if she'll ever listen to me again."

"Hmm. I understand where she's coming from," Dad chimes in.

"Yes, I do too. That's why I don't blame her. The problem is, I don't know where to go from here."

"You still love her, don't you?" Mom asks.

I nod before realizing she can't see me, so I use my words. "Yes, Mom. I thought my feelings had fizzled, but seeing her the last two weeks has only confirmed that those feelings never went away. I still love her."

"Do you know if she reciprocates those feelings?"

I sigh and stare out my window. "I'm not sure, Mom. If she does, she has a good way of hiding it. When we had lunch yesterday, it was nice to sit there and reminisce about all the good times we had. I missed talking to her and spending time with her. Apart from being a loving girlfriend, she was a wonderful friend to me and I blew it."

"Yaw, the past is in the past," Dad speaks. "To move forward from this, you have to stop dwelling on the past. Yes, you made mistakes and hurt her, but let's focus on how we'll move forward from here. What has God said to you?"

I clear my throat. "Well, every time I pray about this, I get the same response, which is that I should trust Him."

"Then do so," Mom says. "*Onyankopɔn renhyɛ wo aniwu da.* Never. God can never put you to shame."

"Amen. Thanks, Mom." Mom and Dad spend a few minutes praying for me in Twi and when they're done, we say our good-byes and end the call.

After looking at the gorgeous view outside my window for a few minutes, the previous doubt that filled my heart slowly fades away, and in its place, hope that God's got this.

So before I can talk my heart into unbelief again, I push myself off the couch and make some omelets and toast. I would've put the eggs to good use if I made *kosua ne meko* instead. It's a Ghanaian snack made from boiled eggs stuffed with tomato relish. But all is not lost. That'll be my adventure for tomorrow.

After breakfast, I shower again and sit on the couch in the living room area of the apartment. Picking up the TV remote, I put it on and scroll through the different TV stations before settling for YouTube and playing some worship songs by the Ghanaian gospel artist Joe Mettle. I pick up my Bible and open it up to the back, which has a list of Bible passages about different topics. Under the title 'trust,' the first suggested story is the story of Abraham.

Opening my Bible to Genesis chapter twelve, I read about Abraham's story, from when God first called him to when God promised him a son, and finally to when God asked him to sacrifice his son, Isaac. In all these circumstances, it must've taken a lot of trust to believe that the outcome would be good, even though Abraham couldn't see the result. I flip through to Hebrews chapter eleven and read the first verse, which says:

Faith shows the reality of what we hope for; it is the evidence of things we cannot see.

. . .

Even though I can't see the end right now, I can rest because I know God can be trusted. If He could heal me from my previous physical and emotional traumas, what makes me think He can't come through for me now?

In the past, I ran away when the going got tough, but this time, I'm staying with God till the end. God brought me here and I refuse to leave without accomplishing what He sent me to do.

22

ALEX
THEN

After ending the phone call with Kwame, the doctors trooped into my hospital room, followed by Mom and Dad. They shared the good news that the surgery was a success and my observations were stable, so I was free to go home.

I thought I'd be more excited than I was, but I couldn't help worrying about the truth that was waiting for me at home. Mom and Dad tucked me in bed as soon as we arrived and Mom warned me to stay in bed and call her on her phone if I needed anything.

My ensuite bedroom is spacious, with a comfortable double bed and desk in the corner. The bathroom is a short walking distance from my bed, which I'm grateful for, especially at a time like this.

"Don't get out of this bed. *Woate me asɛm anaa?*" She wagged a finger at me and waited for me to confirm I had heard her before she left my room half an hour ago.

The pain is much more bearable now and I can walk myself to the bathroom, but Mom doesn't want to hear that. She gave strict instructions to call Dad if I needed to use the bathroom.

I cover my head with my pillow to stop my thoughts from running wild, but it only makes matters worse. I can't stay here. I need answers. Pushing myself up, I swing my legs over the bed before dialing Mom's number.

"Mom?" I speak into my phone when she picks up.

"I thought you were sleeping?" Her alarmed voice cuts through before the sound of approaching footsteps travel into my ears from the stairs. She walks into my room, distressed eyes scanning me from head to toe. "*So wo ho ye?*"

"Honestly, Mom? No. I'm not okay." I stare into the distance as a ball of emotion wells up in my chest.

She rushes to my side and sits next to me on the bed. "*Dɛn na ɛyɛ bɔne, me ba?*" She wraps her arm around my shoulders.

"What's wrong is that I don't think you've been honest with me."

"*Herh*. Honest about what?"

I pause and exhale a long breath before saying something I never thought I'd say. "Whether you and Dad are my real parents."

Her body stiffens, her eyes widen, and her jaw drops open. "What do you mean by that?" She narrows her eyes at me.

"Is there something you and Dad are hiding from me?" I hold her gaze, but she quickly averts it before standing up.

"Why would you ever ask such a question, Alex. Why?" She places both hands on her head as she paces my room.

"Mom, please. I just want you to be honest." I lift my head to look at her, but before I can put in another word, she storms out of the room, crying out Dad's name as she runs down the stairs. For a few minutes, all I can hear are their muffled voices in Twi, but I can't make out what they're saying.

"Abena, let's talk to him." Dad's voice becomes clearer as footsteps travel up the stairs and toward my room. When they both step in, the look on their faces says it all. "Yaw, I heard you have a question."

I nod. "Yes, Dad. I do. Our blood types don't match. Does that mean anything? Are you my real parents?" I think I already know the answer, but it wouldn't hurt to hear them say it.

Dad clears his throat. "Erm...well I think we need to sit down and have a talk like a family."

"Okay." I take a deep breath to slow down my breathing before they confirm my doubts.

Chair legs scratch the floor as Dad pulls out the chair from my desk before signaling for Mom to sit on it.

"Yaw, my son." Dad's weight sinks into the space beside me on the bed. "You know we love you, right?" When I don't respond, he reaches out and squeezes my shoulder. "You know we will never do anything to hurt you, right?"

"I just want to know the truth." My voice comes out in a whisper, and Dad lets out a big sigh before speaking again.

"No." His reply finally comes and I turn my head slowly to look at him, wondering if I heard him clearly.

"What?" I ask, my gaze shifting to Mom, who has tears sliding down her cheeks.

"No, we're not your real parents," Dad responds and just like that, with those six simple words, my life changes.

Mom covers her mouth to quiet her sobs, but her shaky hands are not doing a good job because they escape anyway and fill the room.

I push myself up from the bed with every intention of stomping back and forth across the room, but the pain that shoots up into my groin reminds me to take it easy.

I walk up to my closed window and lean my arm against it. "So, where are my real parents?"

The silence that meets me switches my sadness to anger as I

turn around to look at them. They both look at each other and Mom speaks first.

"Son, we don't know. We adopted you from a children's home in Accra. The owner didn't know your birth mom because she..." Mom's voice trails off and she covers her mouth again.

"She what?" I inch towards them before turning to Dad. "What did my birth mom do?"

Dad holds my gaze for a few seconds, sympathy heavy in his eyes. "She left you in front of the children's home in a basket with a note. We don't know who she is or whether she's still alive."

"And my dad?"

Dad shakes his head. "We don't know who he is, son."

Tears blur my vision and the room spins as I grab onto the wall to steady myself. Within a few seconds, Mom and Dad are by my side, guiding me back to bed.

"But why?" I ask when I'm sitting at the edge of my bed again. "Why did it take you twenty-one years to tell me this?" Tears flood out of my eyes. "Why did I have to find out like this?"

"Son, we wanted to tell you," Dad says. "But we just didn't know when the right time was."

"Yes, he's right," Mom chips in as her voice breaks. "Your dad has always wanted us to tell you, but I wasn't ready." She wipes the tears in the corner of her eyes. "Your dad and I planned to have at least four children. We wanted to have so many children running all around our house." She smiles through her tears.

"But every time we tried, I had a miscarriage. The doctors did tests and scans and they found nothing wrong with both of us. So before leaving Ghana, your father and I decided to adopt a child just in case we never had children of our own. God blessed us the day He gave you to us and I couldn't bear the thought of ever losing you. So every time your dad brought up telling you, I convinced him we should wait longer." She drops her head. "That's why it has taken twenty-one years, son. I'm so sorry."

My chest tightens as a lump builds in my throat. When I open my mouth to speak, pain shoots up my groin again and this time, I double over, clutching my side.

"I told you to rest. Now look at what you're doing to yourself. *Worentie me.*" Mom's voice slowly fades in the background as they both help me get into bed again.

As I lay there, staring at the chandelier above me, everything starts to make sense. That's why I don't share any similar physical features with Mom and Dad. I wasn't just imagining it. That's why our blood types don't match.

Kwame was right. My real parents are somewhere out there and I have no idea who they are. I close my eyes, and tears trickle down my cheeks when the reality of it hits me. I've been living a lie. Everything I've believed about my identity my entire life is a lie.

23

OLANNA
NOW

"When the man I once loved looks me in the eye and tells me he didn't trust me enough to share his vulnerable moments with me, what does that say about the type of girlfriend I was to him?" I ask Heather as I chop the last red bell pepper.

After church today, I told Manny and Heather about my conversation with Alex yesterday and they offered to come back home with me so we could talk about it. As if Heather read my mind, she suggested we cook *jollof* rice, so we made a quick trip to the grocery store before going home.

With Dad not being around, Manny and Heather's presence will give me the distraction I need. It's better than spending the rest of the day watching videos of all the sophisticated events Dad has attended over the last two weeks and wishing I was experiencing all that with him. No, I'd rather spend the afternoon eating some good *jollof* rice.

Heather loves trying all kinds of food and she has fallen in love with Nigerian cuisine since she and Manny started dating. I taught her how to cook *jollof* rice two years ago and it's her favorite meal so far.

Heather takes one piece of the bell pepper and puts it in her mouth before answering my question. "I'm sure you were a great girlfriend, so don't blame yourself for the bad choices he made. I now see that he had a lot of issues to deal with."

"Yeah, I gotta say, it must've been tough for him, but he still should've told Olanna. Don't defend him, babe," Manny chimes in as he takes a break from playing with Ayannah. For the past half hour, the baby hasn't stopped giggling because Manny keeps throwing her up in the air, much to Heather's horror.

"I'm not defending him." Heather turns to Manny and leans on the granite counter. "I'm just saying that cancer is not a joke. I remember when I had a scare in my senior year of high school. It ended up being a benign breast lump called a fibroadenoma, but I was still terrified. It took me over a month to gain the confidence to see a doctor."

"Wow. That must have been scary." I place all the chopped peppers and scotch bonnets into the blender before turning it on. Whenever I'm cooking for people, I'm always mindful of how many scotch bonnets I put into the food, but Heather is a full member of the Nigerian spicy food association, so I've got nothing to worry about.

When I'm satisfied with the texture of the tomato mixture, I turn off the blender and place a medium pot on the hotplate. After pouring some vegetable oil into the pot, I gesture for Heather to check the chicken in the oven.

"Scary is an understatement," Heather says, before walking to the oven and opening it, revealing the golden brown, crispy texture of the chicken thighs and drumsticks. The spicy aroma fills the air as she sticks a fork in them. "Yeah, that looks and smells so good." She turns off the oven and closes the door.

Walking back to me, Heather helps me with the rest of the recipe, while Manny resumes playing with Ayannah. I add in onions, followed by tomato paste and the pepper mixture to the oil, and Heather takes over the stirring while I pull out a high chair and plop myself on it.

"So." Heather looks over her shoulder and lowers her voice. "Now that we've established why he broke up with you, what are you going to do next?"

I shrug and throw a kitchen towel over my shoulder. "What is there to do? He has said his piece. I have closure. Now we both can move on." Saying those words breaks my heart because it's the exact opposite of what I want to happen. But what can I do? He hurt me.

Heather closes the pot, puts the spoon down on a plate, and takes a seat across from me on the granite countertop. "Is that really what you want? For both of you to move on?"

I pause and stare into her green eyes, which bore into my soul as if she's reading my thoughts. When I hesitate to answer, she asks another question.

"Did he say that he wanted to move on?"

I shake my head. "Not exactly." I exhale as memories of our last encounter flood back into my mind. "But he held my hand, and he called me baby, which was his nickname for me when we were dating. He said those words so casually, as if we were still in a relationship. It felt good to let him hold my hand again. But every time I entertain the idea of us being together again, I remember how he hurt me and I shut it out of my head. It's going to be impossible."

Heather leans forward and says, "There's nothing impossible with God, Olanna. Since He brought Alex back into your life, He will work out a way for your love for each other to be restored." She reaches across the counter and holds my hand. "Please, don't let your anger and hurt prevent you from trusting God."

In a split second, all of God's promptings flood back to me as realization dawns on me. This isn't the first time the message is coming to me. "Trust God." I repeat Heather's words.

"Yes, exactly. God can be trusted." She gives my hand a little squeeze before standing up and checking on the food, leaving me to ponder on my thoughts for the rest of the day. After adding seasoning, chicken stock, and water to the cooked tomato mixture, we add the rice and cover with aluminium foil while it cooks.

An hour later, as we sit at the table, devouring the delicious *jollof* rice, chicken, and fried plantains, my thoughts drift back to what Heather said. With the same message coming through different people, I feel like God is communicating something to me.

Okay, Lord, if this is what You want for me, then I don't want to miss out because I'm holding on to anger and hurt. Please help me to trust You with my whole heart.

With the revelations of the weekend behind me, I'm determined to throw myself back into my routine this week. Even though I've been considering the idea of us getting back together, Alex's presence is only temporary and in two months' time, he'll be gone. But I'll still have Madu Health to serve. I can trust God for whatever He has planned for us, but I still have to prepare for the worst.

"Earth to Olanna." Lerato's voice presses into my thoughts as she clicks her fingers in my face. "It's green." She points to the traffic light, which is now signaling for us to cross to the other side of the road.

We both had a busy morning with department meetings, so I treated us to some lunch at Rosa's Café. Heather encouraged me to try their shortbread two years ago and since then, I've been hooked. Today, I ordered a latte as well, and Lerato got a grilled cheese sandwich.

"Sorry," I say to Lerato when we're on the other side of the road. "I promised I won't zone out anymore, didn't I?" I sigh, and she smiles. Since Alex's arrival, I've frequently been lost in my thoughts, usually at the start of the day when I see Alex. Thank God Lerato is the only one who has noticed and I promised her I won't do it again.

"That's okay. I understand," she says as we approach the building entrance. "When you're in love, you can't help it, can you?"

I pause in my tracks and watch Lerato carry on ahead of me. "Wait, what did you say?"

Lerato presses her lips together and responds with, "*Dololo.*" She told me it's a South African slang for "nothing," but with the way she's suppressing a laugh, I'm certain she's hiding something.

I don't remember telling anyone at the office about Alex and I. *Oh no, did she figure it out?*

"Come on, boss. We have to prepare for your two o'clock meeting." She beckons me over to the elevator and presses the button when I enter.

The one minute silence in the elevator feels like a thousand years and, to prevent any awkwardness, I speak. "Lerato, is there something you know about me I don't?"

She shrugs. "No, I only know what you tell me, boss."

I tilt my head. "So, what was that about me being in love?"

She averts her gaze and suppresses another smile. "Well, sometimes other people can notice things you can't," she says and when the elevator dings, she walks out without giving me a chance to respond.

Oh, no. She's figured out I have feelings for Alex? Is it that obvious?

"Lerato, wait." I run after her, but stop in my tracks when I spot a crowd of the employees gathered around Yin and my attention immediately switches. "Oh my goodness, Yin." I walk up to him and give him a hug before holding him at arm's length. "I thought you didn't start until tomorrow."

"Yes, that's true, but I was taking the baby out for a stroll and thought I'd drop by." He moves out of the way to reveal the stroller with the baby sleeping safely inside. Everyone, including Alex, makes way for me to see the baby and when I lean over and set my eyes on him, their reaction makes sense.

He is sleeping peacefully, making cooing sounds with his hands tucked in his full head of dark, silky hair. He stretches his arms and turns his head and everyone *awws*. "He is beautiful, Yin," I say as I straighten my back and meet Alex's gaze.

He smiles at me, but I force myself to look away and turn to Yin. "We have a card and a gift for you and Jess. Lerato will get it for you before you leave."

"Aww, thanks, everyone." Yin places both hands on his chest and looks around. After greeting everyone again, Yin, myself and Lerato make our way to my office.

"How's Jess doing, by the way?" I ask when we're in my office.

"Not too bad." Yin parks the stroller next to the desk and sits across the table from me. "It hasn't been easy making the change. The sleepless nights are a killer, but Jess' mom came over from Hong Kong and she has been super helpful. I don't know what we would've done without her."

"Aww, I'm glad it's going well. I'm so happy for you guys. Let us know when it's all clear for us to visit, but until then, we can't wait for you to be back tomorrow. We've missed you so much."

"We sure have." Lerato walks in carrying a gift bag with an A4 sized envelope. "It's signed by all of us. Congratulations." She hands it to Yin, who takes it gladly before placing it safely at the bottom of the stroller.

"Honestly, I'm so touched. Thank you again, Olanna," Yin says.

"So, have you met Alex yet?" I place my hands on the table, my fingers intertwining.

Yin nods. "Yeah, we had a great conversation earlier about SEO when we were waiting for you. He's so knowledgeable about what he does. No wonder HearCare sent him to us."

Hearing Yin praise Alex makes me so happy and I love that everyone can see how amazing he is. For the last two weeks, I restructured my timetable so Alex and I wouldn't have any one-to-one meetings. Now that Yin is back, I don't have to worry about that anymore.

I thought this would make me feel better because Alex and I will barely see each other unless during our weekly general meetings. That's what I wanted two weeks ago, but I'm not sure what I want anymore.

I clear my throat. "Yes, we have a lot to learn from him about SEO and I'm certain we will set up an SEO department here at Madu Health."

"Amazing." Yin leans back in his chair. "I can't wait."

After a few more minutes of catching up, Yin says goodbye and leaves while Lerato and I get to work, preparing for my next meeting with a potential client. Even though I wanted to ask Lerato what she meant by what she said before, I let the comment slide because I might be reading too much into things. I don't want to end up exposing my feelings for Alex.

"Okay, that looks good." I place my pen down and turn off the iPad before pushing myself away from my desk. "I'm going to take a quick break and then we can bring the client in. Is that okay?"

Lerato nods, and I tug on the sleeve of my yellow pantsuit before walking out the door and toward the restroom. As I round the corner, I spot the subject of my thoughts walking down the corridor toward me—Alex Obeng.

When I saw him earlier in the open-plan office, I spent the

whole time trying to avoid him and I didn't notice how incredibly handsome he looks in his white long-sleeved shirt and gray striped pants.

I fluff my hair, which I'm wearing down today, before clearing my throat. "What are you doing here?" I ask as my heart rate quickens for whatever reason. "You can't just come up here whenever you feel like it. You know that, right?"

Alex slows down and a smile forms on the corner of his lips. "Yes, Ma'am, I do." He lifts up the folder in his hands. "You asked me to bring my report before the end of the day, remember?"

"Oh...right. Of course, I did." I lower my head and tuck a strand of my locs behind my ear. "Please, drop it with Lerato. She's in my office." I continue my walk without saying anything else.

Alex brushes past me, but before I can breathe a sigh of relief, he turns around and walks alongside me. "Since I've gotten your attention, I might as well let you know I need to talk to you."

"I don't think there's anything left to say."

"Olanna, you're wrong. There's still so much I have to tell you, so you understand the full picture."

"I don't know if anything you say will change the past, Alex." I stop walking and turn to look at him. "Don't you understand that you can plead from now till tomorrow, but it won't change the fact that you hurt me?"

His face falls, and he rubs his temple with his hand as he exhales. My heart throbs at the disappointment in his face and I remember the prayer I made to God just yesterday. *Lord, if this is what You want for me, then please help me to trust You.*

"Look, Alex." I sigh, taking one step toward him. "I appreciate that you have good intentions, but all I'm saying is that this isn't easy for me and I..."

Before I finish my sentence, he closes the gap between us,

wraps one arm around my waist, and gently pushes my back against the wall. His hold on me is not restrictive, but I can't bring myself to wiggle out. He leans forward, close enough to have his cool, minty breath mingled with mine as my hands rest on his chiseled chest.

He props his other hand against the wall and drops his voice low as his honey-brown eyes stare directly into mine. "You have every right to be mad at me. But baby, one thing's for sure. I will not give up on us. I love you and love never gives up." He tightens his grip around my waist, and my sense of reasoning flies out of the window. "It just doesn't."

Forgetting everything around me, my gaze slides down from his eyes to his beard, and then his lips. They always tasted like perfection when they were on mine and now I have an urge to taste them again. When he leans closer, I part my lips and close my eyes, waiting for him to kiss me. But then he releases his hold on me, leaving the folder in my hands as he steps back.

"Have a good afternoon, boss." He winks at me before turning around and heading for the elevator, leaving me to slowly wake out of my reverie. His lingering scent on my clothes causes warmth to travel from my stomach up to my chest and cheeks. I touch my lips and a smile breaks forth, my brain trying to figure out what just happened. It's his confidence and persistence for me. I forgot how attractive that was.

24

ALEX

THEN

"I'm really sorry, dude." Kwame removes his baseball cap and places it on the bench we're sitting on. "If I had known things would turn out this way, I would've kept my opinions to myself."

"It's okay, man." I shrug, staring into the distance at the fall leaves scattered over the green grass. "It's not your fault. I'm actually glad you said something because now I know the truth."

Silence passes between us for a few minutes as students walk past to and from campus. Sirens go off in the distance, reminding me about the busy New York streets and how much I miss exploring them with Olanna. She and I used to walk on this side of campus most weekends when we needed a break from studying.

Kwame's apartment is close by, so when I told him I was on my way home from my library shift, he insisted we speak face to face. I've been avoiding human contact as much as possible the last few days because I need the space to think, but Kwame, as usual, has figured it out and he won't let me get away with it.

"Alex, please, don't take this the wrong way, but I gotta ask, man." Kwame looks me in the eye. "Why?"

I shrug before leaning back on the bench. "Why what?"

"Why does this bother you so much? Even if your parents had told you, it's not like they know where to find your birth parents. Your parents have given you everything you've ever asked for. Isn't that enough?"

"No." I raise my voice slightly. "No, it's not enough." I lean forward. "You don't get it, do you? I feel lied to and cheated on. They had twenty-one years to mention something to me. I would've looked for them." I pause before continuing.

"I need to know about my roots and why I am the way I am. I need to know if I share any characteristics with my birth parents and whether I have relatives out there—brothers, sisters, uncles and aunts. I need to know whether there's anything in my family history I should know. I don't want to wait ten years down the line to find out I have a genetic disorder I could've planned for." I turn my head away and stare at the trees in the distance.

Kwame stays silent while I calm down, and then he speaks. "Okay, I get it now. But, dude, how are you going to find all of this information when your parents don't know themselves? It's not like you can just get up and go to Ghana, so why are you torturing yourself?"

A lightbulb moment shines on me, and I straighten my back before looking at Kwame.

When realization hits him, he shakes his head. "Alex, no."

"Yes, yes, yes. That's a brilliant idea." I clap my hands and tap Kwame's shoulder. "I can even go alone."

"Alone? No, dude, that's a terrible idea. You can't just go to Ghana now. How about you wait till summer vacation? Didn't your parents plan on taking you there after college graduation?"

I push myself up and walk the length of the bench. "No, summer is too far away. I can't wait."

Kwame stands up too and puts his cap back on. "But will your parents ever agree to this?"

"Once I explain to them, they will. Fall break is only two weeks away and I've got some money saved up from my library shifts. I have a Ghanaian passport, so I don't need a visa. All I need is to book a flight and sort out accommodation." Excitement surges through me as I whip out my phone and start searching for cheap flight tickets to Ghana.

"Alex, wait." Kwame squeezes my shoulder. "I worry that you're making hasty decisions without thinking about how people around you will feel. Look at the situation with Olanna. You still haven't told her about the surgery and I worry that when this is over, it'll come back to bite you hard. Please, think about this before you make a decision you'll regret." He pats my back before walking away and heading toward his apartment.

I pause my search on flight tickets and sit on the bench again, mulling over Kwame's words. But no matter how much I think about it, the situation remains the same—I need to know the truth.

Back in my apartment later that evening, I sit on the edge of my bed and stare at my phone, trying to give myself some time to change my mind. But the more time I waste, the more certain I become that this is what I want to do. My parents won't like it, but I hope they'll understand once I explain.

I pick up the phone and dial Dad's number before putting it on speaker. He picks up on the second ring. "Hello, son."

I exhale before responding. "Hey, Dad. Is Mom there with you?"

"Yes, she is."

"Son, are you okay? Is the pain getting worse?" Mom's panicked voice comes through the phone.

"No, everything is fine. In fact, the pain is ninety percent gone. I need to talk to both of you."

"Okay, we're listening."

I lean forward and rub my forehead before saying a silent prayer. "I would like to go to Ghana during fall break...alone."

There's silence for a few seconds as I expected, and Mom is the first to break it. "What do you mean, alone?" she asks and when I explain the same reasons I told Kwame, she raises her voice. "What is wrong with you, Alex? Why are you acting as if we committed the greatest sin in the world by adopting you? All we have ever done since you came into our lives is love you like our own child." Her voice breaks and she sniffles. "You are our child, Alex. Our only child. Now you just want to leave us?"

"Mom, I never said anything about leaving you. Of course, you'll always be my parents. All I'm saying is that I need to know the truth about who I really am."

"But you're an Obeng and you always will be," Mom says between sobs and Dad still hasn't said anything. "You just had surgery and you're still recovering. Why would you want to travel alone?"

"Mom, I'm no longer in pain and I'll have my follow up with the doctors before traveling."

"Yaw?" Dad's soft voice comes while Mom's sobbing fades. "Are you really sure you want to do this?"

I nod before remembering they can't see me. "Yes, Dad. It will give me peace of mind."

There's a pause before Dad sighs. "Okay."

Relief washes over me while Mom speaks again. "Okay? Daniel, *dɛn na ɛhaw wo*? Why are you agreeing to this?" she says and then continues in Twi as the sound of retreating footsteps come through the phone, followed by the slamming of a door.

"Please, don't worry about your mom. We never planned for you to find out like this. I'll speak to her."

"Thanks, Dad."

He responds with another sigh. "But son, can't you wait until Christmas or summer break, so we can go with you?"

"I've thought about this and I think it'll be best if I do this now, Dad. Please."

He exhales. "Okay. I may not fully understand your reasons, but I agree you deserve some closure. How long are you planning on being there for?"

"Just the week of fall break."

"Have you looked at tickets?"

"Yes, and I can afford them."

"You also need to sort out accommodation."

"Yes, I've been looking, but I haven't reserved one yet."

"Don't worry about that. We have some vacant apartments in our properties in Accra. I'll sort something out for you."

"Awesome."

"I also have a friend in Accra who has a tour guide agency. I'll ask him to arrange for someone to help you navigate your way around Accra. I'll also send you all the information we have about the orphanage."

"Thank you so much, Dad. I really appreciate it."

"You're welcome. Good night, son."

Getting off the phone, I walk up to my bedroom window and watch the blanket of stars spread across the sky. Soon. Very soon. I'll find out the truth about my birth mom and why she abandoned me.

25

ALEX
NOW

A smile spreads across my face as I stare out the glass wall of my office, thoughts of Olanna dancing around in my head. I know how much our little hallway encounter last week affected her. She would never admit it, but since that day, I've caught her stealing glances at me during meetings when she thinks I'm not looking.

I've also noticed the way her body tenses whenever I get close to her, like it did when I had her against the wall. I don't know what came over me that day, but I'm glad I took that leap of faith. She could've screamed her lungs out, pushed me away, or gotten me fired, but she didn't. Instead, she leaned in toward me and that gave me hope.

The way she reacted when I held her tells me that even in that moment, she could let her guard down and consider the possibility of us being together again. I wanted to kiss her that day, but I promised myself I won't be doing that until I tell her the whole truth. If we're going to do this again—I mean—when we do this again, we'll start on a clean slate with no secrets and *definitely* no lies.

The sound of a ringing Christmas bell drags me out of my

thoughts and when I'm transported back to the present, I spot Melissa and Neil out in the open plan office. Neil is wearing a Santa outfit while Melissa is dressed like an elf, who is ringing Santa's bell.

"What in the world?" I mutter to myself as I walk out of my office before standing next to Yin, who is now back to work in full swing. "Hey, man. What's going on?"

"Well, let's just say it's the most wonderful time of the year at Madu Health," he responds as we both turn to face the front.

"Gather around, everyone. It's that time of year again." Melissa's voice travels across the room as everyone leaves their cubicles and approaches the pair. With the way she's grinning and stomping her little feet, Melissa might burst from excitement if she doesn't share what she and Yin are up to.

Neil leans back and grabs his Santa belly before saying, "Ho, ho, ho. It's Christmas time."

"Nah, it's the first of November. It's nowhere near Christmas," Yin teases and we all laugh until Santa speaks again.

"Silence, children. It's Christmas when Santa says it's Christmas."

I shake my head and smile, welcoming the much-needed distraction from Olanna. But the distraction is short-lived when the queen of my heart walks into the room, closely followed by Lerato.

"Did someone say Christmas?" Olanna says, allowing us to grace the full view of her outfit as she catwalks. Today, she's wearing her locs up in a curly bun and it seems she might be the only one who got the Christmas memo, because she's also wearing a green pantsuit, red stilettos, and a matching red lipstick. *Heart-stoppingly beautiful.*

"Yes, boss," Melissa responds on our behalf. "Santa and I were just about to announce that it's time to decorate the Christmas tree."

"So, what are we waiting for? Come on." Olanna beckons everyone as she leads the way to the first floor in the recreation room. There are a dozen boxes of Christmas decorations neatly arranged on the table and there's also a Christmas tree in the corner. That was definitely not there when I came in this morning.

"Alright, children. You know the drill. Pick a box and start decorating." Melissa claps her hands and after pressing a button on her phone, Christmas songs permeate the air, the first one being "Oh Christmas Tree" playing from the overhead speakers.

Wow, I didn't even know there were speakers in this room.

"Here you go." Yin hands me a box and we both walk up to the tree.

"Thanks, man. So you guys do this every single year?"

Yin laughs. "Yes, we've done it for the last four years that I've been working here." He takes out some ornaments and tinsel while Carolina and Sarah put up the Christmas lights.

"It started when Mr. Madu—Olanna's dad—tried to get us to work as a team during the busy Christmas period," Yin continues. "I wasn't surprised when Olanna kept the tradition. She used to come to our Christmas parties when she was still in college."

"Really?" I smile as I glance at her across the room. Olanna and I only celebrated one Christmas together as a couple, but I vaguely remember her mentioning the Christmas party. I feel so privileged to experience this part of her world and to see for myself all the things she was so excited about.

"Yeah." Yin hangs a snowflake ornament on the tree. "You know, a few colleagues had some reservations when Mr. Madu announced Olanna as the new CEO. They were worried that she was too young and inexperienced. Some people even thought she would quit after a month because of the pressure that comes with the role."

"But she has proved that she's a small girl with a big God roaring behind her, right?"

"Exactly. I couldn't have put it better myself." Yin pats my shoulder before Melissa's bell draws our attention again.

"Okay, friends. Our CEO has a few words to say, so please listen up."

Olanna steps forward and interlocks her fingers in front of her. "I'm going to keep this short and sweet because I promised Lerato I won't be shedding any tears today."

Laughter erupts from the crowd, and Olanna continues. "I'm incredibly proud of every one of you in this room and I mean it when I say I love you all. Thank you for being amazing."

"Aww, we love you too, Olanna." Melissa responds on our behalf, while hugging Olanna, and envy surges through me.

I could've been the one hugging her and standing by her side right now. But I'm here, hoping and praying that not too long from now, that imagination will turn to reality.

"Oh, I can't believe I almost forgot." Melissa holds Olanna at arm's length. "We have to put the star at the top of the tree and turn on the Christmas lights."

"Yeah, and according to the Madu Health tradition, the chief executive and the newest employee have to do it together," Yin says as he gently nudges me from the back of the crowd to the front toward Olanna.

Okay, I would've preferred a less awkward moment to get close to her, and I could certainly do without a dozen pairs of eyes staring at me. But I'll take this because a win is a win.

James and Yin bring two ladders forward and perch them on either side of the fully decorated seven-foot Christmas tree. Olanna and I climb to the top of our ladders and when Melissa hands her the star, Olanna looks at me and says, "Shall we do this?"

I smile at her. "Yes, Ma'am." I reach over and hold the star too, our fingers touching in the process. There might not be any physical sparks on our hands, but I don't need to see them to believe they're there. We pose for a few photos and I climb down the ladder before extending my hand to Olanna and helping her down.

"Don't forget Neil and I will come 'round at the end of the week with the Secret Santa cards," Melissa announces as the crowd disperses and everyone walks over to the table of ginger-bread cookies.

"Thanks, Alex." Olanna's soft voice grazes my ears, almost sounding like a dream. I turn my head to find her looking at me, and that's all it takes for me to get lost in her gaze.

"For what?" I ask, wondering what miracle could've happened in her heart for her to start a conversation today.

"For not giving up," she says, but before I can process what she means by that, Lerato swoops in and pulls her away while chatting about Olanna's next meeting, which starts in ten minutes.

Not giving up? Not giving up on what? On us? Is God really softening her heart again?

As I stand there, watching her walk away and trying to decipher the meaning behind her words, all I can hope for is a sign, some encouragement or something to hold on to for now.

When Olanna reaches the door, just before she and Lerato disappear from my view, she turns her head and holds my gaze for a few seconds. Then she sends me a smile before closing the door behind her.

My heart dances around in my chest the same way it did the day I told her I loved her. I recognize the familiar emotion in her eyes. It's the same way she looked at me when she first told me she had feelings for me. It might only look like a smile to others, but to me, it's confirmation that all hope is not lost. *Thank You, Jesus.*

26

OLANNA

THEN

"**S**o you finally remembered that I exist?" I frown at Alex, who is making his way toward my table at the library. Since his dad got sick, he has been scarce, and seeing him today is a leisure I can't take for granted. I deserve answers.

Instead of responding to my question, Alex pulls out the chair next to me and settles on it. He reaches for my hand and squeezes it, but I turn my face away. "Baby, I'm sorry."

"For what?" I zap my head back in his direction. "For ignoring me? Not answering my text messages? Not picking up my calls or canceling our dates? What exactly are you sorry for, Alex?"

"For everything." He averts his gaze to the bookshelves behind me. "I'm sorry for everything."

"You can't even look me in the eye when you apologize. This is *so* not you." I push my textbooks to the side and lean forward, covering his free hand with mine. "Alex, please tell me the truth. What's going on with you? Is it still about your dad? Is his condition getting worse? Tell me, please."

He sighs and shakes his head. "I can't." His voice is a whisper as tears wet his eyes.

"You can't or you won't?"

"I can't," he repeats. "All I can say is that next week, my parents and I will be traveling to Portland for fall break. We'll be visiting family there, so I might be a little busy. There's so much I'm still trying to figure out about myself and my family. It's a lot to take in for me, and I know it will be a lot for you."

"That's not fair. Let me be the judge of that." My voice breaks, and tears slip from my eyes.

"Baby, when the time is right, I'll tell you everything. I promise."

No matter how much I want to believe him, I can't shake the feeling that he's lying to me. "Alex, what happened to us? You used to tell me everything. But these days, it feels as if you enjoy pushing me away."

He lowers his head and leans his forearms on his thighs before whispering, "I don't enjoy pushing you away. This isn't easy for me. You don't understand."

"Then make me understand." I move my chair closer and take hold of his hands again. "Tell me what you'd like me to do to help. I want to help you. All I'm asking is that you let me in, please."

He lifts his head and looks at me, but when he goes for several minutes without saying anything, I'm convinced there's an internal battle within him. But I don't know what exactly he's battling. *Lord, please help him talk to me.*

He reaches for my face and holds it in his hands, his warmth traveling all over my body. "If you want to help me, then baby, please pray for me. That's all I need right now." And with that, he kisses my forehead, stands up, and walks away.

"Alex, please wait. Alex!!!" I call out to him, but he doesn't respond. I want to run after him, scream in his face, and throw things at him until he opens up to me. But I'll be fighting a lost battle because he has made the decision to keep me out of that part of his life. I don't have the words to describe just how much that hurts.

I've never lived through a more tortuous week than this one. Every part of my body hurts. I can't sleep, I can't eat, I can't concentrate, and I've woken up every morning with surging pains in my chest that have almost sent me to the ER.

Since speaking to Alex on Monday, I haven't taken my eyes off my phone. Every time it beeps, pings, or vibrates, my fingers grab it so fast, I've even dropped the phone twice now, cracking the screen in the process.

"Girl, are you sure you're okay?" India asked me last night when we were having dinner.

"Alex still hasn't told you anything?" Danielle leaned in and rubbed my back.

I shook my head at them as tears rolled down my cheeks and a lump built in my throat. The girls have been by my side since I noticed a change in Alex three months ago. With this being my first relationship, I wasn't sure if I was doing anything wrong, so I opened up to them about my worries.

Hearing India say that it was normal for couples to have challenging seasons was reassuring. At first, it made sense that Alex would be a bit withdrawn if his dad was sick, but I can't shake the gnawing feeling that there's more to his actions than he's letting on.

Every day, when the girls ask me for an update, I wish I could tell them everything is okay now, so they wouldn't think Alex is a jerk. I know he's not a jerk, but as each day passes, I'm struggling to defend his actions.

Today is Friday and I'm going home tomorrow to spend fall

break with my family. I was hoping we would resolve this before tomorrow, but I've lost all hope of that happening.

I've called him three times today and each time he lets it go to voicemail, the intensity of the pain in my chest goes up a notch. At least he still cares enough to respond to my text messages, but his answers to my questions provide no reassurance for me.

Me: Babe, please stop ignoring my calls. 😭

   Alex: typing...

   Me: Why are you doing this to us? Please pick up the phone, so we can talk about this.

   Alex: typing...

   Me: Your actions are really hurting me, Alex. 😫

   Alex: Baby, my flight to Portland is at 9am on Monday. I'll be back at the end of the week and I promise I'll tell you everything then. Trust me, baby. Please.

I throw my phone on my bed before pacing the length of my room. "I don't understand what's going on with him."

India and Danielle are sitting on the edge of my bed, with their eyes following my every movement. I've been crying for the last half hour and my throat hurts so much I'm losing my voice.

"Are you sure Kwame didn't tell you anything?" I turn to India, who shakes her head with sympathy in her eyes.

"I'm sorry, girl. I've been nagging him for the past week about it and he insisted he doesn't know anything and that even if he did, he didn't feel it was his place to say anything."

I stop pacing and rub my hands together. "I can't believe this is happening. I can't believe Alex is doing this to me."

"Do you think he's cheating?" India asks and Danielle

smacks her arm with a notebook. "Ouch! Girl, what did you do that for?" India rubs her arm and frowns at Danielle. "It was just a question, and it's a valid possibility."

India is right. It is a valid possibility, and I have thought about it a thousand times. Even though my head would want to believe something like that, my heart believes otherwise. The pain and hurt in Alex's eyes were too real. There's something genuinely troubling him and he wouldn't share it with me.

"No, I don't think he's cheating. He said it's about his family and I believe him. I also understand if he doesn't want to divulge specific information about his dad or family members. Some people are protective about their family business like that."

"That's true," India agrees. "My mom is like that. When I was ten years old, I told my piano tutor I was late for the lesson because my mom and dad had an argument. When my mom found out I had run my mouth, she gave me an earful for a month about how I need to keep family business within the family."

Danielle chuckles. "And yet, you still run your mouth."

It's India's turn to smack Danielle's arm and as the two girls bicker at each other, my breath hitches, my throat closes up, and stabbing pains travel up my chest as I fight to breathe.

I stagger backward while India and Danielle rush to my side and guide me to the bed. Danielle brings out a brown paper bag from her backpack and hands it to me. After five minutes of breathing in and out, my heart rate calms down and my throat unclogs, but the tears don't stop.

A squeezing headache travels around my temples down to the back of my neck, and I lean forward and groan in pain. India takes out some Tylenol from her purse and gives it to me while Danielle hands me a glass of water.

After taking the pain medicine, I lay my head on India's lap as tears continue streaming down my face and Danielle rubs my back gently in a circular motion. My phone vibrates and when I check the caller ID, it's Manny. I turn the phone on silent and place it on the bed.

"Aren't you going to get that?" Danielle asks, and I shake my head.

"No. Manny would flip if he hears what Alex is doing to me. I don't want him traveling down here and beating Alex up."

"I think Alex deserves a whooping, if you ask me," India mumbles under her breath and Danielle sends her a glare.

"Yeah, I think so too, actually." I smile through the tears and dab the corners of my eyes. "I just wish it hadn't come to this."

"I'm so sorry, Olanna." Danielle squeezes my shoulder. "Is there anything you'd like us to do for you?"

I sniffle. "Pray for me, please. Just pray that Alex should come around and that God should give me the strength to endure this because it hurts. It hurts so much."

The girls hold hands around me, and they sing worship songs and pray for me. Within a few minutes, a sense of peace washes over me and I'm able to fall asleep again for the first time in one week.

27

ALEX
NOW

Melissa's bell goes off again at the end of our Friday staff meeting and our heads snap in her direction at the far end of the table. How she has worn coordinated red and green outfits every day this week is beyond me. I can't help but wonder whether she has a designated closet in her house filled with Christmas-themed clothes.

"It's the moment we've all been waiting for," she sings in a high-pitched voice as she raises a white shoe box wrapped with red and green ribbons. "It's time to pick your Secret Santa for this year." She shakes her head as she speaks, her Christmas tree earrings dangling in the process. I don't think I've ever met anyone that has made me as excited about Christmas as Melissa has.

I can't complain, though. As an adult, I've often yearned for my childhood days when I used to look forward to enjoying Christmas rather than looking at it as a time to spend money on food and presents.

Being here at Madu Health has reminded me of the importance of community, unity, and togetherness. I don't know if Melissa believes in God, but her simple actions have also helped me to reflect on the true meaning of Christmas—the faithful love of God, not just toward me, but everyone else around me.

"Y'all know the drill." Melissa's voice pushes my thoughts to the side. "Can I please ask each of you to step forward and pick a card? I have to remind you not to tell the person whose name you've picked because it ruins the surprise. Even if you pick the name of your arch-nemesis, we encourage you to stick with it because this might actually be a chance to salvage that relationship."

Neil chuckles as he wraps his arm around Melissa's shoulder. "But of course, if you absolutely dislike the person you've picked, you can swap with someone else." Neil winks at us.

Laughter and chatter fill the room as everyone walks up to Melissa and picks a card from the box. Everyone except me. Given that Melissa and Neil are staring in my direction and whispering to themselves, I think they've figured out I haven't picked a card yet, so I better get out of here while I still can.

"Alex." Neil's voice comes from behind me and I pause in my tracks, only a few inches away from the door. *This is why I should've left as soon as the meeting was over.*

"Yeah?" I turn around slowly to look at him as Melissa leaves the room carrying the box with her.

"Were you really going to leave without picking a name? Come on, man, where's your Christmas spirit?"

I shrug and tuck my hands in my pocket. "Well, let's just say gift buying is not my forte. I've only been here a month and I don't think I know anyone well enough to buy them anything."

"Come on, dude. You know it's not a big deal." He walks beside me as we get out of the room. "It's not about getting the perfect gift. It's about the experience. In fact, being part of this will help you get to know people." We pause in the corridor of the open-plan office.

"I'd like to believe you, but didn't I just see Melissa walk away with the Secret Santa shoe box?"

Neil smirks. "Yeah, but that's because we took it upon ourselves to pick a card for you." He sticks one in my pocket and taps it before walking to his desk. I wait until I get to my office before taking out the card and opening it. To my surprise, the name I least expected is staring back at me on the card. *Olanna Madu—The Boss Lady.*

A jittery sensation takes over me and without even thinking about it, the perfect present for her comes to mind. I didn't get the chance to give it to her two years ago, but this is how I know God is at work.

I have to make sure I do it right this time. There's a reason we fell in love the last time and I know she still has feelings for me too, but I don't expect her to admit it anytime soon. I need to earn back her trust. It'll take time, but it starts with this. My gaze drops back to the card in my hand. This is more than just a Secret Santa gift exchange. It's a mission to get back the love of my life.

28

ALEX
THEN

My grip tightens around my backpack strap as Dad and I wait for the escalator, taking us up to the security gate. Unfortunately, Mom couldn't swap her shift at the hospital, so Dad was the only one who could accompany me to the airport. My flight is at nine AM, so we left home two hours ago to allow enough time to check in my bags.

The check-in process was smooth because the line wasn't long and I'm only taking one large suitcase with me. My main priority is to meet my birth parents, but I also plan on visiting some important tourist spots. I planned to only take my backpack and a small suitcase, but Dad encouraged me to take a large suitcase as well, so I'll have space for any souvenirs I find.

Dad connected me with a tour guide from his friend's agency. His name is Stephen, and Dad vetted him before he agreed to link him up with me. Stephen messaged me and he seems like a cool dude. The plan is for him to meet me at the airport and we will make it to the apartment from there.

When we get out of the elevator and climb up the stairs, I cover my mouth to suppress a yawn. My anxious brain kept waking me up every hour last night because I thought I would miss my flight. In the end, Dad was the one who woke me up at six AM after I missed my alarm. Dad bought me a cup of coffee with breakfast on our way here, but I still need a good sleep.

"Don't worry, you'll sleep when you land." Dad pats my back and smiles, as if reading my thoughts.

I toss the empty coffee cup in the trash can and fall in step with him. "What about on the plane? They'll let me sleep, right?"

Dad's baritone laugh erupts from his lips. "Of course they will. But with the uncomfortable seats and the interruptions for food and drinks, I can never get quality sleep on a plane."

"Well, it's a good thing I have a window seat. At least I don't have to worry about anyone disturbing me during their toilet breaks."

We share a laugh as we walk past a family dragging their suitcases in the opposite direction. Their two younger girls are whining about how they need to sleep while the teenage-looking son keeps rolling his eyes and asking the parents to make his sisters stop talking.

An announcement goes out about keeping all belongings with you and also reporting any suspicious baggage. We walk past a line of restaurants, coffee shops, and bookstores as different aromas of coffees and food tease my nostrils.

I would've bought something to binge on while waiting for the plane, but Dad warned about how expensive airport food is and also that they wouldn't let me go past the security gate with any food or drinks.

"Well, here's my last stop. You're on your own from here, son." He nods toward the security gate at the end of the corridor.

I swallow to wet my dry mouth and for the first time, I regret my decision to do this alone. Lowering my head, I ask a question that has been on my mind since I told them about my impulse decision to go to Ghana. "Dad, are you mad at me?"

His brows crease together in a frown. "Mad? Why would I be?"

I shrug. "For taking this trip alone. Mom still thinks it's a bad idea."

Dad clears his throat. "Yaw, not everyone will be on board with some decisions you make in life. Your mom and I had a long talk about the recent events and we agreed it would've been best to tell you sooner. She's not mad at you."

"Are you sure?"

Dad nods. "Positive. You're an adult now and I guess some journeys are better made on your own. I hope you find what you're looking for, son. Just always remember that your mom and I love you very much."

"I love you too."

Dad must have noticed the tears in my eyes because he wraps his arms around me and pulls me close, giving me enough time to blink the tears away. "You're going to be fine, son. Again, I'm sorry that things turned out this way."

I shake my head when we break the hug. "It's not your fault, Dad. Thank you for understanding. You have no idea how much this means to me."

Dad nods and wipes his eyes before touching my shoulder. "Please call us as soon as you land, okay? You know your mom won't let me rest with her questions if you don't."

I chuckle. "Of course. I'll update you about my location at all times."

"That's my boy."

I drag my suitcase to the security gate and when I join the line, I turn around to find Dad still standing there, one hand in his pocket and the other hand waving at me.

My heart rate quickens as I approach the front of the line.

What if they find something in my bag or they decide to detain me in Ghana for whatever reason? Mom and Dad won't be there to protect me.

I clear my dry throat so many times and from the side-eyes the people behind me are giving, I'm sure they're wondering whether I'm bringing a viral illness with me on the plane. The check-in process is seamless and soon I'm through the security gate and sitting in front of my boarding gate with all the other passengers going to Accra.

I take out my phone and send a text message to Olanna to let her know that I'm on my way to Portland—as I had previously mentioned. I could've easily told her we were going to Ghana, but she would've wanted to know why we were going earlier instead of next summer.

How I became so comfortable lying to the girl I love scares me to the core. This is not me, and Kwame was right. But let me see this through to the end and then I can amend my ways and fix things with Olanna.

When I'm all settled in the plane, I try not to think about all the advice Dad gave about not going anywhere alone, being careful about eating street food and also not staying out too late. When the plane takes off, I channel all my nerves into the excitement of what is waiting for me in Accra.

What if my birth mom has other children of her own? Will she know where my dad is? What if she ended up getting married to my real dad? That means there's a whole side of my family I've never met. After living my whole life believing I'm the only child and envying other people with large families, this prospect excites me.

When the turbulence dies down, the flight attendants hand out breakfast, but because I'm still so full from the sandwich and coffee Dad bought me, I decline and listen to some worship music instead.

I turn my head to the window, watching the clouds float below as endless thoughts swim around in my brain. Soon, even my excitement and imaginative thoughts can't keep me awake any longer as sleep finally sneaks in and takes me away to dreamland.

29

OLANNA

NOW

"**T**here you girls are." Melissa's shrill voice interrupts my conversation with Lerato and we both turn our heads toward her. I just finished my last meeting for the day, so Melissa skitters across the room, her heels click-clacking against the floor as she clutches onto her legendary Secret Santa shoebox.

"You left before I shared the Secret Santa cards." She slides the shoebox across the table toward us, the red and green ribbons looking as intact as ever.

"Sorry, I had to drag her away." Lerato straightens her back and plops in the chair next to me as Melissa walks around the table to stand between us. "She was running late for her meeting and you know I don't like it when the boss is late."

"Yeah, I don't blame you. You did what you had to do." Melissa says to Lerato before turning to me. "But it's time to pick your card, Ma'am." She opens the shoebox, which only has two folded cards in it.

"Everyone has picked a card?" I look up at Melissa, who is grinning at me. *Do her cheeks ever hurt from smiling so much?*

"Yeah, it's just you and Lerato," she responds. "Come on, the world is waiting."

"Did anyone tell you you're so dramatic?" Lerato stretches her hand to pick a card, but Melissa smacks it away. "Ouch, what was that for?" She recoils and rubs the back of her hand.

"Let the boss pick first, please." Melissa smiles at Lerato before turning to me again.

Okay, that's weird. "Erm...Melissa, I don't think it matters who picks first." I lean over and peer into the shoebox while Melissa's intense gaze stays pinned on me. When I pick the card on the right, Melissa's smile widens and then she turns to Lerato and hands her the last card. *Very weird.*

"Thank you, girls, for your wonderful cooperation. Remember, you're not allowed to switch with anyone." She winks at us before walking out of the room and closing the door behind her.

Lerato smiles and shakes her head. "She's just a ball of sunshine, isn't she?"

"She sure is." I lean back in my seat before stretching out my arms and yawning. "I'm so glad it's Friday. I need to sleep for thirty hours straight."

"Sis, you need to sleep, period. But *definitely* not for thirty hours, because we have our girls' day out tomorrow, remember?"

"Oh, yes. Shopping and movie night will lift my spirits."

"You can say that again, but until then, you need to check out the name on your Secret Santa card."

I scoff. "Girl, please. You know I don't have time for this."

"But you made Melissa a promise."

"*Nuh uh.* Last time I checked, I made no promises."

"Come on. Don't be such a Grinch. You skipped Secret Santa last year for the same reason. You're not exempt from Christmas traditions just because you're the boss." She leans forward and picks up the card before opening it for me.

"Okay, you're starting to sound a lot like Melissa and—" My

words trail off when Lerato turns the card around for me to see the name written on it. *Alex Obeng—The SEO Star.*

Silence passes between us for a few seconds and my breath slows down as a warm and fluttering sensation travels from my stomach into my chest. "Melissa tricked me." My jaw drops, and Lerato chuckles.

"That's why she was acting all weird and smacking my hand, huh? It was rigged. She's clever. I have to give her that." Lerato supports her head with her hands as she stares at me, her eyebrows wiggling.

"Why are you looking at me like that?" I suppress a smile. *Get yourself together, Olanna.*

"You know, if you were three shades lighter, your cheeks would be so red right now."

"*Pfft.*" I shake my head, choosing my oblivious stance even though I've been caught red-handed. "I don't know what you're talking about."

"*Nuh uh.*" Lerato clicks her fingers in my face. "I love you, boss, but as your friend, I think you're a terrible liar."

"What? No, I'm not. I..." The words catch in my throat as I try to spew out a lie, but I can't deny it anymore. The warm sensation takes over my entire body as memories of all the good times Alex and I spent together force their way into my mind. "Okay, fine. You win."

"Yes! I knew it." Lerato squeals and taps her feet on the ground before running around the table and sitting in a chair close to me. "Please, tell me everything. How long have you had feelings for Alex? Was it love at first sight when you saw him a month ago? Or did you know when your hands touched as you put the star on the Christmas tree? Will you tell him about your feelings? Does he know about your feelings?"

"Lerato, calm down." I grab her hands to stop her flailing them. "You need a chill pill, okay?"

She takes a deep breath in and out. "Yes, Ma'am."

"Actually...we were college sweethearts."

Lerato's eyes widen. "You were what now?" She raises her voice.

"Shh!!!" I place a finger over my lips.

"You two have a history and you never told me?"

I cover her mouth before looking over my shoulder at the door. "Girl, what did I say about keeping your voice down?"

"Okay, sorry. But I'll keep my voice down on one condition. That you tell me *everything*," she says, and that's how I spend half an hour narrating the entire story to Lerato without leaving out any details.

I tell her everything from the first day we met at Ignite Fellowship, to the day he asked me out on a date, the horrendous break up, how terribly I dealt with it, and to the present day where he has made it clear he still loves me and wants me back.

"Aww, that is so cute. I love *love*." Lerato tilts her head and pouts as I round up my story. "Why don't you take him back? It's so obvious that you love him, too."

"Well, he doesn't know that."

Lerato shrugs. "So? Why don't you want to tell him?"

I pause for a second as I consider her question. "Because..." I sigh and stand up before walking to my window and staring at the view of the Hudson River. "I don't think my heart will bear it if he hurts me again."

"Aww, but time has passed and the way he looks at you says a lot about his determination to make things right."

I frown. "You've been watching him?"

"No, I've been watching both of you." Lerato covers her face and giggles. "What did I tell you? I love *love,* so I've been very vigilant."

I shake my head. "You are something else."

"But it's true." She ignores my comment and continues. "It sounds like he really wants to make it up to you. Please give him a chance?" She makes praying hands and juts her bottom lip out in a pout.

"I've been praying about it a lot and something has shifted inside me. I didn't realize how much I missed him until he started working here. But if he wants me back, the least he can do is show me, right?"

"That's right, Queen. Hang on tight, and he'll come to you."

"Exactly." We both chuckle as I pick up the card and stare at his name again. For the first time in two years, I can fully entertain the idea of the two of us being together without reprimanding myself.

If I wasn't so scared about giving my heart away again, I would've kissed him right there in the corridor when he held me against the wall. I would've told him I never stopped loving him and I want to be in his arms.

But he's going to have to show me how much he wants this. Until then, I'll sit tight and keep praying that things turn out exactly the way God wants it to.

30

ALEX
THEN

The first thing that hits me as I walk out the doors of Kotoka International Airport is the heat wave. I'm used to the warm summer days, but even the ninety degree Fahrenheit July heat in New York is nothing compared to what I'm experiencing now. I can't explain it and I have no choice but to embrace it because it's refreshing.

It didn't take long to find my suitcases and the immigration officers were polite and friendly, so the check-in process was very smooth. When one of the airport officials asked how I was doing, it felt like a warm welcome hug and it was as if God was telling me I made the right decision coming here.

Outside in the welcome area, my gaze sweeps through the crowd of people waiting to pick up their friends and family. A family of five walks past me, pushing trolleys mounted with suitcases as my phone pings with a message from Stephen. I swipe up to read, grateful that at least the airport Wi-Fi still works outside, and I respond to the message to confirm that I've retrieved my suitcase.

Stephen texts back to say he's parking the car and will be with me in a few minutes, so I place my phone in my pocket and let my gaze wander. As I turn around and stare at the words *Akwaaba* written in bold white letters on a yellow board above the airport entrance doors, a calming feeling washes over me.

Of course, I have no memory of being here as a baby, but my senses know that I've breathed this air before, traveled these streets before, and lived in this world before. There's something about this space, this environment, the warm air against my skin, the distinctive Ghanaian accent and the Twi language grazing my ears, that welcomes me with open arms. I've been here less than an hour, but I don't need anyone to tell me I'm home.

A hand squeezes my shoulder, and I turn around to meet a familiar face smiling down at me. "Stephen?"

"Alex?" He leans back, tilting his head and squinting before a wide smile spreads across his face. "*Charley*, you're finally here. The *borga* has landed. Welcome to Ghana." He steps forward and hugs me before taking my large suitcase and leaving me with the smaller one. "I hope you haven't been waiting long. It's very busy tonight, so I struggled to find a parking space, please." He points toward the parking lot.

"No, that's okay. Thank you."

Stephen is much taller than I imagined he'd be. With the muscles on him, the guy could take me down in a fight without even lifting a finger. Even his full grown beard puts mine to shame, but the good thing is, he seems even friendlier in person, which works well to get rid of my nerves.

"You packed very light," Stephen says, as he makes a display of lifting my large suitcase with no effort.

"Yeah, there's barely anything in that one. I had to leave some space for souvenirs."

"That's very smart."

"Thank you." I accept the compliment even though it was all Dad's idea. Olanna crosses my mind as we mention souvenirs and I put a reminder on my to-do list to find the necklace she loved. Mom told me she bought it from a vendor at Makola Market, so Stephen added it to the list of places we need to visit after meeting my birth mom.

When Stephen finds his car, he places my suitcases in the trunk before we get in. Stephen was right about how busy it is because getting out of the airport parking lot is a struggle. It would've been smoother if the pedestrians weren't walking on the road and if other drivers weren't blasting their horns every two minutes. But after what seems like forever, we get on to the main road.

Throughout the entire drive to the apartment in Adabraka, a neighborhood in Accra, my eyes stay glued to the new, yet familiar world passing outside my window. Everything, no matter how small it is, fascinates me. From the shrubs and trees growing on the traffic island, to the billboard posters of new products and upcoming events, and the distinctive black and white patterned kerbs. All these little observations build an excitement in me I can't explain. Excitement for a new world of endless possibilities.

"It's so beautiful." I turn to Stephen, who takes a glance at me and smiles.

"It is. But you've barely scratched the surface. When you're well rested, I will show you what Ghana is made of," Stephen says, as he presses on the brakes to make way for a driver who cut in front of him without signaling.

"Whoa, he was so wrong for doing that." I point to the car in front of us, but Stephen only laughs and shakes his head.

"*Charley*, it seems you wouldn't be able to drive in Ghana." He laughs before turning left off the main road and we make it to the block of apartments safely. It's a quiet area with some shops and hair salons on the opposite side of the road.

Stephen asks me to wait in the car while he steps out and

knocks on the black iron gate guarding the block of apartments, which belongs to my parents. A minute later, a young man, who looks to be around my age, steps out and strikes a conversation with Stephen in Twi, which I understand as Stephen saying he is here to check me in.

I've always wanted an opportunity to practice my Twi when I'm not with my parents or Kwame. This would be good exercise since everyone I've met here in Accra always starts speaking to me in Twi first.

The young man opens the gate from the inside and Stephen drives the car into the compound before parking in one of the many spaces available. "I have the key. Let's get you settled in." Stephen carries my large suitcase as we walk into the building and up the stairs to the second floor. He opens the door to the apartment and my jaw drops.

"Wow. Will someone else be living here with me?" I ask, admiring the living room space, the sofas and the smart TV.

Stephen chuckles. "No, please. This is all for you," he says before giving me a tour of the one-bedroom apartment with smooth ivory tiles, a kitchen, living room, en-suite bedroom, and a balcony.

"What would you like to have for dinner? *Jollof* rice or *waakye*?" Stephen asks after connecting my phone to the Wi-Fi.

I shrug. "I'm not really fussed. What are you having?"

"As for me *dier*, anything I see goes."

I smile at the use of his Ghanaian slang. I'd have to get used to hearing them more this week. "Okay, then. I'll eat whatever you bring."

When Stephen steps out to get food, I send a message to my parents to let them know I've arrived. When no reply from Olanna pops up, my shoulders drop in disappointment. The blue ticks confirm she has seen the message I sent her earlier this morning before my flight left New York.

Our last conversation in the library didn't go so well. I wanted to tell her everything. Especially when she started crying and begging me to let her in. I wanted to tell her. But I couldn't tell her what I didn't know.

I couldn't tell her about all my uncertainties and my doubts. I couldn't tell her that this is the first time in my life I've felt completely lost and that pushing her away is my way of guarding her from experiencing the dark twist of emotions that are slowly dragging me into a hole of despair. That's why this trip is so important to me. Finding the answers to my questions will be the start of me making my way back to discovering who I am.

Vibration from my phone interjects my thoughts, and I swipe left to answer the video call from Mom and Dad. After confirming that I'm okay and reiterating their advice about staying safe, I end the call with them, just when Stephen arrives with some *jollof* rice and chicken.

For two hours, we sit in the living room, talking about how Stephen started working in the tourism sector and all the interesting clients he has had over the last five years.

"I spent most of my twenties in the U.S. chasing after the American dream. But on my thirtieth birthday five years ago, I had an awakening that changed my perspective. So instead of spending my life away from home, I returned to my roots and now I'm able to help craft the Ghanaian dream. I'm married to a wonderful woman, with a two-year-old son and a baby girl on the way. I wake up every day doing a job I love while showcasing the beauty of my beloved country. That, to me, is a dream come true and everything I've prayed for."

"Wow, that is such an inspirational story, Stephen. You're making me even more excited about this trip."

By the time ten PM rolls around, fatigue hits me hard, and we bid each other goodnight as Stephen leaves for his own apartment with the promise of returning in the morning, so we can start our adventure.

After taking a quick shower and working out how to turn the air conditioning in my room, my head hits the pillow and sleep takes over. There can only be so much excitement for one day. I'll save the rest for tomorrow, when the true journey begins.

31

ALEX

NOW

There's no better way to show Olanna I still love her than reminding her about the reason we fell in love. That's why I'm going on a love note writing spree. Yes, it's cheesy, I know. But she loved the cheese, and she fell for the cheese, so I'm going to remind her all about it.

In order for me to succeed at this venture, I'll need a partner, and Lerato, to my greatest surprise, has happily agreed to help me. We had lunch together in the communal area last week and we talked about faith and relationships. She told me all about her boyfriend—or shall I say, her soon-to-be fiancé—Paul and how she can't wait for their long distance relationship to end when they get married.

The conversation moved on swiftly to my love life and since she had been open about hers; I thought I'd be honest with her, too. When I told her my love life was complicated, she told me she has been watching me and she knows I like Olanna.

I was so sure no one else knew about Olanna and I—except maybe Melissa—but apparently the word has spread around the office and Lerato claims to have very reliable sources.

Since Olanna and I work on different floors and her

schedule is usually packed with meetings, Lerato has agreed to help me deliver my love notes without Olanna noticing. Today is the first day of our assignment, and here's the cheesy note I wrote for her.

If I could turn back the hands of time, I would turn it
   right back to the first day I met you.
You were shining bright like the diamond you are and
   I couldn't help but keep my eyes on you.
There's something about the beauty you exude that
   can make a man lose the right words to say to you.
But permit me to say that your irresistible charm has
   drawn my heart to you.
So there's only one thing left to do, and that is to never
   stop thinking about you.

After sealing the note inside a blue envelope with a pink heart sticker, Lerato takes it over to the queen of my heart, while I hide behind a wall in the corridor, so I can have a good view of her office. This is the moment where I thank God Olanna's office is on a different floor to the open plan office. If someone was watching me right now, they would think I'm stalking the boss, but you gotta take risks to see results.

Lerato closes the door to Olanna's office, but through the glass walls, I'm able to make out the confused expression on her face when Lerato hands her the note and leaves. When Olanna opens the envelope, my stomach flips inside out and I hold my breath the whole time she reads it.

For a moment, it seems all my efforts have gone to waste when she places the note down and shakes her head. Then, after what seems like forever, that charming smile I know and love breaks through. She leans back in her chair and twirls a loc strand as she reads the note again.

When she looks in my direction, I duck and head for the stairs while victory songs play in my head. Now I can spend the rest of the day thinking about that smile and hoping that someday she'll admit she still loves me.

When lunch time rolls around, my excitement is at its peak and I can barely eat my burrito or listen to the conversation Melissa, Neil and Yin are having at Rosa's Café.

"So, tell us, Yin. What does it really feel like to be the dad to a one-month old?" Melissa asks.

"Well, all I can say is I never knew I could be so obsessed with another human being." He taps on his phone screen and shows us a beautiful photo of their son David on his screensaver.

"Aww," Neil and Melissa say in unison.

"But I also don't know what it's like to have a good night's sleep anymore." He shakes his head and Neil pats his back.

"As someone who has twin toddlers, I can assure you it will get easier as they grow older." Neil sips on his coffee.

"I hope so," Yin says before turning to me. "You alright there, man? You've been quiet."

"Yeah. I'm fine. Just a lot on my mind."

"A lot on your mind, huh?" Melissa leans forward. "Are you sure it has nothing to do with a certain boss lady?" She giggles and Yin sends her a glare.

"Come on, Melissa. Don't tell me you've been sitting there, making up theories just because Alex has been quiet," Yin says before turning to Neil, who averts his gaze and whistles.

Yin shakes his head and looks at me again. "I'm sorry, Alex. The longer you work at Madu Health, the more you'll realize that Melissa and Neil have a reputation for prying into everyone's business."

"Is that so?" I smile, but before I can add another comment, I spot Lerato across the street, heading toward Rosa's Café.

"Guys, excuse me for one second," I say before leaving the table and meeting Lerato outside the front entrance. "So?" I ask, my heart thumping like it would explode any minute.

"She loved it." Lerato squeals and relief washes over me. "She has been smiling all morning, and I caught her reading the note multiple times. She even asked me who sent it, but when I refused to tell her, she said she'll find out herself and then she walked away smiling."

"I noticed the smile too. It means our plan is working, right?"

"Yes, I read the note and I have to say, you have a hidden talent right there."

"Well." I send her a sheepish smile. "Olanna is the only girl who brings out the poet in me."

"Aww, you guys are so cute." Lerato stomps her boots on the sidewalk. "I can see it in your eyes that you love her and I think she loves you too, but I wish she would just admit it."

"I think she'll say it when she's ready. So for now, please calm down and don't ruin our plans, okay?"

She nods. "Okay."

"Thanks for your help, and we'll do the same thing again tomorrow." I bump her fist and we bid our goodbyes before she makes her way back to the office.

When I return to Melissa, Neil, and Yin, their eyes are pinned on me. "What?" I shrug, choosing to play oblivious. They look at each other and then back at me, their eyes begging for me to spill, but when I remain silent, Melissa breaks.

"Oh, come on, Alex. Tell us what is going on between you and the boss," she says over the saxophone music playing from the overhead speakers.

"Could you *be* any louder, Melissa?" I roll my eyes.

"We just want to confirm if what we're hearing is true," Neil explains.

"Oh, really?" I take a sip of my orange juice. "What have you been hearing?"

"That there's something going on between you and Olanna and you've been hiding it," Melissa says.

I laugh and twist the cap back on the juice bottle. "And who else knows about this story?"

"No one." Neil and Melissa respond in unison, but I won't be surprised if Melissa has told everyone.

"Alex, you don't owe anyone any explanations," Yin says. "Please ignore these guys."

"Thanks man, but it's okay. Now that there are rumors going around, I think it will be better for me to set the record straight."

"That's what I'm talking about." Melissa leans forward and rests her head in her hands.

"But just so you know, I won't be giving you any specific details because I respect Olanna too much to share her personal business with you guys."

"Understood." Neil responds for the rest.

"Olanna and I go way back. We dated while we were in junior year at NYU and she loved me with everything she had. I loved her too, but I was too naïve and selfish, so I hurt her real bad. The last two years have made me realize that I never stopped loving her. I made a mistake and I hope that before my contract ends here, I would've given her enough reason to give me a second chance."

"Wow." Neil turns to Melissa and says, "I think you owe me twenty dollars." He stands up and does a chicken dance without caring about the other patrons looking at him.

Melissa rolls her eyes as she opens her purse and hands Neil a twenty-dollar bill. He takes it and changes his move to a Harlem Shake dance.

"You guys made a bet?" I ask, amazed by Neil's display of the running man dance.

"Yeah, Neil said you were the reason you guys broke up and I thought it would be Olanna." Melissa pulls Neil, so he can sit in his chair again.

"And out of interest, why did you think it was Olanna?" I ask.

Melissa shrugs. "Well, because she always says Madu Health is her only commitment, so my theory was that she chose the career over your relationship."

"And you couldn't be more wrong," Neil says, trying to catch his breath.

"Yeah, but if she had chosen the company over me, it still wouldn't have hurt me as much as I hurt her." The silence stretches between us before I speak again. "By the way, cool dance moves." I bump Neil's fist and we stand up, making our way back to the office.

"Oh, by the way, since we're all spilling secrets, I just want to know whether you guys had anything to do with me getting Olanna as my Secret Santa."

"*Pfft*. What? No." Melissa throws her hands up in the air and her voice goes pitchy again.

I turn to Neil, and he gives me a thumbs up.

"Hey!" Melissa smacks Neil on the arm as we cross the road. "This is why you can never work for the Secret Service. You don't know how to keep secrets."

"Oh, and *you* know how to keep them? You'll get caught on the first day of the job," Neil responds and we all burst out laughing.

When we're inside the office building, I pull Yin to the side as Neil and Melissa walk ahead of us, bickering at each other.

"So, can I have Emmanuel's number?" I remind him of the request I made earlier in the week. Yin doesn't think it's a good idea, but I have to do this.

"Okay, man. If you really think it'll help." He swipes his phone and sends me the number.

"Thanks, man."

"Yeah, just don't tell Emmanuel I was the one who gave you his number, alright?"

"I *gotchu*." I shake his hand, and we walk toward the elevator.

I press the doorbell of Emmanuel and Heather's house and wait, my heart beating so fast my chest hurts. I prayed about this meeting last night, but I still couldn't stop myself from watching videos about self-defense, just in case things turn south. The only thing stopping me from bolting is the promise I made to God. *Lord, please help me not to give up.*

Alex, my beloved. Trust Me.

The door swings open and my heart leaps to my throat when Emmanuel's face appears. I freeze on the spot, unable to even extend the friendly handshake I've been practicing all morning. I open my mouth to speak and my voice comes out more croaky than I would like. "Good afternoon, Emmanuel."

He only grunts and rolls his eyes as the door opens wider to reveal an auburn-haired woman carrying a sleeping baby. "Hi, Alex." Her smile is warm enough to break me out of my frozen state as she shakes my hand. "Please forgive my husband's manners." She pushes Emmanuel with her free hand and he walks back into the house without saying a word.

"Please come in." She beckons me in. "I'm Heather. It's so nice to finally meet you."

"Likewise." I smile at her as I take a deep breath and take off my jacket. After placing it on the cloth hook Heather showed me, I walk further into their home, admiring their shelf of plants and the ginger cat touring its way around the living room.

"Ermm...this is for you." I hand them my peace offering of a bottle of wine.

"Aww, that's so sweet of you. Babe, please, can you take it from him?" she says to Emmanuel, who flares his nostrils before taking the bottle from me and heading to what I assume is the kitchen.

"I'm going to put our daughter to bed and I'll be right back. Please make yourself comfortable." She nods to the sofas in the living room before heading up the stairs. Olanna was right when she talked about how nice Heather was. If she can get back down before Emmanuel returns, that would be amazing, because I ain't trying to die today.

"Just so you know," Emmanuel speaks for the first time as he walks back into the living room. "The only reason I agreed to this meeting was because of Heather. So make sure you thank God I married a woman who has more patience for people like you."

I swallow to wet my dry mouth before responding. "Yes, sir."

He squints before taking a seat across the couch from me, and I follow suit.

"I'm back," Heather announces as she joins her husband on the couch. "I hope he hasn't been giving you a hard time?" she asks me as she squeezes Emmanuel's leg.

"Not at all."

"Oh, baby, you didn't offer him anything?" She shakes her head and turns to me. "I'm sorry, Alex. My husband is usually a much better host than this. Would you like anything to drink?"

"No, I'm good, Heather. But thank you."

A moment of silence passes between us before Emmanuel speaks again. "Well? Are you going to tell us why you're here?"

"Babe, please." Heather tilts her head at him.

I clear my throat and shuffle to the edge of the couch. "Yes, but before I say anything, I just want to say thank you so much for having me in your home. It means so much that you agreed to meet with me even with the inconveniences caused." I stare at Emmanuel, who averts his gaze.

The cat walks past us again, purring before disappearing from sight. "I also would like to say that I'm here because of Olanna. I made a mistake which I can't undo, but I still love her."

Emmanuel scoffs but says nothing, so I continue. "Olanna is the most amazing woman I've ever met. She has a kind heart and she would do anything for the people she loves."

"Of course, Olanna's amazing. Now, what's your point?" Emmanuel responds while Heather shoots him a glance.

I look at Emmanuel straight in the eye and say, "I believe God sent me to Jersey City to make things right with Olanna."

"Yeah, right!" Emmanuel's remarks are starting to get to me, but instead of reacting to them, I focus on the task at hand.

"You may not believe that, and that's okay. But I don't believe in coincidences. I believe God is a God of second chances and He can restore broken relationships." I sigh before continuing to tell them the full story of what happened to me in college, the cancer diagnosis, the surgery, the recovery process, and everything I experienced in Ghana.

"I'm telling you all this not because I want your sympathy. But I wanted the truth to be out there because the one thing I think Olanna deserves is closure. My experiences gave me no right to treat Olanna the way I did. I hurt the only woman I've ever loved and I take full responsibility for everything that happened. I know how much she loves and cherishes her family, so I'm here to apologize to you for everything I did."

I lift my gaze to look at Emmanuel, whose head is still turned away as he stares out of their window. Heather smiles and leans forward. "Thank you so much for coming to us, Alex. It was so brave of you to do this."

I nod at her and wait a few moments, but when Emmanuel

doesn't look at me, I stand up. "Well, thank you again for having me. I think it's best I leave now."

Heather stands up and looks at Emmanuel, who doesn't move, so she follows me to the hallway to get my jacket. "It was lovely to meet you, Alex. I pray God gives you wisdom as you navigate this situation with Olanna. I'll be praying for you both."

A warm sensation settles in my heart and even though I'm still in Emmanuel's bad books, Heather's kindness has made this meeting worth it. She hugs me briefly and when I turn around to open the door, Emmanuel's voice stops me. "Alex."

I turn around to look at him and Heather smiles before walking to stand behind her husband. "Thank you for coming here today," he says. "Olanna is one of the most precious people God has placed in my life, and I don't take it lightly when people hurt her."

"I understand."

"But I have to say, what you've done today has shown me you are a man who is leaning on God to make things right. That is very admirable." He takes a few steps forward. "I'm sorry for giving you a hard time. Your story is incredible and you're a living testament to God's unfailing love, so...I forgive you, Alex."

My eyes widen as Emmanuel approaches me. "Really?"

"Of course."

I extend my hand and Emmanuel shakes it before pulling me in for a hug and patting my back. "Thank you so much. You have no idea how much this means to me, man."

Emmanuel steps back and puts his arm around Heather. "Thank you for trying to make amends with Olanna. Is there anything you'd like us to do to help?"

"Yeah, do you want us to talk to her?" Heather asks, and I shake my head.

"No, I don't want her to feel pressured to do anything. But there's something you can do for me that would really help."

"Sure. What's that?" Emmanuel asks.

"I picked Olanna's name as my Secret Santa at work and I have an idea for what to get her, but I need your help." I take out my phone and show them my idea.

"Aww, that's so sweet." Heather squeals. "I'm sure she'll love it."

"I hope so." Joy fills my heart as Heather, Emmanuel and I walk back to the living room to talk more about my surprise for Olanna. This meeting couldn't have gone any better and I only have God to thank for that. I'm glad I didn't give in to my fear and bolt. *Thank You, Jesus.*

32

ALEX
THEN

If I could use one word to describe my first night in Adabakra, Accra, Ghana, it would be *interesting*. The softness of the mattress was a huge stress reliever, and it did wonders to help my jetlagged brain. The air conditioning stayed on for most of the night, but during the early hours of the morning, the room got so warm I had to push the comforter away. That's when I realized the A/C had gone off and when I couldn't turn it back on, I counted my losses and went back to bed.

I could still fall asleep with no problems, but at exactly eight AM, the voice of a singing man snatched the remaining sleep away from my eyes. I thought I was dreaming at first, but when I opened my eyes, there was actually a man outside singing a popular afrobeat song at the top of his lungs.

By the time I drag myself out of bed, throw on a t-shirt, and walk out of my room, the singing man has walked further down the road and turned the corner. On the balcony, there's a drying rack, a small round glass table, and three brown tub chairs. The cool breeze brushes against my skin as I lean against the iron bar, watching the world go by.

It was dark when we came in last night, so I didn't get the

chance to study the environment. But being up here puts me in the perfect position to do just that. The surrounding buildings in the area are similar blocks of apartments and also bungalows with corrugated iron roofs.

Straight ahead of me is a compound surrounded by brick walls, and there are teenage boys playing football inside. I would've joined them if I wasn't tired and hungry, so I whip out my phone and take a video of the environment instead.

Unlike the normal hustle and bustle of New York mornings, the peaceful atmosphere here comprises of random Twi conversations from the passersby walking below and the honking of passing motorcycles.

There's so much to observe, but the sight that steals my attention is the crowd of people waiting to buy *Hausa Koko* and *Koose* from the street seller below. It's a spicy millet porridge served with bean cakes and it's a popular Ghanaian breakfast. My Dad always talks about how much he loves it and watching the woman work hard to make it sends my stomach rumbling in response.

The sound of the doorbell takes me back into the house and to the front door. I look through the peephole to find a smiling Stephen carrying two plastic bags. When I open the door, a spicy aroma teases my nostrils as he lets himself in.

"*Mema wo akye,*" he greets me as we walk back to the living room.

"Morning." I yawn and cover my mouth.

"*Mtchew*, Alex, if you're serious about being fluent in Twi, then you have to stop responding in English." He reminds me about the goal I shared with him last night—to become confident in speaking Twi.

"Okay, okay. *Yaa nua,*" I respond.

"That's very good." He pats my shoulder. "With a lot more practice, your pronunciation will improve."

"Thank you." I smile and resist the urge to pat myself on the back.

"I brought you some breakfast from downstairs. You can start with this, *but* if you don't like street food, we can go grocery shopping to get some food." He opens the plastic bag to reveal the same *Hausa Koko* and *Koose* I've been craving from my balcony.

"No, I'll have this." I take the bag from him as saliva wets my mouth.

After taking photos and videos of the food, I post them in my family's group chat to show my parents. I know they asked me to be cautious about street food, but they are four hours behind, so the food will be long gone by the time they wake up.

Dad wasn't lying when he raved about this meal. I'm already a big fan of oatmeal, but the spicy kick coupled with the bean cakes blends perfectly in my mouth, giving it a burst of flavor. I'll definitely be having this again.

"How was your night?" Stephen asks as he wipes the corner of his mouth and I recount about my adventures with the broken A/C and the singing man.

"I can't believe the A/C stopped working." He shakes his head. "Please, don't worry, I'll speak to the manager on our way out, so he fixes it by the time we're back."

"Thank you." I take another bite of my bean cake.

"Since we're going to the children's home tomorrow, I thought we could do some sightseeing in the local area today when you're well rested," Stephen says, and I nod.

I told him I needed to go to the orphanage to get some records about a "family member." Tomorrow will be perfect for the trip because my jetlagged brain would've reset and I wouldn't be as tired as I am now.

"We need to get you some Ghana cedis. You won't get very far with your American dollars." Stephen chuckles as he points to my wallet on the table.

"Okay. So we go to the bank?" I ask, and Stephen shakes his head.

"No, please. You won't get very much with the exchange rate at the bank. There's a place, a twenty-minute drive from here in Osu and we will get a better deal."

"You mean the black market?"

"Yes. It will save you some money. Trust me." He stands up and clears the table.

"Can we go to Makola Market today as well? I need to buy something for my girlfriend."

"Of course. I'm at your service, remember? Now get ready and you can tell me all about this girlfriend of yours." He throws the plastic bags into the trash can and puts the plates in the sink.

Guilt ravages through me as thoughts of Olanna press into my mind again. She still hasn't responded to my message and I want to call her, but she's still mad at me. I send her another message before taking a shower and getting dressed. It's still very warm today, so a t-shirt and pants will be fine.

By ten AM, we're in Stephen's car, driving to a different part of Accra called Osu and Stephen points out different restaurants along the way while I make a note of all his recommendations, so I can try the food before I leave. He also mentions popular tourist sites like Cape Coast Castle, Elminah Castle, and Labadi Beach. I write the names down for the future because I won't be able to go to all these places in the next few days.

When we arrive at our destination, Stephen finds a parking spot and we walk across the road to some men sitting outside a shop. Stephen collects the hundred and fifty-dollar bills from me before speaking to the men in Twi.

A man carrying a large collection of sunglasses walks past me multiple times, trying to convince me to buy one. At first, I shake my head, telling him I don't need one, but when beads of sweat start running down my forehead, I put on my cap and beckon to the man.

"How much?" I point to the pair of glasses I'm interested in.

"Twenty-five cedis," he says and points to more expensive ones, but I take out some cedis notes Stephen gave me yesterday and pay the man, who thanks me before walking away.

"Here you go." Stephen hands me the cedis notes. "How much did you buy those glasses for?"

"Twenty-five cedis. They're cool, right?" I ask, proud of myself for making my first solo purchase.

Stephen clicks his tongue and shakes his head. "You could've gotten it for ten cedis cheaper. Next time, you wait for me, so I can teach you the art of haggling."

"Yes, sir."

Our next stop is the ShopRite mall, but I stop outside before pointing to a man selling street food. "I'd like to try that."

Stephen raises his brows. "Are you sure?"

"Yes, I want to try it all." I'm clearly still riding on a high after my breakfast experience.

We walk up to the man and buy *asaana,* which is a drink made from fermented corn and caramelized sugar. I also buy *FanChoco*, a chocolate-flavored ice cream, which activates my sweet tooth.

"*Man*, Ghanaian street food is the best."

"I have to agree with you." Stephen laughs.

Inside the mall, I stuff my basket with some eggs, bread, tomatoes, rice, spices, and vegetables. We pay for the groceries and travel back to the apartment to drop them off. Then Stephen hires a cab to Makola Market because he mentioned there were no parking spaces close to the market and we will have to do a lot of walking.

To say that the market is buzzing with people is an understatement. But I love everything about it, from the noise to the sea of different colors, and the display of fresh food, fruits, clothes, and different accessories.

"Where's your phone?" Stephen asks, and I tap the back pocket of my jeans. "I'll put it in my bag." He takes it from me and puts it in his cross body bag, which he wears across his chest. "It's a nice phone and no one will take it under my watch."

"Thanks, man."

Further into the market, we walk past a row of shops selling Kente clothes and after searching a few shops, I find the necklace for Olanna—the same one Mom has with the African map and a cross in the middle. I also buy a necklace for myself, which has the andinkra symbol for *Sankofa*. This symbol teaches that you must go back to your roots in order to move forward. I think that will be the perfect souvenir to remind me about the significance of this trip.

Even though Mom and Dad insisted I don't get them anything, I pick out some Ankara shirts for them before Stephen takes me to the section of the market where they're selling food. I love my mom's food, but this rice and stew with beef and *shitto* is the tastiest meal I've ever had in my life.

We get back to the apartment at around four PM and we're both too stuffed to do any more activities, so we make a unanimous decision to call it a day. This is only the beginning of the adventure and I need to have an early night, so I have enough energy for tomorrow—the day I meet my birth mom.

33

OLANNA

NOW

I t feels so good to be chased and it feels even better to be chased by someone you love. Sitting back and watching Alex jump through hoops for me the last three weeks without fail has not only softened my heart, but it has also reminded me about the man I fell in love with two years ago.

He hasn't read his cheesy love notes out loud to me, but reading them for myself has helped me realize one important thing—he still loves me. It's evident in the way he talks about the memories we had and the way he describes how he feels.

I believe him because his words always leave me feeling like I'm the only girl in the world. Maybe it's time to let my guard down a bit more, put him out of his misery, and finally let him tell me the last piece of his story.

"Morning, boss." Lerato's voice pulls me back into the present as she sashays into my office, smelling like tropical flowers and wearing a smile as bright as the sun.

"Well, someone had fun this weekend with her boyfriend." I tilt my head as my gaze drops to her left hand, which she's hiding behind her bag. "Or should I say...fiancé?" I gasp when realization dawns on me.

"How did you know?" She whips her hand out and we both squeal.

I rush to her side, admiring the shiny rock of a ring on her finger. "Only a newly engaged girl would wear a smile like this." I pull her in for a hug. "Girl, I'm so happy for you. I know how much you prayed for this, and this is proof that we serve a God who answers prayers."

"Amen," she responds as we break the hug and she holds me at arm's length. "He sure does, and I believe the same for you, too."

"Oh, please. We're not talking about me today." I wave a dismissive hand and I take her hand in mine again, caressing the diamond. "You've got a wedding to plan, and I'm here to support you all the way."

"Aww, you're so sweet. But before you whisk your planning powers my way," she looks at her watch and fluffs her afro, "it's lunchtime and time for Secret Santa." She runs in place before linking her arms with mine and we both walk hand in hand downstairs to the communal room.

The last three weeks have been busy with finalizing the plans for HearCare's launch in the New Year. Dad is also back from Nigeria after his extended stay there. I missed him so much and I love having him around the house again.

I love listening to him tell stories about his *Naija* adventures and every time he talks about Mom's charity organization, A Widow's Comfort, I get a tugging on my heartstrings to throw caution to the wind and join Manny and Heather on their next trip to Nigeria. I'm sure they'll be happy to have me on board since I've been declining their invitation for two years.

I also got a message from Heather over the weekend that Amara delivered her twin girls safely. Now Lerato is getting engaged and Christmas is next week. It's good news galore and I have nothing to complain about.

When we walk into the communal room, Neil and Melissa are standing by the lit-up Christmas tree handing out the presents that were laid out beautifully underneath the tree for weeks. Today, not only is Neil back to wearing his Santa suit, but Melissa is matching him with her Mrs. Claus outfit. *These two will never cease to amaze me.*

My eyes scan the room, looking for the one person I know makes my heart skip around like a child in a candy store. When I find him standing next to Yin, our eyes meet and he sends a smile my way, maintaining our eye contact until my shyness takes over and I avert my gaze. Heat flushes my face as Lerato and I make our way to the front of the crowd. *Thank God for melanin.*

"And last, but certainly not the least," Neil and Melissa, say in unison, holding the last present together. "Our one and only chief executive."

Everyone cheers as I step forward and take my present from Mr. and Mrs. Claus. I'm about to step back to my place in the crowd when Melissa stops me.

"Where are you going, boss? You know you have to give a speech."

Of course. This girl loves speeches. I take Neil and Melissa's place at the front before smiling at the employees who have their attention on me. "This week, I've had so much good news and my heart is literally swelling with joy. You already know how incredibly proud I am of every one of you, so thank you again for your hard work this year.

"The last year has tested my character and my faith in different ways, but I'm glad that you all have made this journey worth it. Thank you for believing in me. It has been an honor serving you and I pray that we would have so many more amazing memories here, even as this year ends. I wish you nothing but a merry Christmas, and don't forget our Christmas party tonight. Melissa and Neil have worked really hard to plan this for us, so y'all better be there."

"Woop!!!" Everyone claps and cheers before Mr. and Mrs. Claus announce we can open our presents. Christmas music and chatters fill the room as Lerato and I take a seat at a desk.

"*Psst.* Your knight in shining armor is coming your way," she whispers in my ear. "Nine o'clock." She winks at me and a butterfly feeling settles in my stomach. Before I can say a word, she abandons me and walks over to meet Yin.

I feel his eyes watching me and his scent teasing my nostrils before he calls my name with that voice, which makes my insides melt. "Olanna?"

I turn to look at him, his brown gaze so intense I could stop breathing just to take in the view. Never have I seen someone look so handsome in a Christmas sweater.

"Merry Christmas," he says as he takes the seat Lerato has just vacated.

I'm pretty sure my heart is beating drums in my chest right now, but who cares? *Get it together, Olanna. Come on.*

"I thought I'd come clean and say I picked your name, so I'd love to be here when you open your present, if you don't mind?" he says, still looking at me with those charming eyes.

I smile subconsciously. "Of course, I don't mind." I pull the present close to me. "And I picked your name as well."

Alex laughs and leans back before rubbing his beard. "Don't worry, I figured that out already. Apparently Mr. and Mrs. Claus over there are also playing Cupid." We turn to look at the culprits as they both give us the thumbs up and wink at us.

"And they're not even being subtle about it." I chuckle. "Please, you can start by opening yours first."

"Okay." He gently pulls at the strings and, in one swift motion, unravels the present I spent a long time wrapping last night. He smiles as he takes out the box of his beard grooming kit, complete with a beard hedger, shampoo, conditioner, oil, comb, shaper, and balm. "Wow." He stares at it for a few moments before looking up at me. "You remembered."

I nod as memories of that night come flooding back into my mind. The night he comforted me after I had the nightmare about Mom and how he mentioned on our drive back home that he wanted to get a beard grooming kit to help him grow his beard. "Of course I did. I was hoping you didn't already have one."

"Even if I did, I'd toss it out the window tonight and start using yours right away."

He draws a smile from me, and I bite my bottom lip. "Also, I don't think I ever got the chance to say that I really love your beard."

"Really?" He smiles and leans forward. "Is that your way of saying that you've been checking me out, Miss Madu?"

Is he flirting with me? I suppress a smile. "Maybe?" *Did I just flirt back?*

"I knew it." He laughs and I smack his arm gently before he nods at the present in front of me. "Please, open yours."

"Yes, sir. But before I go on, I want to say that your love notes are cheesy, but beautiful. You even remembered that I love pastel colors when you were choosing the envelope. I love them, but I gotta say, you and Lerato are *terrible* at keeping secrets."

The sound of his laugh soothes my heart as I stare at him. "You can mock the delivery all you want, but we accomplished what we set out to do, so I count that as a win."

"Of course. A win is a win."

"That's right." He concurs and we both laugh.

Unlike Alex, who was more gentle opening his present, I tear through the wrapping paper to reveal two boxes. Starting with the rectangular-shaped one, I untie the ribbons and open it to reveal a necklace, but not just any necklace. It's the one shaped like an African map with a cross in the middle.

"Oh, Alex. This is so beautiful." I lift my head to look at him. "How did you get this?" He told me his mom got it in Ghana, and he promised he would get one for me when he goes to Ghana himself. "Did you..."

"Please," he cuts me short. "Allow me?" He extends one hand and I place the necklace in his palm. He walks behind me and clasps the necklace around my neck before letting the warmth of his fingers graze my shoulders long enough to send tingles traveling down my arms.

"Thank you," I say when he sits down again.

"Can you open the next box, please? I'll answer all your questions after that."

"Okay." I open the square-shaped box and when my gaze lands on the content, the tears that were hanging thick in my eyes finally break free as I bring the personalized snow globe closer to me. It's a photo of my parents, Manny, and me at the airport. The last photo we took with Mom before she traveled to Nigeria. It was the last time we were ever together as a family.

"How...how did you get this photo?" My voice breaks, and I dab the corner of my eyes.

He shrugs and says, "Let's just say I have connections in high places."

I smile through my tears as I try to figure out who could've given him the photo. Only Manny and Dad have it, but Manny hates Alex and Dad knows nothing about him.

"Baby, please stop trying to figure out how I got the photo." Alex takes my free hand in his. "Do you like it?" He shuffles forward and as he gets closer, the warmth of his body radiates to mine.

"I love it, Alex. Thank you so much." I pause as we look into each other's eyes and my instinct is to hug him, but I stop myself.

"You said there was something else that happened after your surgery. I'm ready to hear the end of your story now."

He lets out a sigh and plants a kiss at the back of my hand before looking over his shoulder. "Should we get out of here?"

I nod. "I thought you'd never ask. Let's leave before everyone finds out Lerato is now engaged."

Alex's eyes widen. "She is?"

"Oh, my goodness!!! It's a rock. A huge, sparkling rock." Melissa points at Lerato's finger as her squeals travel across the entire room. In less than thirty seconds, everyone flocks toward the poor Lerato, clapping, cheering and hailing her.

"Here's our chance." Alex places his hand on the small of my back and guides me toward the exit. "Go, go, go."

I feel bad for Lerato and I should probably try to save her from the claws of Melissa and her thousand questions. But I have a date with this handsome Ghanaian prince who makes my heart do *azonto* and I won't miss this opportunity for anything in the world.

Alex and I meander through the crowd, slipping away from the commotion and going up the elevator to my office, where I'm hoping to finally get the closure I've been craving, so this battle between my head and my heart can end.

34

ALEX
THEN

M y second night in Adabraka was a lot smoother than the first. With the A/C working again and me getting a full ten hours of sleep, I've finally overcome the jet lag. Excitement overwhelmed me as I got ready this morning and I could barely eat my breakfast.

But when Stephen reminded me of the long day we have ahead of us, I finished the bread and tea for my own good. After stuffing my backpack with cookies, plantain chips and bottles of water, we left the house at nine AM this morning in Stephen's car.

Not far into our journey, I begged Stephen to stop when I saw street food vendors selling grilled meat. So far in my updates to my parents, I have left out the fact that we bought food at Makola Market yesterday, but if my stomach was accepting of the *Hausa Koko* and *Koose*, then I'm sure I'll be fine with the chicken.

After stuffing my face with the spicy grilled chicken, I drink some water, sit back and settle into my usual routine of watching the passing world outside as Stephen drives us to the Sunshine Children's Home in East Legon. This morning, Stephen asked more specific questions about our trip, but I calmed his curiosity with my vague answers. Well, at least I hope I did.

My Dad mentioned that East Legon, which is only an eleven-minute drive from the airport, is an affluent town in Accra, and home to foreign diplomats, members of parliament, international footballers and the wealthy Ghanaians who have returned from abroad to live in Ghana.

As we drive past some of the sophisticated, extravagant, and luxurious homes, I can say for myself that Dad was absolutely right. Twenty minutes later, Stephen turns left and stops in front of the ten-foot black wrought-iron gate of the children's home. The compound has a ten-foot brick wall surrounding it and barbed wire at the top to deter any potential intruders.

Stephen and I step out of the car to speak to the security guard, a middle-aged gentleman in an all-black uniform. He steps out of his cozy-looking booth at the right-hand side of the gate and Stephen greets him in Twi. I introduce myself too, explaining in Twi that I called yesterday and spoke to the secretary who booked an appointment for me today.

The guard makes a phone call and after getting approval, he opens the gate for us and Stephen drives into the spacious compound, which has palm trees flanking each side of the sidewalk leading to the parking spaces in front of the main building.

On the far left of the compound, there's a playground with kids on swings and slides while others are bouncing on a trampoline. As we approach the main entrance, I notice the signs pointing to the children's living quarters at the back of the main building and I can't help but imagine what my life would've been like living here as a child if Mom and Dad didn't adopt me.

The automatic doors slide open as we walk in and head for the desk. After giving my name to the secretary, she asks us to sit in the waiting room. Fifteen minutes later, a stocky man in a blue suit and gray beard walks towards us. "Mr. Alex Obeng?"

Stephen and I stand up as the older man extends his hand. "Good morning, my name is Dr. James Boadu and I'm the owner of this children's home." He shakes our hands, smiling as a tinge of a British accent comes through. "Thank you for waiting. Please, can you come with me to my office?" He leads the way and I follow close behind him while Stephen stays in the waiting room. We walk past a few offices and storage rooms before settling into his office, and he closes the door.

"So, Alex. How can I help you today?" He adjusts his glasses and leans back in his chair.

I clear my throat. "Thank you so much for agreeing to meet with me. I'm looking for some information about a child who was brought here about twenty years ago."

"Okay?" He tilts his head. "What is the name of this child, and why do you want this information?"

"Erm...because I am *that* child." I fiddle with my fingers and lean forward. "I was only a baby when I was brought to the children's home and I was adopted a few months later by Mr. Daniel and Abena Obeng."

"Wow." Realization dawns on Dr. Baodu's face and he takes off his glasses. "You're the little boy Daniel and Abena adopted?" A smile spreads across his face and I nod. "You've grown so big."

"Thank you, sir. Please, do you have any information about my birth mom? My parents told me she left me in front of the gate in a basket with a note. Do you know who she is?"

Silence passes between us before Dr. Boadu walks up to the filing cabinet behind him and opens the bottom drawer. He goes through the files sorted in alphabetical order and picks out one before placing it in front of me. "This is all the information we have about your birth mom."

My heart skips with joy as I reach for the file, hoping to find some name, address, or phone number that will help me find her. Inside the file is a document sleeve with a photo and a folded piece of paper. The photograph is of a baby wrapped in Kente cloth on a bed with a basket beside him and the note simply says:

Please take good care of him.
Maame.

Disappointment plunges into my heart, threatening to rip it apart as I turn the note over, looking for more clues. I lift my head to look at the older man sitting across from me with sympathy in his eyes. "I'm sorry, son. There's nothing more I can give you."

My stomach clenches as I stare at him. Surely I didn't come all this way just for this. Surely he can dig deeper and figure out who Maame is. "Are you sure you don't have any more information that could help me find her?"

Dr. Boadu sighs and shakes his head. "I've been running this children's home for long enough to know that when babies are brought here the way you were, it's usually because the parents don't want to be found."

My eyes widen and I shake my head, waiting for him to say he's just kidding, that this isn't the end of the road and that he can help me. But he only sighs and says, "I'm sorry, Alex."

I drop my gaze to the floor and take a deep breath before responding. "Okay, thank you, sir." I take the file with me and walk back to the waiting room to meet Stephen.

"You're done already?" he says, looking over my shoulder as if expecting someone else to come with me. "Did you find what you were looking for?"

When we get to the parking lot, I open my mouth to speak,

but can't find the right words. How can he be so sure my mom doesn't want to be found? How does he know he's not wrong?

"Alex?" Stephen's voice drags me out of my thoughts.

"This is all he could give me." I place the file on the roof of the car before leaning my back against it.

Stephen picks up the file and opens it, inspecting the photo and the note. "*Eii, Charley,* is this you?" he asks before reading the note. "Who is Maame, please?"

I swipe away the unexpected tears under my eyes before turning to Stephen. "Yes, it's me and Maame is my birth mom. She left me in a basket at the gate when I was born. This is the only information they have of her."

Stephen pauses for a few seconds. "Okay, but it's still something. We have a name at least. Maybe we can work with that," Stephen says, and I scoff.

"I'm trying to stay positive right now, but having the name 'Maame' will not help. Do you know how many Maames are in Ghana or Accra alone?"

"Did you say Maame?" A voice comes from behind and we turn to find the security guard walking toward us, a bottle of water in his hand. "I'm sorry, I was just passing by and I heard you talking about a baby who was left at the gate in a basket by a woman called Maame?"

Stephen sends a stern look my way, cautioning me with his eyes not to say anything, but I have no other option. I'll take all the chances I can get.

"Yes, that's right," I respond.

The man sighs, places one hand on his waist and shakes his head. "And are you the baby who was left here? Twenty-one years ago?"

I nod and walk toward him as Stephen tugs on my arm. "Yes, I am. My name is Alex Obeng. I was adopted as a baby and I grew up in the US. Do you have any information about my birth mom?"

The man smiles and rubs his stubble. "Yes, Maame was my friend. Please, promise me you'll keep everything I tell you to yourself."

"Yes, sir. Please tell me everything you know."

The man steps closer and lowers his voice. "My name is Joseph Ofei and your mom's name is Maame Mensah. She and I were friends, and I liked her very much. I convinced myself I would marry her someday, but she was never interested in marriage, which is why I was surprised when she told me she was pregnant. She never mentioned anything to me about the father, but because she was struggling financially and trying to set up her hair salon here in Accra, she didn't have the money to look after the baby.

"Since I was already working here when she gave birth to you, she brought you here and asked me to make sure you were well taken care of. She also begged me not to reveal her identity to anyone. After that day, she left and changed her number, so I haven't spoken to her since then."

"Please, sir. Do you know where she is now?"

He shakes his head. "The last time I saw her was in Legon two years ago, and her business was doing well."

"Legon?" Stephen and I ask in unison.

"Yes, she finally opened her hair salon very close to the University of Ghana, so the students in that area make up her loyal clientele. I can give you the address of where I saw her. I don't know if she's still there, but—"

"Yes, please give us the address," I cut him short as excitement builds in my chest again. "We'll start from there. Thank you so much, sir. You have no idea how grateful I am. God bless you."

❧

The sun is setting in Legon by the time we get to the address Mr. Ofei gave us. The hair salon can't be mistaken, as the name *Maame's Hair* shines bright in white letters above the front door. We park outside, and I wait for a few minutes to calm my erratic nerves.

"Are you sure you don't want me to come with you?" Stephen asks for the umpteenth time as I stare at the front door.

This is it. This is the moment I've been looking forward to for the last three weeks. I'll finally understand why she left and never tried to look for me.

"Alex?" Stephen's voice pulls me out of my thoughts.

"Yeah. I can do this on my own, thanks." I glance at the front door one more time, let out a deep breath, and get out of the car.

Inside the hair salon, there's one customer getting her braids done, another one having her hair washed at the sink, and another sitting in a chair with a baby on her lap. Mr. Ofei was right when he said her business was thriving, because the spacious hair salon with a long row of good quality sofas and equipment speaks for itself. The women all turn to look at me as I walk in.

"*Agoo,*" I greet before switching to English because I know my nerves won't let me sustain a conversation in Twi. "Good evening, ladies. I'm looking for the owner of this place—Maame Mensah." I hope she still has that last name.

The stylists glance at each other before turning to me. "Who are you, please?" The stylist at the sink asks, but her use of the word "please" doesn't wipe away the skepticism in her voice.

"Oh, forgive my manners. My name is Alex Obeng. I just need to speak with your boss. Is she around?"

"No, she's not. You can come back tomorrow, please." The stylist doing the braids responds before the girls whisper among themselves. I'm about to open my mouth to speak again when an older woman steps out from the back office.

"What's going on here?" she asks her girls before turning to look at me and my heart recognizes her. All my life, I believed I was one of those children who didn't share any physical traits with their parents, but now I know that is not true.

The woman standing in front of me is wearing a beautiful *Ankara* skirt and blouse with braids that trail down to her waist. Her hands are covered in gold bangles and rings. Even though she is wearing makeup, I can still tell we have the same dark complexion, the same smile, nose, and eyes.

"How can I help you?" she asks, smiling.

"I...I need to speak to you, please," I start, before realizing I've been bitten by the "please," bug, too. "My name is Alex Yaw Obeng. I'm here to find my mom—Maame Mensah."

Her smile fades away, and a frown quickly replaces it. "Excuse me?"

"I've come from Sunshine Children's Home in East Legon and I met your friend—Mr. Joseph Ofei and he..."

"Stop." She raises a hand before looking at the stylists who have their eyes on the clients, but whose ears are surely listening in on the conversation. "Follow me," she says before walking back in the direction she came from.

When we get into an office space, she doesn't offer me a seat, but she paces the length of the room as I stand awkwardly next to the door, watching her chest rise and fall as she punches one fist into her palm.

"Why are you here?" she asks when she stops pacing.

I frown. "Erm...to meet you, of course. I came all the way from the US to find answers. I need answers. *Mom*."

"Don't call me that." She wags a finger at me. "I am not your mother. Your mother is the one who has raised you, so go back to her."

I take a step back as my muscles go weak and numb. A mixture of shock, anger, and confusion surges through me as I try to make sense of her reaction. "Why are you doing this? I thought you would be happy to see me. All I want is to get to know you."

"Why?" She leans against her desk and crosses her arms against her chest, her bangles clinking. "The last time I did my research, I found out that the family who adopted you are wealthy. Did you not have a good life?"

My eyes well up with tears as I soak in the anger in her voice. "Yes, I did."

"Did you ever lack anything?"

"No, I didn't."

"So, why are you bothering me?"

"Because I deserve to know who my real parents are." I raise my voice. "Because I have the right to know where my father is."

She lets out a hysterical laugh and I frown before swiping my tears away. "You can never find him."

"Why not?"

"Because I don't know who he is or where he is," she retorts. "He doesn't know you exist because you were a mistake, okay? It was one drunken night at a club in Kumasi and all I remember about him is that he was a married man. I don't even remember his name and I was so drunk I won't be able to point him out to you in a crowd. I never wanted to have children. Didn't Joseph tell you that when he was running his mouth?

"The only reason I went through with your pregnancy was because I found out when I was already five months gone. This place right here is all I care about and you won't be replacing that. So my advice is that you go back to the US and be content with the life you have rather than dreaming about something that can never be." She walks up to the door and holds it open for me. "I can't help you, Alex. Please show yourself out when you're ready. I'm a very busy woman."

My chest tightens as her words stab at it like a dagger. My heavy legs stand there for a few seconds, waiting for the moment where she'll burst out laughing and tell me this is a prank, and she's really happy to see me. I wait for her to tell me she has been thinking about me too and waiting to finally hold her son in her arms.

But that moment never comes, so I head toward the door. Outside her office, I turn around one last time to look at her, but she averts her gaze and shuts the door, leaving me out in the corridor. As I make my walk of shame through the main salon and back to Stephen's car, a dark cloud hangs over my head, tears blur my vision and all the hope I had disappears.

35

OLANNA
NOW

Silence stretches between us for several minutes after Alex finishes his story and, with tears streaming down both our faces, he lowers his head and wipes his eyes. I squeeze his hand, and he lifts his eyes to look at me.

"I'm so sorry you went through all that." I sniffle. "What she said to you was horrible. You are not a mistake. God planned for you to be here with me and your legacy on earth will be established regardless of whether you know your birth parents or not. God's plans for you still stand and they always will."

"You're right." He nods and smiles through his tears. "I know that now. God has confirmed all these things to me. I know I am His child and that is the most secure identity I can ever have. It took me a while to understand and accept this truth, but God helped me get out of that dark place.

"What upsets me more about this story is that I went to Ghana to get answers, but I left feeling more lost, empty, and uncertain. It was the fear of the unknown that pushed me to my breaking point and I ended up hurting the only woman I've ever loved." He pushes a loc strand away from my face and stares into my eyes.

"I'm sorry for everything I said and did to you, Olanna. I've learned that I need to trust God when I'm uncertain. I don't need to have the answers to everything. It doesn't matter that I don't know my real dad or my paternal family. God is still sovereign and as long as I put my trust in Him, I'll be okay." He sighs.

"I just hope that it's not too late for you to forgive me. I believe God sent me here because He wants to restore what we have and I'm ready to do things right by you if you'll take me back. I love you and I hope you'll give me a second chance to show you that."

I hold his hand against my face, letting him caress my jaw with his thumb. "Honestly, I still wish you had let me be a part of your journey. But if I were in your shoes, I don't know what I would've done. You've been through a lot and God is healing you from your hurts. So, I forgive you."

"Thank you, baby." He kisses my hands, and I savor the warmth of his lips against my skin. "Thank you," he says again.

"But..." I pause as his gaze meets mine. "I still need some time to pray about this. Our break up helped me seek God more and I've experienced spiritual growth just as you have. I love that for both of us, but I need some time to take this all in and think things over. Can you please give me until Monday?"

"Of course," he says. "You don't have to give yourself a deadline. I don't expect you to give me a definite answer in three days. I just want you to take as much time as you need because I want you to be certain about what you want."

"Yeah." I let out a sigh. "Please, let me pray about it over the weekend. I'll let you know on Monday."

He nods, leans forward, and kisses my forehead. It takes a lot of strength for me not to wrap my arms around him, pull him close, and kiss him. He leans his forehead on mine for a few minutes, allowing me to take in his scent.

"Good night, Alex."

"Good night, baby." He stands up and walks out of my office, leaving me alone to my thoughts as I say a prayer to God, asking Him to confirm whether I'm making the right decision.

36

ALEX
THEN

I tossed and turned throughout last night and it had nothing to do with the A/C or the fact that there was a funeral going on in the opposite compound with loud music and singing.

It had everything to do with the fact that my own mother has shattered my heart into several pieces and I don't know if anything or anyone can put it together again.

I wish I had listened to my parents or Kwame about how hasty my decision was to come here. Maybe that conversation wouldn't have hurt so much if Mom and Dad had confronted her with me. They would've stood up for me and been a shoulder for me to lean on when she spewed out those venomous words from her mouth.

But it's too late now. I've already been exposed. I can't turn back the hands of time. I have to live with the consequences. I was supposed to find myself here, connect to my roots, and figure out my identity. But how do I do that when the same woman who birthed me treats me like a plague?

You were a mistake.

I rub my sore eyes and swing my legs over the bed so my feet touch the warm floor. I woke up every hour for the last eight hours, and now that the sun is up, sleep is completely gone.

Slipping my feet into my flip-flops, I drag myself to the bathroom, brush my teeth and take a quick shower, hoping to feel more awake. I put on a polo shirt and pants before heading out to the balcony to get a good view of what's going on outside.

The compound opposite us where the boys were playing football on my first morning at this apartment now has a crowd of mourners, dressed in black and red, with matching black and red frame tents pitched in all the corners of the compound. But not even the dancing people, the beautiful music from the talking drums or the commotion can distract me from the dark thoughts drowning me.

How could she not want her own son? Her flesh and blood. The child she carried for nine months and brought into this world. How could she look me in the eye and say she wished I'd never been born?

Alex, My beloved.

I close my eyes and try to whisper a prayer to God, but I'm too defeated to even form the words. What do I say? How do I start? It's one thing to accept that I've failed at this, but how do I face my parents or Kwame? How do I face Olanna?

Tears blur my vision as I lower myself onto a tub chair at the balcony and sob into my hands. I'm not sure how long I let the tears run for, but a few moments later, the sound of the doorbell forces me to wipe my eyes. After washing my face and drying it with a towel, I open the door for Stephen.

"*Mema wo akye,*" he greets as he enters and I only nod without saying a word. He respects my silence and follows me into the living room.

"Have you had breakfast?" he asks, and I shake my head. "Aren't you going to have anything?"

I shake my head. "No, I'm not hungry." I glance at my phone, reading the text message notifications from Mom and Dad on our family group chat. They asked me to let them know how the meeting went and to call them, but that's the last thing I want to do. I need to gather my thoughts first so I don't break down in front of them. I don't think I'm ready to relive that conversation yet.

"Come on, Alex. Are you going to sit here and sulk all day?" Stephen's voice presses into my thoughts. "I promised you I was going to help you experience Ghana, remember? You have a lot to see."

I clear my throat and lean back on the couch. "I think I've seen enough, actually."

Stephen plops down on the couch opposite me. "Alex, will you really let what happened yesterday ruin your experience in this beautiful country?" He waits for my response, but when I give him nothing, he continues. "Okay, how about this? Why don't I take you to a place that I think will help you clear your thoughts and enjoy nature? If you still don't find it helpful, then I'll leave you alone."

I sit up in my chair. "Where is this place?"

"Are you agreeing to go?"

"I don't know, man. I think what I really need is some time alone."

"*Herh.* So you're going to stay here alone all day? With the funeral going on next door?"

Okay, he's got a point there. I have no idea how long the dancing and singing is going to take.

"Fine. You win. I guess I could benefit from some fresh air."

"That's what I'm talking about."

After a twenty-minute drive, we arrive at the busiest beach in Ghana—Labadi Beach, one of the top places on my list to visit. Although it is a public space, we still had to pay an access fee at the gate. Before getting to the beach, we walked past shops selling souvenirs, clothes and even swim suits for those who forgot to bring theirs.

I'm only here to enjoy the view, the culture, and to distract myself from the war going on inside my head. Stephen and I make our way to the beach, packed with people as I expected. There are several colorful beach umbrellas and chairs along the shore, with some people walking along the beach and others horseback riding.

We take a seat under one of the beach umbrellas as I enjoy the view of the Atlantic ocean while also bopping my head to the music playing behind us. The cool breeze brushes my face and I inhale the scent, closing my eyes and hoping to clear my thoughts.

Stephen orders some food for us, but shortly after digging into my french fries and chicken wings, Olanna pops into my mind and my heart wishes she was here with me. I take out my phone and scroll through our messages. She still hasn't responded to my last text message and now I'm convinced I've messed everything up.

I place my chicken wing back on my plate as a lump builds in my throat and my appetite disappears. Tears blur my vision, but I'm determined not to cry in front of Stephen. So I push myself away from the table and excuse myself while Stephen finishes his meal.

The white sand wedges between my toes as I near the water. I walk past a Ghanaian flag standing erect on the sand and I run my fingers on it before walking further along until my feet enter the water. The waves crash into my feet, cooling it while I stare at the large body of water and the clouds hovering above it.

Being here is a blessing, and I appreciate everything that is God's creation. But I'm sure I would've appreciated it more if I had come out here a few days ago. The damage has already been done and my heart feels numb. There's still so much I want to see and experience, but I can't keep forcing what isn't there. My time in Ghana has come to an end.

"So, my big plan didn't work?" Stephen's voice pulls me out of my thoughts and he pats my shoulder.

"I'm really sorry, man."

"Ah, sorry for what? *Hwɛ abarimaa yi.* Don't be sorry, please." He laughs. "At least I dragged you out of the house, so I count that as a win."

"Yes, you did." I smile. "Thank you for everything, Stephen."

"Please, tell me you will come back to Ghana?"

"If God wills, then I definitely will."

"Amen to that. And you promise to keep in touch?"

"Always, my brother." I hug him and we pat each other on the back before returning to the car and driving back to the apartment.

37

OLANNA
NOW

I plant another kiss on Ayannah's cheek and bounce her up and down on my lap before letting her slide down to the floor. I came over to Manny and Heather's for our weekly Bible study, which we finished half an hour ago. Heather stepped out to get some snacks for our movie night, so Manny and I will have to choose the movie.

Ayannah grabs her dark-skinned doll and crawls over to Manny, who is sitting next to me on the couch. She pulls herself up and sends me a smile, which warms my heart.

"Aww, look at how strong she is. I bet she'll start walking soon," I say as Manny lets her play with her dolls.

"I won't be surprised." He smiles at his daughter before turning to me. "So, what's up with you?"

I sigh and pick up one of Ayannah's dolls before lowering my head. While playing around with the doll's textured hair, I replay the last conversation with Alex in my head.

"I spoke to Alex yesterday, and he finally told me why he broke up with me."

"And?"

"He wants us to get back together. I told him I'll pray about it and give him an answer on Monday."

"Do you know what you'll tell him?" Manny asks, and I shake my head.

"No, but I know I still love him," I admit out loud and instead of Manny taking his usual stance to talk me out of it, he pauses and replies.

"I know you do. And I know he loves you, too."

I look Manny in the eye. "How do you know?"

"He told me."

I lift my eyebrows and lean forward. "What do you mean, he told you? You spoke to Alex?"

Manny shuffles closer to me and nods. "Yes, he came here two weeks ago and spoke to Heather and me."

"What?" My eyes widen. "How did you and Alex end up in the same room together without you breaking his face?"

"Oh, come on, cut me some slack." Manny chuckles and elbows my side.

"You were the one who promised you would do that to him if he ever broke my heart."

"Yeah, yeah, yeah." He rolls his eyes. "I know what I said, but I've changed my mind about him." He takes the comb Ayannah hands over to him and starts combing the doll's hair at the instruction of his daughter. That's what he gets for being a girl Dad.

"Okay, I'm really curious." I turn to face him squarely. "What exactly did you guys talk about that made you change your mind about him?"

Manny shrugs. "Everything. The cancer diagnosis, how he found out he was adopted, and how he took a solo trip to Ghana to find his birth parents but ended up experiencing rejection, which threw him into what he described as the darkest season of his life." He pauses before continuing.

"I wanted to fault him. I really did. But I could tell he was being genuine. He jumped through a lot of hoops to get my number from Yin. Then he reached out to me multiple times and even when I ignored his messages and calls, he came over here when he knew there was a possibility it would not end well. He asked me to give him your favorite family photo so he could make a Secret Santa present for you. People don't go through that amount of trouble for anyone."

Wow, so that's how he got the photo.

Manny reaches out and holds my hand. "I know you're scared. But it's just like Heather said. What if God has really granted you a second chance with Alex?"

Heather walks in carrying a bag of snacks and Manny helps her take the bags to the kitchen while Heather joins me on the couch. After planting a kiss on Ayannah's cheeks, she turns to me. "Aww, honey, are you okay?" She catches me swiping a tear away.

Stupid tears.

"Yeah." My voice cracks.

It's Heather's turn to hold my hands now as Manny sits next to her on the sofa. "Is this about Alex?"

I nod, sniffling. "I still love him."

"Oh, honey." Heather touches my cheek and thumbs a tear away. "One thing God has taught me so far in my journey with Him is that there's nothing too irredeemable that He can't restore. He doesn't make mistakes with things like this. Don't close your ears to what God is saying. Listen to Him."

Restoration. The word echoes in my heart as I ponder on it and the more I think about it, the more it makes sense. The main thing holding me back from saying yes to Alex is that I'm afraid things won't go back to the way it was. But a lot has happened in the last two years and we've both grown closer to God—who can restore and make things brand new—including my relationship with Alex.

"Push away our opinions and your fears, sis," Manny adds. "It's important to stay in the secret place where there's quietness and solitude. I'm sure God has already been speaking to you. Listen to Him, obey Him, and trust what He says to you. He'll never lead you wrong."

38

ALEX
THEN

My trip back to the U.S. was a lot longer than I wanted it to be. By the time we landed in New York, I had given up. Nothing made sense, and I didn't see the point of pretending like my life was going to be okay when it was a big, shambled mess. After narrating the story to Mom and Dad, they tried their best to comfort me, but all I wanted to do was hide away in my room and never come out again.

I spent the rest of the fall break mostly in bed and when I got out, I was moping around the house and trying to find different excuses to give Mom and Dad for not wanting to eat. Day and night blurred into one. I was confused, disoriented, and forgot how to pray. Nothing made sense, but instead of fighting to find meaning, I let the darkness consume me.

When I got back to college, even Kwame couldn't get me to talk about how I was feeling. I couldn't form the words because my life didn't feel like my own. I didn't know who I was or what the point of anything was.

"Come on, man. You have to stop this." Kwame places his snapback hat on my desk with a sigh. He showed up at my apartment after I missed three calls from him earlier this morning. "You've been moping around like this since you got back. You won't talk to anyone about it, not your parents, not me, and not even Olanna. She called me this morning crying because you haven't reached out to her since you got back. She thinks you're mad at her for not responding to your text messages while you were in Ghana. You're destroying all the relationships around you, man. You have to do something about it."

"What can I do?" I lift my head to look at him. "Tell me, what can I do to change the fact that the woman who brought me into this world looked into my eyes and told me she preferred I had not existed at all?"

"Bro, her opinion doesn't matter," Kwame interjects. "Since when did your life's worth start depending on a woman you barely know? Would you have felt this way if you had never found out you were adopted? Maybe this is the reason your parents didn't want to tell you."

"Well, the truth is out there now, and there's nothing I can do about it."

"Bro, stop it. Look at what this is doing to you. Look at the way you're treating Olanna and your parents who have sacrificed so much for you. You're acting as if you're in this alone. Why are you choosing to inflict pain on yourself when there are so many people around you who love and support you?"

"Bro, I appreciate the concern, but please I need some time alone."

"Alex, are you sure? You haven't—"

"Please, bro." I cut him so short, so he sighs and picks up his snapback hat again.

"Okay, then. Whenever you're ready, you know where to find me. I'll be praying for you, brother." He taps my shoulder and leaves the apartment, closing the door behind him.

I stay at my desk, head in my hands, alone, and ignoring the silent notifications popping off on my phone. When I'm about to return to my bed, the doorbell rings and I let out a sigh before walking to it and opening the door without checking the peephole.

"Kwame, I told you, I need some time alo—" My voice trails off as my gaze lands on her, the sight of her teary eyes ripping out pieces of my heart.

"So you can only open the door when you think it's someone else?" Olanna's voice breaks and without waiting for an answer, she lets herself in and places her backpack on the couch in the living room.

Wiping the tears underneath her eyes, she turns around to face me as I shut the door. "Didn't you promise you'd tell me everything when you come back from Portland? I'm not leaving until you explain."

I lower my head and rub my forehead. "Olanna, you don't understand."

"That's all you keep saying and I'm sick of it." She raises her voice. "Alex, I'm asking now and I won't ask again. What is going on with you?"

I remain silent, not because I don't want to answer her questions, but because I don't know where to start. Olanna takes a few steps toward me, tears streaming down her face now. She touches my chin and lifts my head so I can look at her.

"Alex, please," she whispers. "Talk to me."

My heart breaks as I stare into her eyes. I want to tell her everything, but she doesn't deserve these broken parts of me. I'm lost and I don't know what to do to help myself. She deserves someone who is not a liar and someone who won't make her cry. "I'm sorry, Olanna. I don't think we should see each other anymore."

"No." She shakes her head and takes my hand in hers. "No,

you can't do that. I won't let you. You have to tell me what's going on."

"I'm not the same guy you fell in love with. My whole life is a lie. I don't know who I am anymore and I don't deserve you." I shake my head at her, but she refuses to let go of my hand.

"Baby, what are you talking about? What do you mean you don't know who you are? What happened?"

"It's better if you don't know the details."

She groans and rubs her face with her free palm. "What makes you think you alone can decide what's best for us? You can't just break up with me without telling me what happened. This is so cruel." She brings her hand up to my chest, then my neck, and finally, she holds my face and stares into my eyes.

I squeeze her hands and plant a kiss on them. "I'm sorry, Olanna. I can't give you what you want. I can't be who you want me to be."

With those words, she steps back, lets go of my hand, and picks up her backpack. She wipes her tears with the sleeve of her sweatshirt and exhales before saying, "Alex, I'm tired. Tired of praying and waiting on the sidelines for you to come around. I'm tired of waiting for you to see that I'm trying to help. That we're all trying to help you. If you let me walk out the door today, I'll be walking out of your life for good. I can't keep waiting around for you to come to your senses. If you let me leave today without an explanation, I'm never coming back."

Just like my parents, just like Kwame, Olanna waits for an answer from me and when it doesn't come, she turns her back and marches out of the room, slamming the door behind her as she leaves. I stand there for a few minutes watching the door, hoping maybe she'll come back and I'll get the courage to face my fears, to reopen my wounds and lay out my vulnerabilities.

But true to her word, Olanna doesn't come back, so I return

to my bed, laying my head down and letting the silence and dark thoughts once again become my companion.

39

OLANNA

NOW

"Daddy, I'm home." I shut the door behind me and make my way to the living room, where Dad usually spends his evenings relaxing. As I expected, he's sitting on the couch, a glass of SuperMalt in front of him and his nose buried in a book.

I never thought I would ever see the day where my Nigerian dad reads a book for pleasure. He started off reading memoirs about successful business executives, then before I knew it, he transitioned to thriller novels. I don't know how or when that transition happened, but those books have him in a chokehold.

"Hello, Princess." He places his latest thriller novel on the table when he sees me and I plant a kiss on his cheek before sitting on the couch next to him. "How was your Bible study?"

"It was good. We also watched a movie, which was fun as well." I place my bag on the central glass table and lean against his arm. "What are you reading this week?"

He takes off his glasses. "It's a book about two siblings who set off to find their missing mother and they uncover some deadly secrets about their family."

"Ooh, that sounds very interesting. Maybe I'll read it after you if I have time." I take a seat next to him.

Since his retirement two years ago, Dad has picked up all the hobbies he didn't have time for when he was the CEO of Madu Health. Apart from his newfound love for reading, he has been having more golf battles with Manny and one time he even tried fishing. He is having fun and I love that for him.

"What are you thinking about, Princess?" Dad asks and my mind wanders again to Alex.

I open my mouth to voice out my thoughts when realization dawns on me. I've been speaking to Heather and Manny all this time about my love life, but I've never brought Dad into the loop. He and Mom were happily married for thirty years before she died. I'm sure he'll have some words of wisdom for me.

"Dad, can I ask you a question?" I sit up as he gives me his undivided attention. "How did you know Mom was the woman you wanted to spend the rest of your life with?"

"Hmm." He smiles. "That's an excellent question. You see, marriage, my dear, is something I've never taken for granted. God gave me a lot of dreams and visions and I knew I needed a companion to fulfill those dreams with."

He turns his head and looks at the photo frame on the bookshelf behind him. It's the same photo Alex put inside the snow globe. When the stranger at the airport took that photo of us, we never knew it would become our family's favorite photo shortly after.

"I left Nigeria at twenty-five," Dad continues. "But as you know, your mother and I met when we were studying for our Masters at NYU. We had only been speaking for a week when I knew I was going to marry her."

"Really?" I raise my eyebrows, wondering if Dad is stretching the truth. "What made you so sure after only a week?"

"We had the same vision for life. We shared the same interests, we served God together in the business world, she was a wonderful friend to me, she made me laugh, she brought out the best in everyone around her, and she encouraged me when the world thought I was a failure." Tears well up in his eyes and his voice breaks. I've only ever seen Dad cry when we're talking about Mom.

"I remember when we were struggling to set up Madu Health. The first year was so difficult. I wanted to give up, and I would've if she wasn't there with me. We hit so many roadblocks, but she reminded me that there is no problem God cannot solve. She always believed God would help us find a solution."

"That's what Manny said. Mom always told him that, too." I say, tears streaming down my eyes.

"She was a woman of faith, an exceptional mother, and she loved me—not just with her words, but her actions, too. I saw a lot of those attributes as I got to know her that first week, and that's how I knew I wanted to marry her."

"Wow." I dab my tears away. "That's so sweet. I miss seeing the two of you together, and I miss her so much."

And I miss Alex too. Hearing Dad speak so fondly of Mom reminds me of that night Alex first told me he loved me. I still remember how elated I felt and how his eyes sparkled when he looked at me. The beautiful thing about this is that when Alex told me yesterday that he still loves me, that same sparkle in his eyes was still there.

Dad holds my hands, bringing my thoughts back to our conversation. "I had a wonderful life with your mother and my prayer now is that both my children will also win when it comes to marriage. God has already done it for Emmanuel by bringing the wonderful Heather into his life. I know He will do the same for you. You just have to trust Him, okay?" He pauses before tilting his head. "Or has God already answered my prayer?"

If I were two shades lighter, this would be the time where my cheeks flush with embarrassment. "Daddy, stop." I avert my gaze and try to stand up, but he holds my hands.

"Should I tell my designer to start sewing the *Isi Agu* I will wear to celebrate?" He chuckles and I join him.

"When the time is right, I'll let you know."

"Okay. If you say so." He puts on his glasses again, sips on his SuperMalt, and picks up his book. "I'll be right here waiting patiently. It's not like I have anything else to do." He laughs and I kiss his cheek again before hanging the ornament Alex gave me on our Christmas tree and going up to my room.

As soon as I put my bag away, I get on my knees in front of my bed and whisper my prayers to God. "Lord, it's me again. Give me assurance that You are in this. Just like You gave Alex confirmation that this is what You want for both of us. Speak to me, Lord. I don't want to hold on to past hurts anymore. I want to move on from it because I love Alex. Please speak to me, Lord." And in that moment's stillness, my God speaks.

Olanna, My beloved.

I am your Restorer.

I am your glory, the One who lifts your head high.

I make a way for you in the wilderness.

Open your eyes and see the new thing I'm doing.

Trust Me.

Thank You Jesus, my Restorer. Words of thanksgiving leave my mouth because at this moment, I know without a doubt that God has answered all my prayers.

40

ALEX

THEN

I thought I would've gotten over it by now. That I would've finally found some peace within myself. But it's been two weeks since my return from Ghana and things couldn't get any worse than this. Not only have I broken up with Olanna—the only girl I've ever loved, but I still can't bring myself to let anyone else in—not even my parents.

I force my eyes open as the sun's rays filter through the curtains in my bedroom and into my eyes. My alarm went off an hour ago. It's Saturday and I should be at my shift at the library, but I called to cancel it. Instead, I drag myself out of bed, put on my running gear, and make one lap to campus and back.

But even with the sweat pouring down my face and my heart beating erratically, the tension in my muscles and joints is far from gone. Back in my apartment, I jump in the shower, put on clean clothes, and settle behind my desk.

Since I keep canceling my shifts, I should use the time to study. This session starts off better than all the ones I've attempted over the last few days, so I put my earplugs in and open my notebooks. But it only takes one text notification in our family group chat to send my brain into another spiral.

Mom and Dad have either called or texted me every single day since I came back to college, but I keep giving them vague answers when they ask me how I'm doing because I can't describe this pain that keeps jabbing at my heart. How can I describe those poisonous words that knock the air out of my lungs every time I think about them?

You were a mistake.

I swipe all the books off my desk and they land on the floor as a scream escapes my lungs, followed by the tears blurring my vision. Burying my head in my hands, I let the tears flow until my throat hurts from the lump I'm trying to force down. I lift my head and my gaze lands on my Bible on the floor, together with the rest of my books and pens.

I stare at the leather Bible Mom bought for me when I started college, remembering how she told me to always cherish it because the words written inside it are precious, from God's mouth to our ears, and in that book lies all the answers I need.

I lower myself to the floor and bring my knees up to my chest. The unexplainable urge to open the Bible is strong, but what draws me even closer is the still small voice—the One that has persisted and that always comes at the right time.

Alex, My beloved.

At first, I want to blame God for letting me experience all this. But I can't do that because I acted on my own accord. I never asked God whether He wanted me to go to Ghana. Even while I was there, I never asked Him to guide my decisions or keep my emotions in check. So no, I can't blame Him now that I've hit a wall because of my own actions.

"Lord, I'm sorry." I bow my head in prayer, my heart ready to spill out everything I've been holding in for the past two weeks. "I'm sorry for not seeking your direction. The cancer diagnosis really shook me up and I thought I needed to act with a sense of urgency. But what I really needed to do was slow down and look at You. I'm sorry, Lord. Please forgive me."

I pause before continuing. "When will it end, Lord? I'm tired of feeling sad. I'm tired of feeling guilty for all the mistakes I've made. Is this all You made me for? Is this all that I am? A mistake?"

Alex, My beloved.

You are My child. Not a mistake.

I knew you even before I formed you in your mother's womb.

I have set you apart for Me.

You will always be loved by Me.

A calming presence washes over me, first like a wave, then it towers over me like a cloud, shining a light down into the black hole I'm sitting in.

Nothing can separate you from Me.

You are mine.

I ponder on those words, letting them sit with me, meditating on them and repeating them to myself until the poisonous words fade into the background. "I'm still Yours, Lord?"

You have always been mine.

"But Lord, what happens next? What do You have planned for me? What does my future hold?"

Your future is in My hands, beloved.

I hold you securely with My victorious right hand.

No one can snatch you away from Me.

Trust Me. I will help you.

I pick up the Bible and place it on my knees before flipping the pages to the book of Isaiah, chapter forty-one verse thirteen. Leaning over the book, I read through the words repeatedly, using it as an anchor to hold on to hope.

"For I hold you by your right hand—I, the LORD your God. And I say to you, 'Don't be afraid. I am here to help you.'"

41

OLANNA
NOW

Today is the day, and Lerato has not let me rest since I came in this morning. "So, did you pray about it?" she asks as she hands me my usual Monday morning chai latte from Rosa's Café.

"Yes, girl. I sure did." I sip on the hot drink as we walk into my office.

"And?" She plops herself in the chair opposite my desk. "Are you going to give him another chance?"

"No comment." I force down my smile and then pretend to zip my mouth shut before throwing away the imaginary key behind me, just like Melissa does when we call her out for talking too much.

"Oh, come on, sister." Lerato switches her accent. "Why would you do that to me? I've been rooting for you two and praying all weekend."

"Aww, you're such a wonderful friend, you know that, right?" I lean forward and squeeze her hand. When I first hired Lerato as an assistant, I never imagined we would end up being good friends like this. She has been a blessing all along. "Don't worry. You'll find out what my decision is by lunchtime."

"*Phew*, okay. I wish I didn't have to wait that long, but I'll take it for now."

"Thanks for understanding." I flip open my Filofax planner as Lerato and I go through the agenda for the day. Then when we're done making our to-do list, she stands up to leave, but then stops at the door.

"Oh, by the way. There's something I've been wanting to ask you."

I straighten my back as she sits down again. "Sure, is everything okay with you and Paul?" Worry wraps around my voice and squeezes my heart tight as I search her face for clues. Paul and Lerato are so perfect for each other, and my heart won't recover from it if something goes wrong.

"Yes, everything is fine."

Phew. Thank You, Jesus.

"Olanna, would you like to be one of my bridesmaids?"

I press my lips together as my eyes water. "Aww, girl. Really?" I reach across the desk and hold her hand.

"Yes, really. You know my story about my previous employers and how horribly they treated me. When I first applied for this job, I was so lost about what I wanted to do with my life and I prayed for God to put me in a place where I could grow and get closer to where He wants me to be. I not only got an amazing boss, but I got someone who I can genuinely call a sister and a friend."

"Stop it, girl. You're gonna make me cry." I dab the corner of my eyes.

"Oh, not today." Lerato picks up a notepad on my desk and fans my face as we both try to fight off the tears so I don't ruin my makeup. Today is a special day.

"Honestly, Olanna, you are the definition of a queen. Your attitude toward serving in this company has been so inspiring. I don't know how you do it, but you inspire me so much." She stands up and I walk around the table to meet her.

"Aww, you're the sweetest person ever. Of course, I'll be one of your bridesmaids. It'll be an honor. I've never been to a South African wedding before, so I'm looking forward to it."

"*Aye*, sister. Prepare yourself because it'll be lit."

"Yes, I can't wait." We hug each other again before Lerato leaves and I get ready for my Monday meeting with the department managers. At face value, I'm concentrating and listening to everything that is being said, but God sees my heart, and He knows I want to be with the man I love.

So when the clock strikes twelve, I push myself away from my desk, and Lerato joins me on our mission. While in the elevator, Lerato adjusts my curly puff, which I got by doing a twist-out on my locs last night. I touch up on my Monday black matte lipstick and Lerato sprays my underarms with the perfume she always carries with her.

After getting off the elevator, it only takes a few steps into the open plan office before Alex comes into my view. He is wearing a black, gray, and brown sweater, black jeans and suede high tops. He got a fresh trim over the weekend and he looks even more handsome than the last time I saw him. *It should be illegal for someone to look this good.*

Alex lifts his head and locks eyes with me, and that warm, fuzzy sensation returns, making me all jittery like a little girl. Yin, who was speaking to Alex when I walked in, walks away when he sees me. Lerato drifts away to meet Melissa in the digital marketing section of the office and Neil, who I can spot at the far left of the office, is on the phone, but craning his neck in our direction.

"Hey." Alex smiles when I stop in front of him. It's the one smile I've been looking forward to all weekend.

"Hey." I return his smile and when I realize how many pairs of eyes are on me, the shy little girl inside me takes over.

"Do you want to get out of here?" he asks, but I feel having this conversation here would help dispel all the rumors.

"No, I think I'm okay here. Unless you are…"

"No, I'm fine." He pauses, waiting for me to speak.

We stare into each other's eyes and I block out everything and everyone around us as memories from all the times we shared in college flash back in my mind.

A lot has happened between us, but he still looks at me with the same kindness in his eyes, the same kindness I saw in the guy who stayed up all night with me to distract me from missing Mom.

A lump builds in my throat as emotions well up in my chest. "You're leaving Madu Health in two weeks." I inch forward and he does, too.

"I can always ask my bosses to extend my stay here." His response is quick, as if he already knew what I was going to say.

"Yeah, but eventually, you'll have to leave. What will happen then? What about the days when I'm all moody and sad and all I want is a hug from you to make everything better? What are we going to do about days like that, huh?"

I know I'm being dramatic because we'll only be less than an hour away from each other, but I think I'm allowed to do some *shakara* like the true *Naija* babe I am.

My antics do not fluster Alex, though. With his hands in his pockets, he towers over me and holds my gaze. "If you say yes to me, baby, you won't have to worry about me giving my all. Distance is not a problem because whenever you need me, I'll be there."

He caresses my cheek with his thumb. "You won't have to worry about me having your back or about me staying or leaving. I'm not the same Alex who broke your heart two years ago.

That man has done a lot of maturing. That man has encountered God in ways you can never imagine and that man is standing in front of you today—a new person who would do anything to put a smile on your face and love you the way you deserve to be loved—like the strong, beautiful and relentless queen you are."

As I stare into his brown eyes, standing this close to him and listening to his words, my heart accepts what has always been. This is the moment God was telling me about. He told me to trust Him to bring us back together, and He did.

"I love you, Alex." My hands rest on his chest and he wastes no time in kissing them. He cups my face and leans closer. When I don't move away, he takes it as a sign and kisses my forehead. I stare at his pink lips, waiting and expecting them to meet mine again.

He closes the gap between us and plants his lips on mine. The surrounding crowd erupts in cheers, but we're not moved by their applause. His arms run down to my neck and I wrap my arms around him, pulling him close to me and inhaling every scent he exudes. He kisses me softly and gently—the same way I remember, and when we're both running out of breath, we break the kiss.

"I love you, Olanna." He leans his forehead against mine. "You have no idea how much I've wanted to kiss you again," he whispers.

"And you have no idea how much I've longed to be in your arms again." I plant his arms around my waist as we both sway side-to-side to the unheard music that our hearts are dancing to. "So, we're really doing this again, right?"

"Yes, baby."

"No more lies, right?"

He nods vigorously. "Baby, I'm done being stupid."

I chuckle. "You really want this as much as I do?"

"With every fiber of my being." He leans close, sensing the desire in my voice.

"Then kiss me again."

"Yes, Ma'am." He pulls me close and plants another kiss on my lips. His arms, his lips, his closeness are familiar. It feels right. It feels safe.

42

ALEX
THEN

By the time winter break rolls around and exams come to an end, enough time has passed for me to think things over and decide to right my wrongs. Kwame was right. No matter how much I push everyone away, I still don't have the power to change the past. But I can choose what I do right now, and work toward making my future better.

Pushing everyone away helped me realize how much I needed God. All those times when I ditched class and stayed in my room feeling sorry for myself, God didn't abandon me. He tugged at my heart to pray, and eventually, He softened my heart to listen to His voice.

My birth mom doesn't want me. That's a situation I don't have control over, but instead of accepting that and moving on, I turned that feeling of rejection into anger toward everyone around me. I let my desire to belong consume me so much that I forgot God has already blessed me with a family who loves and cares deeply for me.

How could I have forgotten what truly matters? Why did it have to take pushing my parents, friends, and girlfriend away to help me realize this? I hurt their feelings because I was only thinking of my own. I hope it's not too late to gain their trust again. Now it's the time to get up and change the status quo.

"That's alright, bro. No hard feelings at all," Kwame says on the other end of the line as I glance at Dad, who is in the driver's seat. He came to pick me up from college because my car is currently at the mechanic's.

"Thanks, man," I respond to Kwame. "For always telling me the truth and calling me out. Thanks for not giving up on me."

"You know I *gotchu* always, my brother. I'm glad God helped you realize that. Now you have a lot of work to do to mend the bridges you've burned."

"True dat."

"I'll be praying for you, though. Holler at me anytime, alright?"

I nod. "Thanks, man. See ya." I end the call and enjoy the silence of the rest of the ride home. I grab my suitcase from the car, dragging it across the driveway and inside the house. The spicy aroma of Mom's cooking hits my nostrils as I walk in and the familiar sound of her singing to Twi gospel songs is very comforting.

I hang my coat up before taking my suitcase up to my room and returning downstairs to greet Mom. As soon as I call out to her, she turns around and rushes to my side, engulfing me in the hug she usually gives.

"*Wo ho te sɛn, me ba?*" She holds my cheeks and squeezes them.

"*Me ho atɔ me kɛse,* Mom." I smile down at her, and her eyes widen before she looks over my shoulder at Dad.

"*Eii.* Daniel, is this our son speaking Twi, or did you bring home someone else?"

"It's definitely your son, Abena," Dad responds and we all laugh.

Stephen would be so proud of me. "What are you cooking?" My gaze shifts toward the source of the glorious aroma.

"Only one of your favorites." She waves her hand over the kitchen island, letting me catch sight of the makings of *Banku* and grilled tilapia fish.

My mouth waters and I want to jump in and start eating, but there's something I need to do first. "Mom, Dad, please, can we talk?"

They look at each other before Mom responds. "Okay."

In the living room, I sit opposite them and, after clearing my throat, I shuffle to the edge of the couch. "Mom, Dad, I'm really grateful for everything you've done for me over the past twenty-one years. The last few months have been a roller coaster ride for me, but God made me realize that I've taken the love you've shown me for granted. I was chasing after illusions when God has already given me all I need right here."

Mom's eyes water as she squeezes Dad's hand.

"If Maame Mensah hadn't left me at Sunshine Children's Home, I would've never met wonderful people like you. As much as I sometimes wish that things had turned out differently, I can't deny the fact that God brought me exactly where I needed to be.

"After hearing her say all those things to me that day, I shut everyone out because I was scared of dealing with the anxiety of not knowing about my family history. But God reminded me that my identity is in Him and He holds my future. So I have no reason to worry because I can trust Him."

Mom stands and walks over to me, followed by Dad. They each hold one of my hands and help me stand up. "We hold no grudges against you, my son," Mom says. "We have loved you since the day God gave you to us and even though we won't be able to give you certainty about your family history, we can encourage you to trust God for your future."

"Yes, and God can be trusted," Dad adds. "He knows you, He sees you, and He loves you very much."

I nod and smile at them. "Thanks, Mom. Thanks, Dad."

Mom plants a kiss on my cheek and they both wrap their arms around me in a tight hug. This moment right here is priceless and indescribable. I wouldn't trade it for anything in the world.

43

OLANNA

NOW

If I wasn't so unstable on my feet, then Alex and I would've recreated the iconic scene from *Titanic* right here on the ice rink. But no matter how much Alex plants his firm hands on my waist, my feet can't stay together and glide smoothly on the vast sheet of ice around us. If I didn't love Alex so much, I would be sitting in the corner with my butt glued to the chair, watching everyone else risk breaking their bones.

"Yes, baby. Come on, you can do this." Alex lets go of my waist and lets me glide, one foot in front of the other like he taught me half an hour ago. But soon, my confidence takes over and when I try to go faster, I lose my balance yet again. Before I drop to the floor for the umpteenth time today, my man's muscular arms wrap around my waist and lift me until I regain my balance.

I smile up at him and he leans in and kisses my lips. "I love you, but you're a piece of work." He rubs his nose on mine.

"Yeah, I'm *your* piece of work." I wiggle my eyebrows at him and he laughs.

"I thought I was the master of cheesy lines."

"Yeah, and an excellent teacher too, so well done."

"Thank you very much." He glides with me to the bar and with the way I grab onto it, you would think I'm hanging on for my dear life.

Alex leads me slowly to the bench next to the giant Christmas tree and we watch the other people glide past us, in pairs, in groups, and some on their own. My hands are cold and my muscles hurt from the thousand falls I've had tonight. But you know what? There's no place I'd rather be.

As soon as we got back together a week ago, Alex pulled out our A-Z date ideas list from wherever he was keeping it safe the last two years, and he squeezed in this date two days before Christmas because he's so amazing.

Being here with him, risking breaking my bones and enjoying the laughter and small talk, is a blessing, and I'm going to savor every moment. I think I now know how Dad feels when he describes his relationship with Mom.

It took me much longer than a week to know, but God confirmed Alex was the one for me when we first dated in college. That's why our break up devastated me because I thought I'd heard God wrong. But now I know better. It just wasn't the right time. We both needed to mature in our faith and character. Now God has brought us back together again at the perfect time.

"Can I ask a question?" I lean toward him as he wraps his arm around my shoulder.

"Sure." He nuzzles my neck.

"So when people ask how long we've been dating, do we say one week, or nine months and one week?"

"Hmm, that's a good question." He tilts his head and taps his chin with his forefinger. "We can't say we've only been dating one week because that would make the first nine months invalid."

"Yeah."

"So we can say nine months and one week with a much needed two year pause in between?" He leans in and kisses my forehead.

"That sounds perfect." I laugh as my phone vibrates in my jacket pocket.

When I take it out, messages chime in from my *Boss Chicks* group chat.

"India and Danielle?" Alex peers over my shoulder. "I didn't realize you girls were still in touch."

"Well, we weren't until last week." I place my phone back in my pocket.

"Really? That's cool," he says. "If you don't mind me asking, what happened between you girls? Kwame had no clue because India didn't say anything to him. I didn't ask India because I didn't think it was any of my business."

I tuck a loc strand behind my ear. "Well, after our breakup, Danielle started dating one of the seniors from Ignite, and it was difficult to engage in conversations when they kept referring to their boyfriends. Living with them those last two years was hard, so after college, I kept to myself and focused on my healing journey."

"I see." He nods and pauses. "So, what happened last week?"

I shrug as a girl glides past on one foot. "When Lerato asked me to be her bridesmaid and she started talking about our friendship, it reminded me of the amazing friendship I had with India and Danielle. We stuck with each other through so much and it wasn't fair that I let my personal issues get in the way when they did nothing wrong. I'm in a much better place now and God has taught me how to be genuinely happy for others, even when I'm still in the waiting season.

"I reached out to the girls on the group chat last week and it turns out they have no hard feelings. We've been chatting nonstop and we're already planning our next meet up. As you probably know, India teaches in New York and Danielle works as a marketing manager for a tech company in Florida. She got engaged to that senior from Ignite. His name is Derek and they're getting married next summer. Danielle asked India and I to be her bridesmaids, so we have a wedding to plan."

"Wow, congratulations to her! I'm so happy that you have your friends back."

"Thank you. I missed them so much. I can't wait."

"Did you realize all three of you are in relationships with guys you met at Ignite?"

I tilt my head. "Oh, yeah. That's so true. I miss Ignite fellowship."

"Me too. Maybe in the future, when we're married, we could open up our home to hosting worship and Bible study nights, too."

"Yes, that's a brilliant idea. God is going to do amazing things. I can already feel it."

"Hallelujah." We both laugh as my phone vibrates again. India is sending some inspirational photos for Danielle's wedding dress. "India has been looking forward to one of us getting married for so long. I can imagine what her own wedding will be like."

"I can imagine too. Kwame is planning on proposing as soon as he's done with med school."

I grin as my heart swells for my friend. "Aww, really?"

"Yes, he already bought the ring, but baby, don't tell her I said that."

"Oh, please. India is smart. I'm sure she has already figured it out. But please, show me the photo of the ring."

He laughs and kisses my nose. "I wish I could, babe. But unfortunately I ain't got it. Even if I did, I would reconsider showing you right now because you're so close to bursting with joy."

I swat his arm playfully and rest my head on his shoulder. "I'm going to miss working with you when you leave." I sigh before looking up at him. "We're going to set up the SEO department at Madu Health after the HearCare launch. If you want to take the lead on that, just let me know and it'll be done."

He smiles. "Is this my interview and job offer, Miss Madu?"

I chuckle. "I think it's okay to say you get a free ride since you're the chief executive's boyfriend."

He laughs and shakes his head. "I'm honored that you want me on board permanently. Would you give me some time to pray about it? Working for HearCare over the last two years has been an invaluable experience, but I think God wants me to start my own SEO agency when the time is right."

"Aww, of course. I'm so excited for you."

"Thank you, baby. I'm excited for us." He caresses my ring finger. "How do you feel about us raising a family right here in Jersey City after we get married?"

"Wow, you are rolling with ideas today, babe. It's what I've always wanted as well. The city is all I've ever known. So we agree to stay here for now until God says otherwise?"

"Fine by me." We shake on it. "What do you think about a penthouse?"

I squeal. "Yes, I'd love that. It'll have a balcony and a swimming pool."

"Yes, and a view of the Statue of Liberty and the Hudson River."

"And a dog—a miniature poodle called *Missy*."

Alex laughs before standing up. "Okay then, *Missy*. I'll give the dog a thought if you give me one round on the ice without falling."

"But...but." I whine as he pulls me up. "Do I have to?"

"Yes, baby. Let's do one more round and then we can check out the bumper cars."

"Yay, that sounds fun." I cling to him as he places his hand on the small of my back and we glide together on the ice rink in perfect sync.

44

ALEX
NOW

I t's strange being back inside a doctor's office, but this time is different. After getting back together three weeks ago, Olanna and I quickly developed a routine of texting each other throughout the day and then catching up on video call in the evenings.

On Christmas Day, our parents met each other on video call and I can already tell Dad and Mom have found a new best friend in Mr. Madu. I can't wait for them to meet in person. We still have a lot to do on our A-Z date list, so Olanna is in for an adventure. But we have some important things to get out of the way first.

On New Year's Day, we spent three hours on the phone talking about our future and one thing we both agreed on was getting a medical screen to check for any genetic, infectious, or transmissible diseases we might have. I made some calls and booked our blood tests when I returned to Jersey City.

HearCare's launch was last week and now that we've finished celebrating its success with the rest of the team, we're back at the doctor's office today to get the results of our tests.

Olanna reaches for my hand under the table and squeezes it

as the doctor settles in her chair across the desk. I thought I had some experience reading doctor's faces, but here I am again, completely clueless about what she'll read out to us from the computer.

"Thank you for fitting us in today, Dr. Jackson." Olanna smiles at the middle-aged African American doctor with short gray hair and a white coat. The receptionist told us that the clinic has very limited appointments on Saturdays, but Dr. Jackson was kind enough to book one in for us.

"It's not a problem." She smiles at us and clicks on her mouse multiple times before pushing her glasses closer to her face. "I'll just get it out of the way by saying it's all good news."

Oh, thank You, Jesus.

"Really?" Olanna almost jumps out of her seat as her grip on my hand tightens.

"Mmm hmm." Dr. Jackson nods as the printer comes alive and prints out multiple sheets of paper, which she hands out to us. "Olanna, your blood group is O positive and Alex, you're O negative. Alex, you can donate blood to Olanna, but unfortunately she can't donate blood to you because she has the rhesus protein, which you don't have."

We both nod as Dr. Jackson continues explaining the results. "You both don't have any blood clotting disorders and you had negative results for hepatitis and HIV."

"Awesome," Olanna says.

"Alex, your blood group is AA, which means you don't have any sickle cell or thalassemia traits. However, Olanna, while you're clear of the thalassemia trait, your blood group is AS, which means you have the sickle cell trait."

"Oh." Olanna's shoulders drop and she turns to look at me with fear in her eyes. "What does that mean?"

"Don't worry." Dr. Jackson raises her hand. "All that means is that you both have a twenty-five percent chance of having a child who also has the sickle cell trait. But you can't have a child with sickle cell disease because Alex doesn't have the sickle cell gene."

"Oh, okay, good." Olanna exhales, and it's my turn to squeeze her hand.

"It's important to know," the doctor continues. "That if any of your children gets the sickle cell trait and has children with someone who also has the sickle cell trait, they'll have a twenty-five percent chance of having a child with sickle cell disease. Does that make sense?"

We both nod. "Yes, doctor."

"Perfect. Any more questions for me?"

We look at each other again for a few moments before turning to the doctor and shaking our heads. "No, doctor. Thank you so much for taking the time to explain this to us," I respond and we shake her hand.

The older woman grabs a few more leaflets from the shelf behind her and adds it to our pile of test results as we stand up to leave. When we step out into the cold January weather, leaving the big white building behind us, I hold her hand as we walk down the concrete sidewalk, covered by patches of snow.

"Can you believe she was actually talking about our future children?" Olanna says. "Isn't that crazy to think about?"

I smile and pull her close. "Yeah it is. Sometimes, I feel like I'm not even done being a child myself."

"I know," Olanna concurs, and silence passes between us before she speaks again. "But I already know we're going to be amazing parents. God willing."

My heart sinks as she adds the last part to her statement. This was the part I was dreading speaking to her about, but I have to get it out of the way so I know where she stands.

"Baby, can I ask you something?" I say when we're sitting inside the car.

"Yeah, sure."

Lord, please help me. "Erm...what if we're not able to have children of our own because of the surgery I had?" I muster up the courage to look into her eyes, but instead of sadness or regret, her gaze is still warm and loving as she strokes my beard with her free hand.

"And what if we do?" she asks simply. "Remember, we said we're going to trust God, right? I still believe in miracles, so God will do it." She pauses for a moment. "But even if He doesn't, I'm never leaving you."

"Really? You're okay with that?" I hold her hand in mine. I would never want Olanna to settle for a life she doesn't want.

"Of course. There are options. We can start saving now for IVF. We will even adopt if we need to. I'm sure there are plenty of children out there who need love, the same way your parents showed love to you. Actually, scratch that. Even if we have children of our own, can we adopt a baby, anyway?"

"Really? You'd do that?"

"Yes." She nods. "Speaking to your parents and seeing how much they love and adore you, even though you're not their biological son, was so inspiring. If you are up for it, I think it'll be amazing to pass that down to another child who needs a love like that."

"Wow." I lower my head, in awe of the woman sitting in front of me and the God who brought her into my life. "You're such an amazing person, Olanna. I love you."

"Aww, I love you too."

"Now that you bring up adoption, can I convince you to come to Ghana with me? I'll show you the children's home in East Legon, where my parents adopted me from. Maybe we can adopt a baby from there, too."

"That sounds like a plan." She nods and I raise my eyebrows.

"Really? I didn't think it'd be that easy to convince you about a Ghana trip, given what happened to your mom and..." My voice trails off.

Throughout the time we were dating in college, Olanna told me about how she didn't like the idea of going back to Nigeria because she only saw it as the place that took her mom away from her. I didn't think she would change her mind so soon.

"When my dad got back from Nigeria last month, he shared with me so many experiences he had there, both good and bad. Hearing you talk about all the things you experienced in Ghana and how you felt connected to your culture awakened a hunger in me. I've spent the last four years complaining about all the misgivings of my home country, but I forget that there's no perfect country.

"So I could either keep complaining until the day I leave this earth, or channel all those emotions to make a change. I'm choosing to be on the side of change because there's hope for any country. My mom and dad came to the US decades ago searching for the American dream. God was faithful enough to bless their hard work and turn it into generational wealth. But God didn't make a mistake by putting me in this position of influence and affluence. I feel strongly that he would like me to give back as much as I can."

"Yes, that's what the Bible teaches in Paul's first letter to Timothy. The charge is for the wealthy to be rich in good deeds, generous and willing to share," I say, before sharing Stephen's testimony of leaving the US and going back to Ghana to craft the Ghanaian dream.

"Exactly. I'm tired of wasting time. That's why this summer, I've decided to join Manny and Heather on their yearly trip to Nigeria and I want to volunteer for my mom's charity, A Widow's Comfort. Mom understood this concept, and that's why she was so passionate about what she did. I would love to experience for myself the impact she made before she died."

I squeeze her hands. "I'm so proud of you, baby. This would be a monumental step for you. Would you like me to come with you to Nigeria?"

"Of course. Then we can go to Accra and visit all those places you couldn't visit two years ago."

"Awesome. I'll send Stephen a message now, so he can add us to his calendar."

After sending the text message, I take a moment to reflect on what Olanna and I just talked about. When I prayed for God to restore our relationship, I didn't expect Him to blow my mind like this. What God has been preparing us for is so much bigger than ourselves, and I can't wait.

"Baby, are you okay?"

"Huh?" I look up from my phone. "Yeah, sorry, I just can't believe how blessed I am to have you. I don't deserve you, Olanna."

"Aww, please don't say that. I don't deserve you either. But this beautiful love story has God's name written all over it."

"It sure does." I cup her face in my hands and kiss her, and before I know it, I'm whispering prayers to God, thanking Him for bringing us back together, and the entire time, Olanna is rubbing my back, pecking my cheek and answering, "Amen." I trust God that, indeed, it shall be so for the rest of our lives.

EPILOGUE
FIVE MONTHS LATER

Sometimes I think Nigerians use every single excuse to throw a party, but there's no better reason to celebrate than welcoming not one, but two bundles of joy into this world. So when Amara invited Manny, Heather and me to the dedication ceremony of their twin girls, I couldn't say no. Of course, Alex is my plus one and Dad tagged along since he now has all the free time in the world.

After the service at church, we proceeded to the reception venue. The purple and white decor at the venue blends beautifully with the gold centerpieces and I'm already taking photos for the *Wedding Inspo* album on my phone. I need to ask Amara for the name of the decorator because I'm a huge fan.

Alex and I are at the same table as Dad, Manny, Heather, Teeyana, Jayden—Teeyana's husband, and Zion, their two-year-old son. The master of the ceremony just announced that Amara, Raymond, and the twins will do their entrance into the hall in five minutes. Heather, Teeyana, and I use those five minutes to catch up because every second counts.

"So, is this *the* Alex everyone has been talking about?"

Teeyana says over the Nigerian high praise music playing in the background.

Heat flashes to my cheeks as I drive my elbow into Teeyana's side and she chuckles. "Shh!! Way to be subtle." I glance at Alex, who is smiling and pretending to be lost in the music. *Of course he heard that.*

"Oh, come on. You don't have to hide anything. Heather already filled Amara and I in on all the details," Teeyana says as we both glance at Heather, who is bouncing Ayannah on her lap and hiding her smile.

I squint at Heather. "Of course she has." We all chuckle and I turn to Teeyana again. "Yes, that's my boo."

"Aww, I'm so happy for you," Teeyana says as Zion reaches for her necklace and plays with the heart pendant.

"I'm so glad it all worked out for you, Olanna." Heather hugs me. "God can be trusted, right?"

"Indeed, He can," I respond and hug the girls as the gray-suited MC calls for everyone's attention.

"Ladies and gentlemen. God has been so good and now we have the pleasure of welcoming Dr. and Mrs. Raymond and Amara Aderinto and their beautiful twin girls."

Everyone rises to their feet with rounds of applause as the doors to the venue open. Raymond and Amara dance to the beats of a fast-paced Nigerian gospel song, each of them carrying one of the girls dressed in pink sequin dresses and matching bow headbands.

The couple's outfit is made of beautiful purple lace, with Raymond wearing an *agbada* and Amara wearing a beautiful dress with sequins–like her daughters—and a matching *gele*. Her train swoops at the back as she sways to the rhythm of the music, but Raymond steals the show with his dance moves.

Amara's mom and dad dance behind the couple together with Raymond's mom, who I heard flew all the way from Nigeria to celebrate with them. The joy on their faces warms my heart. I can't wait to share this with Alex someday.

As if he heard my thoughts, Alex wraps his arm around my shoulder and plants a kiss on my temple before whispering in my ear. "That'll be us soon, baby. God willing."

"Amen to that." I chuckle.

When the procession ends and the music dies down, we sit down while the couple share their testimony and the labor and delivery story. Amara went through so many complications with gestational diabetes and hypertension during the pregnancy, so in the end, she had to be induced when they couldn't bring down her blood pressure. One twin was breached, and they almost had to do a C-section. In the end, God came through and both babies and parents are well.

Everyone claps as the pastor takes the mic and starts speaking encouraging words to the crowd. Then he explains that because close friends and family couldn't make it to the naming ceremony because it was during the holidays, Amara and Raymond have requested that they announce the names of the children again and pray for them.

The pastor takes the oldest twin from her dad and reads out her names from an A4 sheet of paper in his hands. "This is Grace Adaego Taiwo Oluwadarasimi Omolade Oluremi Joy Blossom Shola Aderinto."

"Whoa, are all those names going on her birth certificate?" Alex asks, and I laugh at the shock on his face.

The pastor takes the second twin and does the same. "Faith Adaeze Kehinde..."

"No, they won't all be on their birth certificates," I respond. "Raymond is from the Yoruba tribe in Nigeria and in their culture, different people in the family usually give names to the child. A lot of those names—especially the latter ones—were probably given by family members."

"Ah, I see. That makes sense."

The pastor lists out the names again the second time and asks everyone in the crowd to repeat each name after him. Then he prays for the children and hands them back to the parents. The pastor also prays over the food and the music resumes.

Alex and I walk over to greet Raymond and Amara when they pass the baby to their parents.

"Congratulations to the newest parents in town," I say to them, and Amara squeals and pulls me in for a hug.

"Guys, meet Alex, my boyfriend."

"Welcome, Alex. It's so great to finally meet you," Amara says with a wide grin and they both shake Alex's hand.

"It's nice to meet you both, too," Alex responds. "Olanna has told me so much about you two. Congratulations on your twins and I was just saying you have a long list of names to remember now."

Raymond laughs. "*Omo,* I can already see myself getting confused." He scratches his head. "For the first few months, we had to put different colored ribbons around their wrists to differentiate them. It wasn't easy."

"But you can do all things through Christ," Alex adds.

"Amen. Thank you so much for coming, my brother. We should all hang out sometime," Raymond says and I nod.

"Yeah, don't worry, me and the girls are already planning something," I say and we talk for a few more minutes before Alex and I leave them to greet their other guests.

Holding hands, we walk over to get food from a selection of pepper soup, *jollof* rice, fried rice, *gizdodo, ayamase,* white rice, *egusi* soup, *eforiro,* pounded yam, yam porridge, peppered fish, *moin moin,* assorted meat and salad. Alex goes for *jollof* rice and peppered fish, while I choose the *ayamase* and white rice with a side of *gizdodo* and *moin moin.*

"So, Alex, I hear there's still some beef between Ghana and

Nigeria about who has the best *jollof* rice?" Teeyana asks, and everyone's gaze flies to him.

"Wow, girl, you just go'n put my man on the spot like that?"

"Yeah, actually. I'd like to hear his opinion," Dad concurs as he sips on his pepper soup.

"Come on, Dad, not you too. Whose side are you on?"

"The side of victory, my dear, and you know *Naija no dey carry last*."

"Bro, you gotta choose your answer wisely, because you're at a Nigerian party, after all," Manny says and I shake my head at him.

"Don't let them pressure you, Alex," Jayden chimes in.

"Thank you, Jayden. You're the only other man at this table not annoying me right now." I send him an air hug.

Alex exhales slowly, and then, with his entire chest, he responds. "I'm sorry, guys. It's Ghanaian *jollof* all the way."

Voices roar at his response, talking over each other, trying to convince Alex he's wrong, but he just carries on eating his food, smiling at them all.

"You go, babe." I wink at him. "*No gree for anybody*."

"What was that, babe?"

"Never mind." I pat him on the back.

"Don't worry. When you taste Olanna's authentic *jollof*, you'll change your mind," Dad says, refusing to give up the fight.

"Yeah, Olanna taught me how to cook *jollof* rice. She does it so well," Heather adds. "Maybe you will change your mind."

"Maybe," Alex says before looking into my eyes. "Until that day, Ghanaian *jollof* all the way."

The voices at the table fade to the background and all I can see are those big brown eyes I love.

"What?" I push his arm as I lick peppered sauce off my fingers. "You know my insides melt when you look at me like that. Are you trying to embarrass me?"

"Never." He chuckles. "I would never do anything to embarrass my queen. I still can't believe God gave us a second chance."

"He's so good, isn't He?" I wipe my hand on a napkin and lean into him, lost in his gaze and choosing to ignore Mr. Chijioke Madu's eyes on us.

Even if there are aunties watching us right now, waiting to use our story as the topic of their next gossip session, I couldn't care less. I'm exactly where God wants me to be, and that's all that matters.

"You can say that again." Alex closes the gap between us and kisses me, my heart warming and skipping around in my chest, but also thanking God, who kept us, held us, and worked this all out for our good.

A PLEA

Thank you so much for reading this book. I would be very grateful if you could please take some time out to leave a review online. Reviews are very important for independently published authors like myself. They help the book become more visible to others so they, too, can be blessed by it. Thank you again and God bless you.

GLOSSARY

Kedu ka i mere?- How are you?

Adi m mma- I'm fine

Ezigbo m- my dear

Eish- A South African exclamation used to express surprise, pain, annoyance, agreement, disapproval, etc.

Gele- A traditional head tie that comes in different shapes and designs. It is native to Nigerian women of the Yoruba ethnic group.

Amala- A staple swallow food originating from the Yoruba people of Southwestern Nigeria and it is made with yam flour.

Ewedu- A green slimy Nigerian soup of the Yoruba ethnic group made from cooking jute leaves.

Ggbegiri- A bright yellow Nigerian soup of the Yoruba ethnic group made with peeled honey beans.

Buka stew- A popular Nigerian stew made with assorted meat cooked in a tomato base and palm oil.

Eii- A Ghanaian slang used when surprised or in awe.

Herh- A Ghanaian term usually used as a preceding word in a sentence to give more emphasis.

Dɛn na ɛregye wo bere tenten saa?- What is taking you so long?

Waakye- A Ghanaian dish made of cooked rice and beans.

Shito- A Ghanaian sauce made of blended fish, ginger, prawns, dried fish, peppers, spices, fried in vegetable oil.

Gari- Granular flour made from cassava flakes.

Nyame boa yɛn o- God help us o.

Aseda nka onyame- Thanks to God.

Jollof rice- A spicy rice dish from west Africa typically made from long grain rice, tomatoes, chillies, onions, spices, vegetables and/or meat in a single pot.

Wowɔ awerɛhyem?- Are you sure?

Onyankopɔn renhyɛ wo aniwu da- God will never let you down.

Woate me asɛm anaa?- Have you heard me?

So wo ho ye?- Are you okay?

Dɛn na ɛyɛ bɔne, me ba?- What's wrong, my son?

Worentie me- You won't listen to me.

Dɛn na ɛhaw wo?- What's wrong with you?

Akwaaba- Welcome

Charley- A Ghanaian slang which means 'friend' or 'buddy' or 'dude' or 'bro'

Borga- A Ghanaian slang used to refer to people who have come from abroad.

Dier- No direct translation but it is a Ghanaian slang mainly used to give more emphasis to statements.

Mema wo akye- Good morning.

Andinkra symbols- Symbols from Ghana which represent proverbs, concepts and aphorisms.

Naija- Nigeria

Kente- A Ghanaian textile which is made of hand-woven strips of silk and cotton.

Ankara- African fabric made of vibrant pattern and colours

Hwɛ abarimaa yi- Look at this boy

Isi Agu- A vibrant and colourful traditional outfit worn by the Igbo people of Nigeria, so called because of the lion head pattern on the fabric. It is usually worn on special occasions like weddings.

Shakara- In this context, it means playing hard to get. It also means to show off.

Wo ho te sɛn, me ba?- How are you, my son?

Me ho atɔ me kɛse- I'm feeling much better.

Banku- A swallow food from Ghana made from fermented corn, cassava dough, salt and water.

Agbada- A free flowing robe traditionally worn by the Yoruba people of Nigeria.

Omo- It means child but when used as a slang it is used to express shock or stress or as a precursor to the beginning of a conversation with a friend.

Gizdodo- A Nigerian dish made from fried gizzard and fried plantain mixed in spicy pepper sauce.

Ayamase stew- A Nigerian dish made with green bell peppers, onions, chillies, assorted meat, boiled eggs and palm oil.

Egusi **soup**- A west African soup made from ground melon seeds, assorted meat and palm oil and spices.

Eforiro- A vegetable soup native to the Yoruba people of Nigeria. It is made from two main vegetables– Celosia argentea and Amaranthus hybridus.

Moin moin- Steamed bean pudding eaten across west Africa.

Naija no dey carry last- It means Nigerians do not easily give up.

No gree for anybody- A popular slang in Nigeria which means to stand up for oneself and not to give in to opposition or pressure.

AUTHOR'S NOTE

The inspiration for this story came to me while I was writing the third book in the series—The One Who Sees Me. I was so sure the Sovereign Love series was only going to have three books. I was ready to move on to another series, but Olanna's character kept tugging at my heart. Her character came about when I was planning out the side characters for TOWSM. I wanted Emmanuel to have a younger sister because I wanted to show-case a cute brother-sister bond—one I would have loved to have myself if I had an older brother.

I didn't initially plan to write about Olanna's heartbreak in TOWSM. The idea came to me as I was writing the first draft of the book. When I finished the first draft of TOWSM, God confirmed to me that Olanna will need to have her own story. The beta readers for TOWSM also kept asking about a fourth book because they were so invested in Olanna's story and wanted to know why Alex broke up with her.

While planning out The One Who Holds Me, I knew from the get-go it was going to be a second chance romance because of the breakup in TOWSM. But this was a challenge for me because I had never written a second chance romance before. I didn't even know the reason Alex broke up with Olanna, but I knew it had to be a good one, for Alex's sake. During the research stage, I had to ask for suggestions in a Christian readers Facebook group to get ideas about some good reasons for couples to break up. I also read a few second chance romance stories and then God started putting the story together for me.

As I continued to plan out the story, I knew that the best way to show the readers what actually happened between Alex and Olanna was to do a dual timeline story. This was also a new challenge for me, as I had never written a dual timeline story. I had to pick up some dual timeline books as well to see how other authors have done it. My aim with the dual timeline was to keep the suspense going and to keep the reader's interest piqued. I hope you enjoyed that format of the story.

The central Bible verse for this book was taken from **Isaiah 41:13** and it says *"For I hold you by your right hand—I, the LORD your God. And I say to you, 'Don't be afraid. I am here to help you.'"* This theme was mainly for Alex as I believe God wanted me to show through his story that **even though life can take unexpected turns sometimes, God holds us safely in the palm of His hands and He will always help us navigate every uncertainty we have about our future.**

The inspiration to write about adoption came after I watched an episode of *Paternity Court* on YouTube. For those of you who don't know this show, it is based in the US and people can have DNA tests to find out the real father of a child or even an adult. There was one particular episode I watched last year which stayed with me. It was about a boy who came with his family for a paternity test and he sadly found out that not only was he not the son of the man he thought was his father, but the woman he thought was his mom was also not his birth mom. He found out he was adopted and his birth mom had passed away while he was young.

I still remember the pain on this young man's face and the tears that fell from his eyes as they broke the news to him that for almost 20 years of his life, he had been living a lie. I wanted to explore that feeling in this book with Alex and, of course, show what the word of God tells us about this. The powerful message to takeaway is that we belong to God. **We are children of God first.** What Alex also needed to learn was that even though it wasn't possible for his birth parents to be involved in his life, God had already blessed him with his adoptive parents. Of course, it's always great to have the acceptance of our birth parents too, but **the confidence we have in our identity is knowing that the Sovereign God has accepted us into His family and He calls us His children.**

I definitely enjoyed the little part of Ghana I could infuse into this story. I went to Ghana in 2022 for a friend's wedding and I remember how amazing that trip was for me. During that season of my life, I had so many life stressors and, being in the country, experiencing the culture and the kindness of the people, provided solace for me during that time. So when writing Alex's story, I knew it was going to be a fun experience to showcase the beautiful Ghanaian culture. To all my amazing Ghanaian readers, I love and appreciate you, and I hope you enjoyed that part of the book.

The key lesson that Olanna had to learn in this book was trusting God to help her overcome grief and also to open her heart to give love a chance again. Alex encouraged her a lot while they were in college and after the breakup, she put a guard around her heart, as she didn't want to be hurt again. Going through heartbreak can be very devastating, but the healing journey begins when we learn to trust God again. **Trusting God is not easy, but it's always worth it.** He always knows what is best and just like Emmanuel told Olanna, God will never lead us wrong.

Finally, if you're reading this and you're yet to surrender your life to Jesus Christ as your Lord and Saviour, here's an open invitation to do so today. It is not too late. The Lord's open arms are waiting, and He is calling you to come home. There's no pain He can't heal. Jesus has already paid the price for you. He wants you to abandon your pride today and run to Him. He has loved you from the beginning of time and He always will. If you want to take that bold step today, please say this prayer with me;

Dear Jesus, I come before you today with thanksgiving in my heart. I accept that you are God and I am not. I am a sinner, but You alone are the Forgiver of sins. Please come into my heart today. I surrender my all to you as my Lord and Saviour. Make me clean and teach me how to love and obey you. In Jesus' name I've prayed. Amen.

If you've prayed this prayer of faith and are willing to walk into your new life with Jesus, congratulations. Welcome to God's family. Please get plugged into a local church if you haven't already done so. Commit to studying the Bible with fellow believers and find a spiritual mentor you trust who will help you along the journey. If you would like to share a testimony with me, please reach out to me on social media or using the contact form found on my website: www.joanembola.co.uk.

Until the next book,

Lots of love,

Joan.

FREE SHORT STORY

Subscribe to my free monthly newsletter here to stay up to date with book news and to also get a free short story called *A Promise To Keep*, which follows a Nigerian couple—Dayo and Dara as they navigate the challenges of life while learning about endurance and what it means to experience the goodness of God.

ACKNOWLEDGMENTS

Thank You Lord for the inspiration of this book and for helping me finish this story. I dedicate it back to you, oh Lord. Please use it for Your glory.

To my love and wonderful husband, Oladunni. Thank you *ife mi* for always encouraging me and championing all my ideas. I can never thank God enough for the gift of you. I love you so much.

To my beta readers, Blessing and Nicole. Thank you so much for your amazing feedback and for helping me strengthen this story.

To my editor, Michaela Bush, thank you for your amazing ideas and feedback and for helping me shape this story into its final form. I always appreciate you.

To my cover designer, Elle Maxwell, I'm always in awe of your talent. Thank you so much for perfectly bringing Olanna and Alex to life.

To you reading this book, thank you for giving it a chance. I hope it gave you hope and taught you to believe in the God of second chances who loves you very much.

Finally, I'll have to go back to my Heavenly Father—the One who holds me. My Lord, I started this journey with You and I'm finishing it with You. To You be all the glory, honour and praise forever and ever. Amen.

ABOUT THE AUTHOR

Joan Embola is a UK-based Cameroonian-Nigerian Christian author who aims to share God's love one word at a time. She writes books about diverse characters whose hope-filled stories point to the love and goodness of God in our broken world. She is a qualified Physician Associate and also the founder of Love Qualified, a ministry dedicated to encouraging others to experience the sovereign love of the one true God who has qualified us to be His beloved ones. She is a passionate lover and teacher of God's Word, as shared on her YouTube channel and other social media platforms. When she's not writing or curled up with a book, you'll find her watching movies, YouTube videos, or making memories with her family and friends.

You can connect with her at www.joanembola.co.uk and on instagram, TikTok and YouTube. Subscribe to her newsletter to stay up to date with exclusive behind-the-scenes book news, cover reveals, how to sign up for advanced reader copies, and fun giveaways.

DISCUSSION QUESTIONS

1. At the start of the book, we see Olanna in a place where she has built walls around her heart and she is struggling to put her defenses down because of how badly she was hurt by Alex? Have you ever experienced heartbreak before? How did you deal with it?

2. How would you describe the relationship between Olanna and her Dad? How would you describe the relationship between Olanna, Emmanuel and Heather?

3. In the book, we also see that Alex almost gives up trying to tell Olanna the truth because of how hard it was opening up his old wounds. Have you ever been in a position like this?

4. How would you describe the relationship between Alex and Kwame?

5. How would you describe the relationship between Alex and Olanna? Did they have a good foundation from the beginning?

6. What did you think about Alex's reasons for ending their relationship in college? Were you rooting for them to have a second chance at love?

7. What roles did the side characters (Heather, Emmanuel and Kwame) play in the lives of Alex and Olanna? How did these people influence them?

8. What lesson did Olanna have to learn to get her to where God needed her to be?

9. What lesson did Alex have to learn to get him to where God needed him to be?

10. Does the title of the book make sense to you? Do you get the overall theme that the author was trying to portray?

Milton Keynes UK
Ingram Content Group UK Ltd.
UKHW030629061024
449204UK00004B/189